DELECTABLE

ANN GRECH

Edited by: Hot Tree Editing
Formatted by: Sloan's Design Stop
Cover design by: Simply Defined Art
Cover models: Korey Williams, Tara Jiggins and KC
Cover Photography: Melissa Mackley and Rachael Wilson

Ann Grech may be contacted via the following email address:
<u>ann@anngrech.com</u>

�֍ Created with Vellum

BLURB

Connor

I owe everything to Levi. Everything. So when I fell for his girl, I did the only thing a good mate would do. I left. Ran. Six years in that hell hole trying to forget, trying to let them live and love each other. But I couldn't stay away any longer.

And now I'm realising it wasn't just her I'd fallen for.

Levi

He left us—spent years defending our country. He's far more honourable than me. While I was living in paradise, happy, and in love with my gorgeous girl, he's been facing horrors I can't even imagine. It nearly broke me knowing he was there, and Katy and I were here.

Twenty years we've known each other. I've grown a lot in those years. But one thing hasn't changed from the first day we met: we're still inseparable.

Now I'm beginning to understand how, in another life, we could have been so much more.

Katy

Levi's the love of my life, my soulmate. And life is good. We're so damn lucky... blessed to have found each other. But there's a "but". There always is.

We've spent six years waiting, in limbo. Connor was fighting to make the world a better place, and we were incomplete without him. When he left, he took a piece of my heart.

Now he's back.

To all of you who have joined the good fight, who are voting 'yes'. And please vote. Tick the 'yes' box and post the survey back before it's due.
Make this one count, Australia. We need marriage equality.

ACKNOWLEDGMENTS

I'm blessed with a group of people around me every day who are amazing in every way. To my hubby and boys, I love you. You guys put up with so much scatterbrainedness (yes, I know that's not a word) from me and you do it with a smile. I love you always and forever. You are my world.

My gorgeous friend Kariss Stone and the ladies from Hot Tree Editing for your critiques and editing and the ever stunning Maci Dillon for everything you do to keep me in line and professional-looking. I adore you ladies; I'm privileged to work with you.

Ann Grech's A-Team (it's crazy that I even have one member of this fan group, never mind how many of you there actually are), I love all of you. You make me smile, inspire me, motivate me and keep me honest. And the amount of promo you all do astounds me every day. I'm so honoured that you'd take the time out of your day to do that for me. Thank you guys and girls from the bottom of my heart. I hope that this one makes you proud.

To Tara, Korey and CK for your modelling and Mel and Rachael for your insane photography skills. Thank you for the awkwardness, the laughs and most of all a set of photos that I'm so in love with it's not funny. And Jay Aheer. Ever since I laid eyes on one of your covers, I was desperate to work with you. And the magic you weaved, made it totally worth the wait. My cover. Sigh.

Also, a special thanks to three readers who helped me out of a tight spot in choosing songs that were perfect for Nick's birthday scene—Jacqueline Thorgood, Natallie Miernicki and Susan Reeves—you ladies came up with the goods!

There are so many other people who I'm grateful to—the bloggers, readers and fans just to name a few. Your support, your selfless help blows me away every time. Thank you.

Ann xx

GLOSSARY

This story is set on the Gold Coast, Australia. It uses Australian English. There are some terms that you wouldn't have heard of before, so I've set out a few for you. If you come across more, let me know and I'll try to explain our slang. You might also want to take a peek at my website – I'll add more there as they come up.

Arvo – afternoon
Barbie – barbecue. Outdoor griller for meats
Cockroach supporter – one of those sad sacks who support the New South Wales Blues (or Cockroaches) in the Origin
Dole – financial aid paid by the Australian government for people who are out of work
Esky – a cooler for drinks and food that you fill with ice
Footy – rugby league, a full contact sport played between two teams for two forty minute halves where the objective is to score more than the other team by carrying the ball over the 'try line' and, after making a try, kicking the ball between the posts to add an extra two points to the score (called a conversion)
Goldie – Gold Coast

Kitchen bench – kitchen counter or countertop

Mobile – cell phone

Origin – a footy match between New South Wales and the almighty Queensland Maroons (or Cane Toads) in which Queensland kicks New South Wales arses regularly (because we're that much better ;-)). With every year's competition, the entire state of New South Wales whinges about how the referees unfairly gave away too many penalties to Queensland (they don't —we're just better. The record doesn't lie—since 2000, Queensland has won thirteen of the eighteen series)

Pj's – pyjamas

Saltie – saltwater crocodile

Smoko break – morning or afternoon tea

Snags – sausages

Starkers – naked

Straddie – South Stradbroke Island, a sand island that forms the eastern most boundary of the Broadwater on the Gold Coast

The King – Wally 'The King' Lewis. The King is known as Queensland's greatest ever Origin player captaining the Maroons in 30 matches

Thongs – flip flops

Track pants – sweats

Tough Mudder – one of the world's toughest mud runs. See https://toughmudder.com.au/ for the Aussie version

Ute – a pickup truck

1

CONNOR

CONNOR GAVE A BARELY PERCEPTIBLE NOD AS HE GREETED ROB, AS the other man snuck through the doorway of the crumbling stone building. Following orders to find and neutralize the terrorist insurgents in the area, Connor's unit had fanned out and crept around the dusty shell, scoping out the landscape.

He pushed his combat helmet up a little and wiped a bead of sweat from his forehead with the back of his hand. He'd never get used to the Afghan heat. And it'd been a scorcher. The dry desert wind was so hot it was like breathing in fire, and over summer, it didn't quit for months on end. The long days were always the same—sun beating down on them from dawn to dusk. The nights were just as bad, with temperatures hardly dropping. Connor often lay under the squeaky fan in their bunk room—the same one that barely circulated the oppressive hot air—and dreamed of the ocean breezes back home.

Drawing his assault rifle up high, Connor looked through the scope, methodically checking the roofline and each of the windows of the squat buildings surrounding them. Even though air support had confirmed there were signs of recent activity, nothing out of the ordinary was visible from the laneway.

While Rob double-checked the same line Connor had just scoped out, he whispered, "You rocked 'Everlong' last night." The Foo Fighters classic was one of Connor's favourites, but he'd only managed to nail it the night before, sitting in the mess hall of the Allied Forces compound. He grinned. They'd had fun—Rob playing a jerry-rigged set of drums and him on an acoustic guitar singing their hearts out.

"You've got mad skills on the buckets, but that singing? Damn, it was shithouse." At Connor's playful jab, Rob snickered, the unit falling silent once more as they continued their watch.

Connor shuffled forward a little and pivoted, Rob mirroring his movement so they checked each other's lines before spinning back around so he could move again. Taking that single step put him in front of what used to be a window, the building now open to the elements. Through it, Connor saw another window and beyond that, the alleyway around the corner where they would regroup with the other half of their unit.

In the eerie near silence, he heard the click of a firing pin being cocked. It echoed through his brain as loud as a gunshot, setting every nerve ending on high alert. Who did it? And then he spied him. The person—he guessed a man—was covered with a sand-coloured blanket. The slightest movement of the malleable material caught his attention. Almost directly ahead, two stories above them. Silently, Connor signalled for the others, pointing to where he had seen the enemy. Hyperaware of his surroundings, he didn't take his eyes off the target. Time slowed, as did his heartbeat while Connor readied his weapon, flicking off the safety. His hands rocksteady, he waited for the order to engage. It would only be given when they were certain no unarmed locals would be caught in a gunfight.

Next to him, Rob dropped to one knee and raised the gun

scope to his eye. "Insurgent, rooftop, at one o'clock," he whispered, his throat mic transmitting the broadcast to the other men in their unit.

"Hold your cover," their commanding officer ordered.

A couple of barely audible shuffles on the hard-packed earth behind Connor was the only indication that the men in his unit adjusted their positions, covering their six. More locations were given, more of their foes identified. They weren't surrounded, but they might as well have been. And his unit had been given a hold order. Powerless to do anything but wait until they got more intel, this was the part he hated.

The wait and see game they were playing had Connor on edge, ratcheting up the tension. Their commanding officer's shouted order, "Fire at will," shattered the relative calm before the storm. His timing couldn't have been any better scripted, barely a second before the coordinated movement of blankets sliding off weapons happened before their eyes. The insurgents made the mistake of exposing their positions, leaving Connor and the other soldiers to pick them off. Strategically hidden, their Australian Army unit was as protected as they could be in a war zone. The mud and clay houses surrounding them took the majority of fire as the deep boom of their assault rifles rent the air. The recoil from each shot Connor let loose was enough to dislocate an inexperienced shooter's arm. But Connor had been trained by the best. And the six years' experience he'd had in hell holes just like this one kept his shooting arm rocksteady under fire.

All hell broke loose as their fire was returned, the unmistakeable tinny clatter of the enemy's AK47s drowned out by the boom of their more powerful weapons. The acrid smell of cordite filled his nose until he could taste it, dust and smoke creating a haze around them. The danger and adrenaline were like a shot to his heart, kick-starting it into a pounding rhythm.

His brothers and sisters in arms let rip with their full arsenal, and Connor panned his gun, searching for his next target. Instinctively, his sight was drawn back to the spot where he'd initially seen movement only moments earlier. The glint of metal winked in the sunlight, capturing his eye. It wasn't the weapon he'd seen. It was something else—a ring perhaps, or a watch. But there was no mistaking the outline of the launcher and the rocket attached to it.

"RPG." he yelled, depressing the trigger on his rifle to neutralize the target.

"Take cover," his commanding officer yelled, rounding his weapon and firing with Connor in the direction of the rooftop. Their bullets hit their mark, a patch of scarlet blossoming out over the sand-coloured clothing worn by the enemy shooter. Bullets zinged past Connor, his latest shot exposing his position to the insurgents.

An almighty explosion tore through the alley before them, the shockwave launching Connor into the air. He hit the wall hard, driving the air from his lungs. His body reeled from the impact. The instant thump of his head and his vision—foggy around the edges—told him his combat helmet had taken a hit that would otherwise have scrambled his brains. The ringing in his ears was a piercing scream, increasing in frequency until it made him nauseous. Winded, he struggled to take a breath, panic involuntarily welling inside him. Sure, he'd been injured before, but never incapacitated. And he was a sitting duck until he could think straight and get his body to cooperate. Disoriented, Connor fought the fear and took stock of his surroundings. Now inside the building he'd been using as shelter, he was safe for the moment. But he was also trapped, having to traverse past the open windows to get back to his former position. Connor lifted his gun—held to him with the strap attached to his flack vest—checking it would still fire. The screaming pain of flesh tearing had him gasping for breath and looking over his shoulder. He was impaled on a piece of jagged glass, wedged in tight under the Kevlar protecting his body.

The gunfight continued around him, but it faded to white noise when the dust cleared enough that he could see Rob's convulsing form. Limbs splayed at an awkward angle like a ragdoll had been dropped onto the floor, Rob's muscles spasmed. *No. No, no, no.* Connor gritted his teeth and fought another wave of nausea when he pulled away, dislodging the glass from his shoulder.

Still dizzy, he then crawled over to his friend, forgetting about the danger lurking outside. Blood oozed from Rob's neck, the crimson stain on his uniform growing unchecked with each beat of Rob's heart. Horror filled Connor. He couldn't lose his friend. He wouldn't. Rob struggled, fighting to take a rasping breath as blood pooled around him. It was like a horror movie, but one that Connor couldn't press Pause on, one he knew he'd never forget. Every memory of Rob laughing, of the warm glow of pure love Rob got when talking about his wife, of every prank and every serious moment they'd shared over the years hit Connor with the force of a Mack truck. He had to save him. "Stick with me, mate. I'm gonna get you outta here." Connor frantically pressed a hand down on Rob's bloodied throat, trying desperately to stem the bleeding while he searched for a safe exit. He needed to get Rob out of there, needed to get him to safety. *Oh God, no. Please, please let him be okay.*

"Con, left pocket. For Molly." Rob's voice came out with a distinctive gurgle, blood pooling in his wind pipe, quickly drowning him. Tears sprang to Connor's eyes, his heart shattering into a million pieces. This man had been his brother and his confidant since basic training. He couldn't lose him. Connor loved him like family. A piece of him died as the light in his friend's eyes began to fade.

"Live. Go home to them," Rob gasped, forcing the words out while his body shut down. He stilled slowly, but Connor knew the instant he'd lost him. With shaky hands, he closed Rob's eyelids. Taking a steadying breath, Connor nodded, psyching himself up. He took the folded note from Rob's top left pocket—the one directly over his heart—and stuffed it in his jacket. He kissed the other man's forehead, resting his own against it.

"Rest easy, my friend. I'll take you home."

Sucking in another breath and compartmentalising the pain of loss so fresh it hadn't properly sunk in yet, Connor raised his gun again and crept to the nearest window. It wasn't revenge pulsing through his veins, but justice. Rob's killers weren't going to get to face court though. He'd pick off each and every one of them, leaving them bloodied in the dirt to protect his other brothers and sisters. Through the magnification on the scope, he made out shadows inside the building closest to the other half of his separated unit. He fired, pausing only to check that his target dropped before moving onto the next.

The return bullets aimed at them slowed, then stopped and with it, the ache in his arm intensified. Connor found his throat mic, which had dislodged when he'd hit the wall, and reattached it, answering his commanding officer's status check. Rob wasn't the only loss they'd suffered. Two more of their team were down—one with minor injuries and another in need of emergency treatment.

The *thwap, thwap, thwap* of helicopters in the distance grew louder until the noise drowned out everything else. He peered out of the window to see two gunships covering the hovering medivac chopper, paramedics zip-lining down ropes. A stretcher followed them down on the winch into their waiting arms. Their commanding officer and Blair, another member of his unit, carried Ross to the medics, lying him down on the stretcher. Another stretcher followed, and Connor knew this one was for Rob. He waved them over before kneeling by his friend. "Medics are here to take ya home, Rob." Connor lifted his protective glasses and wiped the tears forming with the back of his dirty hand. "I love you, man."

Six months later

Connor stepped out of the plane door onto the mobile steps and looked around. Twilight was falling, the sky a wash of pinks and oranges as the sun set over the Gold Coast hinterland. He couldn't see it from the airport, but Connor could picture the rolling waves of the Pacific to the east. He couldn't wait to lay eyes on the ocean again.

Walking across the tarmac toward the terminal, the salty sea breeze teased him—he could smell it even over the avgas—the balmy breeze caressing his skin. The warmth was a welcome change from the out-of-season chilly weather in the Adelaide hills, and before that, the icy winter in the Afghanistan desert.

He'd been discharged from active service. He was done, a civilian now, a scary thought.

The automatic doors whooshed open and the air-conditioned comfort greeted him. The building was jam-packed, the noise from the crowd a low hum. He passed straight through, heading for the luggage carousel and his two bags, trying his best to dodge the crowds milling around waiting. Spotting his duffle, he snatched it up before collecting his guitar case. Connor then joined the line for a taxi. He was tired—it'd been a hard journey so far. Seeing Rob's widow, Molly, was as heart-breaking as he'd dreaded it would be. But he couldn't come home without seeing her. He'd long since sent her Rob's note, but he owed it to her, to Rob, to tell her as much as he could about Rob's death.

He took a steadying breath and let a smile play on his lips. He couldn't wait to see Levi, his big blond mate again, and the girl who'd captured his friend's heart. Their house wasn't far from the airport. Barely thirty minutes had passed when they pulled up in front of Levi and Katy's 1970s cottage. Connor sat and stared at the house. *Am I really doing this? I left because of them. Why am I back? Because they're my family and I couldn't stay away.* The taxi driver's words roused him. "Mate, you all right? This is it, yeah?"

The house had been partly renovated since he was there a few years earlier. Instead of the reddish-brown bricks, the walls had been rendered and were painted taupe and black. The garden had been cleaned up too, but there was no mistaking it was Levi and Katy's place. "Yeah, we're here. Sorry, spaced out for a sec."

He paid the driver and hauled his gear from the taxi. Finding himself standing at the bottom of the front stoop by the front door, Connor froze. Voices and laughter carried through to him. His heart clenched. God, he'd missed that, missed being so light-hearted. His unit hadn't laughed much in the six months after Rob had died. His absence had hit them hard, Connor especially.

Despite being always surrounded by people, Connor was lonely, and hearing the happy sounds of his oldest friend, Katy, and their visitors conversing, only reminded him of how much he'd lost, and of what he'd had to give up when he was discharged. Six months without one of his brothers had been hell, and now he was out of the army, he wouldn't see any of the men or women in his unit. Not regularly anyway. Sure, he'd keep in touch with them, pay forward the kindness Katy and Levi had shown him when he was posted in that hell hole, but it wasn't the same as being there in the thick of it with them. *But everything had changed after Rob died anyway.*

The sound of a car backfiring startled Connor out of his reverie. Instantly, he was transported back to the little village he'd patrolled with Rob by his side, every one of his senses conjuring up a picture so real it hit him like a freight train, making him stagger back under the weight of it all. The click of the firing pin being cocked had him reaching for his gun, its weight comforting. Time slowed as he lined up the shot, the bullet passing through the chamber when he'd squeezed the trigger and finding its mark. The deep boom of his rifle and the clatter of the AK47s. The cries and screams of agony from his bullets. The dust in his eyes, kicked up by each bullet ricocheting, and the acrid smell of the cordite, so strong he could sometimes taste it for days.

The noises escalated—the hiss of the rocket propelled grenade followed by a thundering boom as it exploded, drowning out even the rushing of blood in Connor's ears. He waited for the shockwave to hit him, but it never came. The pain didn't either. The fear in the air—of extremists, of death, of living a life after the war—enveloped him, his body instantly switching to fight mode. The absolute and utter terror in which he'd lived, forced to face his mortality when he was on the wrong end of a weapon and fight for his life had his training kicking in—they'd taught him to win or be buried. There was blood everywhere, splatters on walls and in the dry, dusty dirt, pools of it spreading over the hard-packed soil, literally draining the life out of Rob. He lunged forward ready to strike, but instead, Connor tripped and hit a hard surface stopping him short. Blinking, his vision cleared. What the fuck? He was on his knees on the middle step, his guitar case having hit the front door when he fell.

"Oh, God. No," he breathed, horrified at himself. He tried to suck in a breath, but he couldn't. His vision darkened around the edges and his heart slammed in his chest.

Connor sagged, the fight draining out of him. What the fuck was he doing? There was no threat here. No, that wasn't right. He was the danger. He wasn't even fit to meet his friends again. He shouldn't have gone there, shouldn't have believed that he could re-enter civilian life. He was putting at risk the two people he'd give his life to protect. There was no way he'd do that. Connor pushed to his feet, picked up his guitar and turned, the weight of the world on his shoulders. He blew out a breath and took the first step away from Levi and Katy. They needed to be protected from him. They were better off without him. Knowing that, though, didn't make it hurt any less.

Levi

The bang at the front door had Levi getting up to investigate. The sight before him shocked him to his core. Connor was unmistakeable, but the man he saw wasn't the fun-filled, quick-to-laugh boy he'd known. No, the Connor walking away from him, not even slowing his stride when Levi called out, "Hey," to him, was a shell of his former self. Even from behind he looked entirely defeated, beaten down. Lean shoulders hunched, hands in his pockets, head lowered, he took another step away. But his oldest friend—the man who took a piece of Levi with him when he'd joined the army six years ago—wasn't supposed to arrive for another day.

Was he really real? Actually home? Nervous energy assailed him, excitement filling his veins. "Con?" he called, wonder in his voice. Connor stopped midstride, and Levi wanted to laugh and cry, to grab hold of the man before him and make him giggle like they'd done as children. Unable to help himself, he launched himself off the steps and reached out, grasping his elbow and drawing Connor to him.

When he turned, Levi's breath caught. He was crushed by the sadness radiating from Connor—his normally imposing six-foot-five frame turned in on itself. The light in those deep, dark eyes had faded, his forehead marred by a deep crease. Melancholy surrounded him like a fog, squeezing the life out of him. The sight had a lump forming in Levi's throat. Wishing he could take away Connor's pain, all the evil he'd seen and lived through, Levi's heart broke. His friend's life had changed far too much over the years they'd been apart. His hair—a buzz cut—gave him a rough edge, highlighting the war machine the army had turned this gentle soul into. Anger filled him, mourning for the hardships Connor had endured while Levi lived the easy life.

"You're here," he murmured as he pulled his friend into a hug, crushing Connor in his grip. Lean muscle met his hands, unyielding even as Levi pulled him closer. Levi's grip practically begged the other man to hug him back. Relief and the love borne of two decades of friendship overwhelmed him. It'd been far too long since he'd seen his best friend, since he could judge with his own eyes that he was safe. Levi didn't let go until Con sagged against him and returned the embrace.

"I'm sorry," Connor mumbled in his ear. "I need to go."

"No," he challenged. His friend was back with them, and this time, Levi wasn't letting him disappear. Connor was going to stick around whether he liked it or not.

Levi loosened his hold and pulled back. Wrapping his fingers around Connor's biceps, he assessed his friend. "We've missed you, Con. This is your home. You can't leave. Hell, Katy'll have my balls if you do."

"Where is she?" He watched as Connor's eyes flicked to the house and filled with something he didn't recognize. Trepidation? Nerves, perhaps?

"Inside." Levi pointed to the door. "You made it just in time. We've got Katy's cousin Nick and his wife over for dinner."

"I'm sorry, I didn't mean to interrupt. I'll...." He trailed off. Eyes glazing over, Levi could see him slipping away from him. What horrors were pulling him back, drowning him?

"Con," Levi prompted.

Connor looked down, not meeting Levi's gaze as he spoke. "A car backfired and it took me back to one of the battles. Right into the thick of it." The other man shook in his arms, and Levi held him tighter, drawing him back into his embrace.

"It's okay, Con. You're safe here." Levi loosened his grip on Connor and squeezed his arms before dropping his hands. "Come on, you're not leaving." Levi motioned to the front door and smiled. Neither of them moved though. Levi could tell Connor still needed a moment before facing the others.

"You haven't changed your aftershave," Connor murmured, wonder evident in his voice. "In all these years, you've still got the same one." He was shocked Con even knew the smell. Then again, it was always the small things his friend had noticed.

Levi's cheeks heated as they walked toward the front steps. With a hand on the door, he smiled sheepishly, embarrassed at his own predictability, and ridiculously happy that Connor would remember something so insignificant. "What can I say? Katy thinks it suits me." Truth be told, he just bought the same one—a blend of orange and cedar—whenever he needed a new bottle. He'd never even thought of changing it.

"Reminds me of our summers together as kids. Remember when we first started shaving and your dad got us the same kits?" Connor said as he smiled and reached up to pat Levi's scruffy cheek. The stubble he hadn't bothered to shave that morning was certainly thicker than the fuzz he had as a teenager, but he still couldn't compete with Connor's thicker stubble.

Levi threw his arm around Connor's shoulder again, playfully rubbing the top of his head with his knuckles as he laughed. "How could I forget? Best days ever. Beach cricket and bonfires. God, my bed always had so much sand in it whenever we crashed. Mum used to go nuts at us more for trailing grit through the house than breaking curfew." He'd always been close to Connor. They'd done all the important things together; his childhood was filled with memories of the two of them side by side. Then when Connor's drunken father had disappeared without a trace, he'd just moved in, and Levi's parents had fought it out with Child Services. There had never been a question of him staying; his parents had made sure that Connor never had to leave.

But things started to change in their final year of uni. Levi knew exactly what he wanted to do. He had the grand plan mapped out, and believe it or not, he'd managed to achieve most of the things he'd set out to do. But Connor was never so sure, and then bam, he dropped the bombshell that he was giving up his studies. It was like he was running from something, dashing away to join the army to fight a battle he'd never seemingly cared about before. Levi and Katy were left in his dust trail, waiting for him to come home to them. That was the worst thing about his being away—the waiting to hear, the never knowing where he was and whether he was safe. Levi's need to know had turned into an obsession, religiously checking the Defence Force's media releases every day and watching the news morning and night. Every day he didn't hear of an injured or killed soldier filled him with a sense of relief, knowing they were one day closer to Connor eventually coming home. But the relief was always short-lived, knowing his best friend would be out there, doing God knew what the very next day.

To top it off, Levi still had no idea why Connor had left. *It doesn't matter. He's here. He's back.* Giddy excitement filled him, and he couldn't help but grin. It widened when Connor reflected his smile, his perfect white teeth a stark contrast to his deeply tanned skin. Levi pulled him closer, hugging him hard. "Welcome home, mate."

"It's good to be here, Lee. I missed you guys."

Connor hefted his duffle bag up his shoulder, and Levi reached out to take it. It occurred to him that he hadn't seen any other luggage. Connor only had his duffle and his guitar case, not that the presence of the guitar was a surprise—he never went anywhere without it. "Is this it?"

"Yeah. When you spend a few years on deployment, you only travel with the essentials. Apart from Dad's car, this is everything I own."

"Katy's gonna have a field day taking you shopping." Levi faked an exaggerated shudder. "Can you tee it up when I'm filming though? I've been exposed to that kind of torture before."

"There's this thing called the web. Great for shopping." Levi couldn't help but laugh at Connor's playful patronising.

Jumping back to his reference about filming, Connor asked, "How is work by the way?" as he leaned against the brick wall outside.

"Good. You got the pics we sent from the award ceremony, didn't you?" Katy always made sure to update him every day. He'd often go to bed to find her sending a bunch of pics to Connor, emailing him with whatever they'd got up to that day. It was her way of letting him know they were waiting for him to come home.

"Yeah, looked like fun."

"It was." Levi nodded. "What about you? What do you think you'll do now you're out?"

"Honestly, I dunno. I'm gettin' a new tat, and I'm gonna fix up my dad's car so it's running again. Then I s'pose I'll find a place." Connor shrugged and shook his head. "Maybe go back to school? I don't exactly have many marketable civilian skills."

"Well, I'm glad your tat is a top priority." Levi laughed and pulled open the door.

Connor paused before entering and looked back at the driveway. Levi's car was parked out there, together with Katy's cute hatch and her cousin's BMW. "Your bike in the garage? Show it to me later, yeah?"

He sighed. "Never did it up. It's still sitting in the garage in pieces. The producers offered me a company car, so I drive that." He pointed to the white sedan sitting in the drive. It was boring as shit, awful to drive and so not him, but it was also free.

"Huh," Connor remarked. A bike was the one thing Levi had always dreamed of having, and sure, he'd bought the frame and most of the parts to put together a sick Harley, but he'd never done it, never managed to take the step of assembling it. Part of that was because of Connor. Levi could have easily sent it to a mechanic, but it was always something the two of them had planned on doing together.

But Connor had lived his life, not holding onto old dreams. Maybe Levi should have done the same. Levi was kind of disgusted with himself that he'd never even started fixing the bike, but every time he saw the parts in the garage, thought about starting it, he missed his best friend so damn much. It was easier avoiding it than facing the possibility that they'd never get the chance to do it together.

Levi held the door open, ushering Connor through first. He couldn't help but admire the man who stepped past him. When he'd left, he was a boy. They both were. Connor had always been good-looking, always a ladies' man, but he'd lost his baby face, and now that Levi had gotten over the shock of seeing his friend again, he could appreciate just how commanding he was. Dark features and a tall, lean frame, he moved with feline grace— almost like he prowled. And Levi was captivated, unable to tear his gaze away from his friend. *God, it's good to have him back.*

"Everything okay?" Katy called out, poking her head into the hall. He smiled at the unmitigated glee that quickly overtook her shock upon seeing Connor. Then the whirlwind that was Katy as she sprinted up the hall hit. Dropping his guitar case off his shoulder, Levi watched as it hit the floor and Katy launched herself into Connor's arms. She wrapped around him like a monkey, holding him tight as she whispered something in his ear. Connor towered over her, but wrapped in his arms, they were perfect together; the two most important people in his world. Her long dark hair, silky soft to the touch, was almost the same colour as Connor's, and their tans were alike too. Levi knew from intimate experience that hers covered every inch of her body. *Does Connor's?* Surprised at his train of thought, he focussed on Katy again. Her curves and those blue eyes, which sparkled with mirth, had drawn him in at first. She was, in his mind, the most beautiful woman on the planet, and he wasn't ashamed to admit he'd fallen hard and fast for her. As he'd gotten to know her, that love had strengthened. Her talent and zest for life, mixed with her spunky attitude livened up his soul. His cock didn't complain either—she was a wildcat in bed, and he loved every minute they were together.

At first, Levi had been jealous of the ease of Connor and

Katy's friendship. Connor had never particularly liked any of the girls he'd dated previously—he'd begrudgingly put up with them, but never made much of an effort. Yet with Katy, it was different. The two of them had clicked and become fast friends. Levi recognized the same thing had happened when Connor befriended him as a kid—it was as if Connor was a sun and Levi had become snared in his orbit, the light from his cheeky personality illuminating Levi's world. But it was different too— Katy had fallen for Levi, not Connor. Yet their connection was undeniable. It was an easy friendship, one that quickly morphed into the three of them becoming inseparable. It took a bit of adjusting after Connor had left, but his and Katy's relationship was rock solid. Now that Connor was back, he selfishly hoped they'd pick up where they left off—that he'd have his best mate back. But Levi had to stay focussed in the present, not the distant past or where they were heading. He couldn't, wouldn't plan every minute detail of his life. If Katy taught him anything, it was to live life to the fullest.

Levi pushed the door closed and turned back to follow them into the living room. Connor had already made it halfway down the hall, arm in arm with his girl. *Live in the now, dude.* He smiled and quickened his step, not wanting to miss out on a thing.

Hanging back, Levi watched from the edge of the room as Connor looked around, taking in the renovations he and Katy had made to the living space of their little house. Everything had changed inside, but it wasn't until about a year earlier when they'd finally hung all the pictures on the wall that it became home. Seeing all of his and Katy's most memorable moments always made him grin. But for every photo of them together, there was another one of Connor—a few with him and his army brothers and sisters, his graduation from basic training, the last pic they'd taken together before he flew out for the first time, and the selfie they'd snapped lazing down on their favourite beach the last time he'd visited. That one—with arms wrapped around each other and bright smiles—held pride of place as the biggest photo in the middle of the wall. Levi remembered the day like it was yesterday.

"Smile," Katy ordered as she sat down between them, still topless from her sun bathing. She was half sitting on his lap while leaning into Connor. And damn, the chemistry was flowing hard. Levi's dick had been half-hard all day and now was no exception. Handing her phone to Connor—who had the longest reach of them all—she playfully squeezed Levi's package as she innocently smiled at the camera and snuggled into their friend. Levi's moan was followed by Connor's rough intake of breath, and Levi's dick pulsed harder.

"Done," Connor murmured, his voice a rasp as he lowered the mobile. Katy looked at the picture and smiled, turning to Connor and brushing her hand over his face.

"You've got sand in your beard, boo." The adoration in Connor's eyes as he stared at Katy was obvious, even to Levi. The tender, lingering kiss Connor pressed to her lips had Levi's heart skipping a beat. Every time he saw a similar moment between the two of them, it always roused the same reaction.

Startled out of their moment by a bird chirping, Connor jerked back, and Katy smiled sheepishly at Levi. He didn't hesitate as he pressed his lips to Katy's, teasing the seam of her lips with his tongue. It wasn't staking his claim as it was a desire as deep as the oceans and as vast as the universe to connect them together again. She opened to him, and Levi deepened the kiss, making love to her mouth. Finally breaking the kiss, he turned to Connor. It surprised him that Connor hadn't pulled away until he realized why—Levi held onto his shoulder, stroking his thumb along the smooth skin of Connor's collarbone. Drawing him closer, Levi hugged them both tight, breathing in the smells of the ocean and summer, his lips ghosting over Connor's cheek when he couldn't hold on any longer.

That was the last time they'd seen Connor. And watching

the look on his face, his gaze flipping between him and Katy, his smile soft, it was obvious that he remembered taking the photo too.

"You kept it," he voiced to Katy, turning her face toward him with a finger under her chin. Wonder laced his tone. "Feels like yesterday and another lifetime ago all at the same time."

"I never would have deleted it," Katy replied, her arm still tightly wrapped around Connor's waist. "Now come on, dinner's ready."

Remembering they had guests, Levi startled when Nick spoke. "Con?" Nick laughed and hugged his friend.

Emma reached out to shake Connor's hand. The slight tremor Levi saw when Connor reciprocated made a knot twist hard in his gut. Emma's smile was warm when she introduced herself adding, "So nice to meet you."

"You too, Emma. I'm Connor."

"Been a long time, Con." Nick took him into a one-armed hug, worry written in his pulled together brows as he stepped back. "Bud, you okay? You're shaking."

"He had a flashback." Levi explained as he wrapped his arm around Connor's shoulder, silently supporting him. With Katy on one side of Connor and him on the other, Levi knew they were bracketing him, the three of them united, showing him they'd always support him. But that's what they did—stood together strong. It's what they'd always done. Even if Connor had left them and was facing demons in his own head because of the horrors he'd lived through, Connor had come back to them.

"Yeah, I have good days and bad ones. The memories kick my ass sometimes, but the counsellor I had before they discharged me helped. He referred me to someone local so I can keep going. I've got my first appointment coming up, so...."

Katy

"Boo, you're exhausted." Katy smiled down at Con, sitting half asleep on the couch. The pet name had started as a joke when Con had copped a busted up nail by slamming his thumb in the door of a car he'd been tinkering with. When Katy saw the Band-Aid around it, she'd teased him about having a boo boo, and it'd stuck.

"I've set you up in the spare room. Wanna come get settled?"

"Thanks, Cupcake." He stood slowly, taking a moment to shake the sleep beginning to take over. "Lead the way."

After she'd shown Con to his room, Katy entered the one she shared with Levi and closed the door gently. She leaned back against it, closing her eyes. She could sense her man close to her —he was always so warm, such a rock-solid strength. "He was hurt, Lee. His shoulder is all scarred up." A sob hitched in her throat, and she leaned into Levi's embrace.

"He's here with us, and he's safe now. We don't have to be scared for him anymore."

"I missed him, babe. I know it sounds ridiculous, but a part of me was missing when he was gone." Levi smiled softly at her, and Katy knew she'd just voiced exactly what her boyfriend had thought so many times before. Levi had taken Con's enlistment hard. He'd grieved for months for his best friend, and it hurt her watching him missing his partner in crime so desperately. They'd been inseparable for such a long part of their lives that suddenly apart, Katy knew he'd felt alone, lonely, even though their relationship was strong.

All her friends were getting married—it was all they talked about. They'd asked her time and again why Levi hadn't proposed, why she wasn't pushing him. It only took one of them to see the wall of photos in their living room to have a go at Levi saying that there were three people in their relationship rather than two. Katy had brushed it off. She was never in competition with Connor for Levi's affection; it'd never been like that between them. How could she be jealous that a piece of Levi's heart was missing, gone with the man who was his childhood best friend? In the short time she'd known Con, he'd captured her heart too. She loved him as much as Levi did, and the count-less emails they'd shared, secrets they'd revealed, and fears they'd spoken of had strengthened that friendship over the years.

And now the light in Levi's eyes was back. The man holding her wasn't worrying anymore. He wasn't scared that his best friend could easily die by the enemy's hand. Levi had come to life again in those few hours since Con had arrived, and the joy of seeing it made her heart explode with love for her man.

She cupped his face, and he pinned her against the door, kissing her deeply. A slow melding of their mouths, while he undressed and worshipped every inch of her body over and over again, had Katy breathing hard, quickly taking her to the knife's edge of bliss. Sensation ricocheted around her body, stealing her breath. Levi down on his knees, his gaze filled with pent-up desire and need, had Katy catapulting off the edge. She couldn't keep her eyes open as her orgasm washed over her. Moaning Levi's name, she floated as her heartbeat thundered in her veins, her breath sawing in and out of her lungs. The endorphins crashed around in her body, reviving her orgasm when Levi lifted and pressed into her in one slow stroke.

Her second orgasm was a slow burn, consuming her as it went on and on. Levi was right there with her, stilling as he found his own ecstasy. Grunting, he pressed his face against her shoulder, brushing his lips over her collarbone. It made her shiver, and when he did it again, she laughed.

Carrying her, Levi staggered towards the bed, and they collapsed on it, a tangle of sweaty, satiated limbs. Curled around her, Levi was soon fast asleep, but it didn't come as easily for Katy. Her body still tingling, she lay awake thinking about the man in their guest room and the scars marring his shoulder and back. He'd never told them he was injured, and it came as a shock seeing the angry red lines when he'd peeled off his snug black T-shirt. Her heart broke knowing neither she nor Levi could have helped him. Had he been in hospital? How long had he suffered in pain? She knew he suffered from PTSD; he'd told them that was the reason he'd been discharged. But seeing the physical signs as well as how shaken up he was after his flash-back, had every instinct telling her that their friend, their brave, loyal warrior needed them more than ever.

Katy jolted awake, her body suddenly on high alert. Blinking her tired eyes and waiting for her sleep-addled brain to catch up to her tense muscles, she heard the noise again. Groans and mumbles. *Is it Con?* "No, Rob, stay with me. Keep focussed on me. Come on, open your eyes. Stay with me." His pained sobs were getting louder and more distressed, crying out, "No, no, no, buddy, no."

She threw off the covers and shook Levi awake. "Lee, babe, get up. Con's having a nightmare." It only took him a moment before he launched out of bed, pulling a pair of boxer briefs from his drawer and tossing Katy his T-shirt that lay discarded on the floor. Dashing into the hallway, they were both still pulling on their clothes as Levi twisted the knob and stumbled into Connor's room.

Katy flicked on the lamp and sat down on the bed, running her fingertips down Con's injured arm. Drenched in sweat, the sheet tangled around his naked hips, Connor tossed and turned.

"Con, you're safe. You're home. Wake up, boo," Katy crooned, fighting back tears. Seeing him like this destroyed her, ravaged her heart like the bloodied aftermath of a battle. Levi sat down on the other side of the bed, and gently shook him awake. The pain etched on Levi's features was as deep as Con's anguish. She couldn't erase his memories, but she would do everything in her power to help him heal. Katy gently wiped the tears staining his cheeks with her thumbs and Con blinked open his eyes.

In the lamplight, she saw his pupils blown with pain and fear as Con looked sightlessly around. His muscles were locked tight, and tension radiated from him as he struggled to get up, fighting their gentle touches. Katy understood in that moment how much his fight-or-flight impulse had kept him safe. Even half awake, his body was primed to attack whoever stood in the way of his survival. But she wasn't scared of him. She didn't see him as dangerous, or broken. No, this was Con, *their* Connor. Levi laid a steadying hand on Con's chest, not holding him down, just connecting them together while she kept touching him, continued speaking softly to him. Letting her gentle caresses bring him fully awake, it took a moment for Con to focus on her. And when he did, Katy's heart stuttered. His heartache was right there, visible in the slumped set of his shoulders, his watery eyes. His vulnerability—so different from the strength of her soldier—was like a knife to her heart. She didn't hesitate as she took him into her arms. "It's okay, boo. It's over. We've got you."

"Oh God, I'm sorry," he breathed, hugging her hard. Levi's strong arms wound around both of them, protecting them in his embrace as Con's chest heaved, his heart hammering against Katy's ribs while he cried on her shoulder. She ran her fingers through Con's spiky hair doing the only thing she could while his tears fell—she comforted him. Slowly, he settled, but she didn't stop playing with his hair. Levi's arms still around them both and her ministrations had Con's tense muscles slowly relaxing.

"Lie down, boo. I'll stay with you until you're asleep," Katy whispered to him.

"We both will, Con. You're home now, we're here for you," Levi rumbled, his voice still sleep roughened.

"I'm sorry." Con shook his head. Katy didn't understand why he kept apologizing. How could he be worried about waking them? "I didn't want to stick you with my problems, but I was being selfish. I should have stayed away."

"We're here for you, Con. You aren't alone anymore." Levi rubbed his hand over Con's shoulders. The remaining tension melted from the other man's body, leaving him trembling in Katy's arms.

"Do you want to talk about what happened?" she probed gently, kissing his temple. His head against her shoulder, his big body curled around hers, he stiffened when she asked the question.

"I can't tonight, Cupcake." He shook his head and wiped his eyes again. "It's too raw."

Levi rubbed the other man's arms, soothing him. "Close your eyes, Con. Get some sleep. We'll stay as long as you want."

Con laid down and took a deep breath, letting it out slowly. But he looked like a deer in headlights, terrified to close his eyes. She knew she had to be strong for him, but she couldn't hold back her tears. She was so very grateful he'd come back to them. But he was hurting, and seeing it so raw and unfiltered, ripped her heart open, leaving a great gushing wound there. She wanted to share his pain, to relieve some of his burden. *But can I?* Katy curled into his warm body, resting her head on his shoulder, petting his chest, giving him what little comfort she could. She was on top of the sheet, Con under. Levi was the same— stretched out on the other side of him above the covers. She caught Levi's eye and smiled sadly as he kept a hand on Con's shoulder.

2

CONNOR

A SHEEN OF SWEAT COATED HIS SKIN, TYPICAL FOR SUMMER NIGHTS in the desert. But something was off. Half asleep and dazed, Connor's head pounded out a beat like he'd partied far too hard at a nightclub. He moaned. Hangovers were a bitch. But he didn't remember drinking anything. Memories of the previous night's dinner party flooded back—good food, great company, albeit a bit uncomfortable to begin with because of his episode, and later lots of laughter. The stress, the self-doubt had faded away in the safety of his friends' home. But that'd been over-shadowed by his nightmare. It was so damn vivid. He could practically taste the cordite hanging in the air from the gunfire, smell the copper tinge of blood blooming out over his friend's throat and pooling on the ground below him. Watching his brother in arms die before him again never got easier. Seeing the light fade from his eyes, the spark of life dying with him clawed his heart out every time he experienced it. Connor wished it was the first time, but the nightmares were persistent bastards. The counsellors said that was normal. Didn't make him feel any better about it though.

He sighed. The migraine-like headache he always ended up

with after one of those dreams took a while to kick. Lifting his hand from its warm pillow of soft skin, Connor pressed his fingertips against his temple and rubbed. He opened his eyes after a time, squinting against the light. Luscious brown, silky hair glowed softly in the morning light and filled his vision. Katy was sharing his pillow, and this close, he could make out the auburn in the fine strands. Her back pressed to his front; he'd held her close as they'd slept soundly. But the fact that he was holding Katy didn't surprise him; he'd been drawn to her the first time they'd met. The surprise was to have Levi's arms wrapped around his own body. Plastered together from nose to tangled feet, the solid wall of muscle embracing him tight was grounding. He relaxed into Levi's touch and leaned in a little more, pulling Katy closer. It wasn't sexual—although his and Levi's morning wood and his hand on Katy's bare hip might suggest otherwise—it was comfort, a safe place from the world.

It was home.

As much as he should leave, as much as he knew staying to watch his two best friends love each other while he was alone would likely break his heart, he couldn't. Losing them again would be worse.

Lips against his shoulder, followed by a sensuous bite on muscle and Levi gripping his hip and grinding, had Connor sucking in a breath. He'd heard Levi and Katy the night before—how couldn't he? Fucking up against the door in the next bedroom over wasn't ever going to be quiet, and he'd felt like a total perv listening. But he'd laid there, stunned and torn over what he was feeling. Too tired to get up and put some music on his headphones, but suddenly too awake to fall asleep, Connor had listened to Levi and Katy make love, wishing he shared a connection like theirs. Had begged the universe for that kind of forever with someone. Now, the press of Levi's cock against him had Connor imagining what it would be like being with him.

The shock of it jarred him fully awake, and he lurched forward trying to get up but unable to because of the sheet trapping him in place. His movement jostled Katy.

"Hmm, yeah, I'm awake. What's wrong?" she rambled as she roused, sitting up.

"Shh, it's okay. Nothing's wrong." He reached out and took her hand as she looked around wide-eyed. "I got a fright when I woke up," Connor soothed, trying to play down the jackhammering of his heart and the reason why he'd practically thrown her out of bed.

"What time is it?" Levi mumbled from behind him.

"Oh, shit," Katy breathed. "We're late, Lee. You've gotta get outta here in twenty minutes, and I should already be at the shop. I've got a cake being picked up this morning, and I still need to do the finishing touches to it."

Connor tossed off the sheet and stood as Katy and Levi dashed out of the room to get ready, relieved they weren't going to stick around to dissect the clusterfuck of his nightmare and earlier flashback. "I'll get coffee on," he called out, walking to his bag to get fresh underwear. He didn't expect Katy to stick her head back in, and when she did, she copped an eyeful.

"Oh, um, thanks, boo. Coffee'd be great. Um," she stuttered, still staring at his semi-hard, pierced cock, "help yourself to whatever you...."

Connor laughed self-consciously, kind of flattered that Katy had lost track of what she was saying. "Cupcake, eyes up here." He pointed to his face. Her shock from hearing him and the deep blush staining her cheeks a rosy pink, made him laugh harder as he bent and rifled through his bag to find his last pair of clean underwear. Holding them against his groin, he watched her with interest. His skin pricked with awareness, her eyes on him setting every one of his nerve endings alight. Desire curled low in his gut. He tried to fight it, but the flush on Katy's cheeks had him wondering what other parts of her would grow pink when she was embarrassed or better yet, turned on. Oblivious to his inner turmoil, Katy ploughed on, trying desperately to save the conversation.

"I don't know what time I'll be finished. Do you want my car? You'll be stuck here. I don't want you to be stuck here." And her rambling was cute.

"I'm fine. I'll Uber to my tattoo guy and back." Checking the time on the alarm clock next to the bed had Connor moving. Levi was going to be late, and Katy already was. If they wanted coffee, he needed to get dressed.

Katy paused, waiting in the doorway as he slipped on the tight boxer shorts. Connor knew she wanted to say something more, but she was hesitating. Did he make her uncomfortable? Should he be sleeping with clothes on? Maybe he should, especially while he was bunking there.

"You have a Prince Albert." Her words were quiet, filled with surprise. "I didn't know you were pierced."

Connor gave her a lopsided smirk, trying to ease any discomfort she had around him. "Only the girls I've slept with know that."

"That's probably a long list. It's not exactly top secret information."

"It's not as long as you think, Cupcake. I don't exactly get around much." He wasn't defensive—never defensive with Katy —but he was a little sad. The truth was he hadn't even kissed a woman in a year.

She could read him well. But instead of pity at his sadness, she opted for humour, salaciously wiggling her eyebrows as she said, "Well, I know your secret now." He loved that about her— her playfulness never failed to make him smile.

"One of them." He shrugged, feigning a casual air and concentrating on willing down the thickening of his shaft.

Despite how damn inappropriate it was, his dick enjoyed the attention. It was nice to have a little for a change, even if it went with a healthy dose of guilt for even speaking with his best friend's girl about his cock.

"One? There's more?"

"Two others." Connor ground his teeth together, willing his dick down. If they kept this conversation up any longer, he'd be sporting a boner that he couldn't hide behind his underwear. Almost desperate to get her out of there without making either of them any more uncomfortable, Connor cut the conversation short. "But we'll have to talk about those another time. You're late." Katy nodded, smiled and sprinted away, giving Connor a chance to breathe. He sat on the end of the bed, resting his elbows on his knees. The last twenty-four hours, hell the last hour, had been surreal, like he was living in the twilight zone. A sexed up one at that. Both Levi and Katy had thrown him. He was kind of glad Levi hadn't woken up to find himself rubbing off against Connor. He could handle it, but he wasn't sure whether Levi could. And knowing his best friend had Connor's taste on his lips, that Levi had sunk his teeth into Connor's muscle? Connor shivered. That bite was hot as fuck, but what the hell? *Why am I even thinking that?* And then Katy checking him out? Her eyes were like velvet sliding over his skin. Decadent and taboo. Connor adjusted himself and took in a breath. Yeah, his head was spinning; he was overwhelmed.

Levi

"That's a wrap, everyone," Sam called out. Levi rubbed the towel over his face, wiping away the sweat from his brow, before stretching his tired arms above his head. He'd been filming at

Village Roadshow's studios that day, in front of the green screen. Wearing a Lycra body suit and enough sensors to detect the slightest muscle twitch, Levi was literally a science experiment for the day. They were filming a series on how muscles reacted to stimuli—he was demonstrating the effect of exercise on the body.

The show, *Challenge Accepted*, was aimed at young teens to change perceptions of body image, encourage physical activity and steer them away from drugs and alcohol consumption—all things Levi was passionate about. He was the host, the face of the show, and most of the time the guy who put his body on the line to accept the daily challenge. Every activity they filmed was in controlled conditions, minimising any risks, but it didn't reduce the physicality of his job. And that's what he loved about it—the rush. He wasn't just some personal trainer turned TV host. He was out there jumping out of planes, swimming with sharks, abseiling and whatever else DJ, his location manager, could think of to challenge Levi with. Whatever it was, it was usually a blast.

Levi pulled the last of the sensors off his skin, wincing at the tug on the hair of his inner thigh and pulled on his shorts and tee. "Thanks, Sam. Lemme know if you wanna re-shoot that last segment." Levi shook his head. *What a nightmare.* His guest host wouldn't stick to the script, kept adding in extra lines, and when Levi was cued in to speak, would talk over him. "I can come in anytime if you need me."

"I think we'll be right once it goes through editing. We can tidy up quite a bit of it. I think we'll be able to use enough to get this segment wrapped up."

The vibration in his back pocket had Levi holding up his index finger to Sam, asking him to wait a minute. He didn't recognize the number of the person calling, but that wasn't anything out of the ordinary. In his line of work, he often had friends of friends calling asking him for advice. "Hello."

"G'day, mate, it's me." Connor's deep voice resonated through the phone and Levi smiled. His friend was settling in, and it pleased Levi to no end. "This is my new number."

"Okay, cool. Whatcha up to?" Sam motioned to Levi in the direction of the staff car park. He nodded and followed, walking side by side between two of the tall industrial-looking steel sheds. Giant numbers were painted on the side of each building, a nine on the one closest to him. It was the largest sound stage in Village Roadshow's studio—the southern hemisphere in fact—and already had an impressive résumé of blockbuster films in its first year of operation.

Their shoes crunching on the loose gravel lining part of the asphalt road, Levi enjoyed being outdoors for the first time that day. The late afternoon sun shone down on them, the slight breeze cooling down the muggy weather. It'd probably rain later that night. It was steamy.

Connor replied to Levi's question, saying, "I've picked up my rental. It's as bad as your piece of shit." Levi could just picture the smirk on Connor's face as he rolled his eyes. "I got my phone and just finished getting my tat. Now I'm hungry. Wanna get some food?"

Levi looked at his watch. "Katy should be finished soon too. Was planning on going past her shop on my way home. We can pick her up and grab a pizza down the beach if you like?"

"No worries, I'll meet you there," Connor replied happily. The line clicked off and Levi smiled.

"I'd say that smile was for Katy, but...." Sam trailed off.

"It was Con, my best mate. He's finally home for good."

"He's the one who was serving in the Middle East, wasn't he?"

"Yeah." Levi couldn't help but smile again. He'd done a lot of that during filming too. What wasn't there to be happy about? Of course, he was a little confused if his reaction that morning was anything to go by. But he was wholeheartedly choosing to ignore the niggling in his gut that there had been some kind of fundamental shift in him. Things that he'd been trying to deny for a long-arsed time had seemed to click into place the night before with an ease that scared him. There were parts about himself he wasn't sure he wanted to give voice to yet, or ever. Things that would, no doubt, affect a lot more people than just him.

He pulled his car into the small strip of shops housing Delectable, Katy's cake shop and bakery. She'd started the little shop three years ago, and it'd grown in leaps and bounds since then. Learning her art from the best pastry chefs in the south-east, she quickly found her passion. It wasn't luck that'd made her such a roaring success. No, it was the hours she spent labouring away, perfecting each element of every cake she'd ever made. It didn't take long for her reputation to grow, leap-frogging her to the number one wedding cake bakery on the Gold Coast. And while she was working on growing that aspect of Delectable, she and Dylan, her new pastry chef, had managed to addict every person within a ten-minute drive of the shop to their delicate sweet tarts and cakes, and complex flavour combinations of the specialty macaroons they baked.

The building housing Katy's shop wasn't anything special, pretty nondescript actually—a single-storey, deep-red brick structure with white awnings. The handcrafted signs adorning those awnings and random collection of businesses somehow gave the centre a quirky character and irresistible charm. Who would have thought that a bottle-o, newsagent, a boutique dress store, antique furniture and Delectable would work? Katy had known it was the right spot the moment she'd seen it. And it hadn't let her down.

Unlocking the door to Delectable was like entering gustatory heaven. The cakes Katy baked were always to die for and the shop smelled just like her: sweet, with hints of vanilla and chocolate. Levi crossed the consultation area on his way to Katy's work area. The candy-striper feel to the waiting room was perfect for the shop. Decorated with light and dark pink satin striped wallpaper, the walls contrasted against the black couch and silver floor rug. The soft light from the understated chandelier and warm oak flooring gave the room some class. He loved it there. It was totally Katy, totally her work—feminine, bold, sexy, and sophisticated.

He paused to admire the latest mock cake before the window. The four tiers covered with preservative-laced icing was designed to look like it was draped in silver satin. Tiny roses, so intricate in their detail, ran along the base of each tier, each one a piece of art in itself. Love flooded his chest, leaving a warm tingly feeling in its wake. His girl had achieved her dream, and he was damn proud of everything she'd done. The awards, thank-you letters, and photos hanging on one of the walls showed just how much her hard work had paid off.

Levi headed to the back of the store, letting himself in through the pin-code protected door to see Katy. Unlike the consultation area, the kitchen she spent most of her time in was monotone—gleaming floor-to-ceiling stainless steel. Katy stood along a stretch of bench working on a partially completed cake which sat on a small trolley, her pastry tools on the only part of the workspace which hadn't been cleaned yet. Her eyes flicked up to his, and they held, Katy flashing him a grin before she turned her attention back to her project. Levi paused to admire her in her element, watching as she smoothed out a fold in the icing. The latest masterpiece she was working on was coming along. The sketch pinned to the wall showed him what the final design would look like—a champagne-coloured round hat box covered in a bow almost the same size as the cake. There was another sketch showing the detail on the brooch—silver antique filigree and pearl— pinned to the centre of the bow. Once finished, the walls of the cake would be covered in what looked like lace and crystals, which he knew from experience would be delicately sweet and crunchy.

He couldn't resist going to her then. Wrapping his arms around Katy's waist from behind, he kissed her temple. "You know, every time I pass through the front of the shop, I wanna tell you just how amazing you are."

"Feel free to. Can't hurt the ego." She leaned into his touch and tilted her head back to meet his lips in a soft kiss, never losing the goofy smile she wore.

"You are, you know? Amazing." Levi brought a hand up to her face and ran the backs of his fingers along her cheek. Looking into her bright blue eyes, he marvelled at how perfect she was. "I love you."

"I love you, too." Katy smiled, and his brain melted. She was beautiful. Tiny and feisty, crazy talented and, although a little piece of him wanted to beat his chest and growl *mine,* the truth was, he was hers.

"Have a good day?" he asked, resting his hands on her hips.

"It was good. The two cakes for this Saturday's weddings were delivered okay. This one is for Sunday afternoon, so I've got a little time up my sleeve to finish it off." She dropped the tiny spatula she was working with and stretched out the kinks in her neck.

"I was hoping you'd say that." Levi smiled and nipped the exposed skin on her throat, licking away the sting. "Was thinking we're about due to have a day at the beach."

Katy hummed contentedly. "I'd love that. Have you asked Connor yet?"

"No, he hasn't." Connor's voice startled both of them as he leaned over the counter where the register was. *When did he get here?* "But I'd love to come, unless I'm gate crashing." Levi may have been surprised, but the spark of... something—excitement, happiness, heck who knew—from seeing Connor surprised Levi more. Ignoring it, he smiled.

Connor motioned around the shop. "Can I take a walk around?"

"Sure, I'll give you a tour." Katy smiled again, glowing with happiness as she moved to the door Levi had just entered through. Levi loved seeing her like that—radiant, excited about finally having Connor see her business after all the renovations. It was a strange sense of satisfaction that he got knowing it was Connor's return, not him that had done it. *How screwed up is that?*

"This place is amazing, Cupcake." The wonder in Connor's tone as he surveyed the space was exactly the same as Levi's reaction every time he walked through. "The refurb looks great."

Levi smiled as Katy took Con's hand and led him around, giving him the story of how the expansion came to be. Her cousin Nick fronted up the money. She'd be able to pay him back in a few months when she turned twenty-five and came into her trust fund, but Nick wouldn't insist on it—he had seen something in her when she'd confessed her dream to do wedding cakes full time. So he'd stepped in and given her the push to break out on her own. Katy had worked hard to prove his instinct right by building the business, taking on Dylan so he could bake the everyday line of sweets, and Ashton, the budding pro-surfer, to work the checkout.

They re-entered the kitchen and Levi was still smiling. It turned into a laugh when Connor's belly rumbled loudly. He flushed red and smiled at them sheepishly. "Sorry, haven't eaten much today."

"Here, take one of these. They're good." Katy tossed him one of the last two muffins. "It's banana and oat bran, no added sugar." Katy moved over to the trolley and wheeled it into the cold room. "I'm just about done here. Gimme five to clean up and we can go and get dinner."

"Can I have the other muffin?" Levi called out to her retreating form.

"Help yourself. It's blueberry."

After shucking her chef's whites in the office—which doubled as a change room—Katy walked out wearing jean shorts, her unlaced steel capped boots, and a tight red tank. Levi took his time admiring her curves. She pulled off hot and sexy effortlessly, and his cock responded. Adjusting himself discreetly, he shot his gaze to Connor and saw the same pained look of desire he knew he was wearing. At least Lee wasn't the only one who was powerless to resist her. Why it didn't bother him that another man was so openly adoring his girlfriend was something Levi would have to return to another time.

"So whose car are we taking?" Katy asked, completely clueless at the state she had both of them in.

"Con can drive," Levi volunteered. He couldn't think straight with no blood in his brain, and he was at the point of being so hard he wasn't sure if he'd be able to walk, never mind drive.

"Ah, yeah sure," Con hesitated, before turning on his heel and quickly walking out.

Katy

Levi adjusting himself and Con looking like he was about to swallow his tongue had Katy reconsidering her getup. She'd thrown them into her bag that morning not realizing that it'd have that kind of effect. She wasn't close to being naked, but their eyes on her caressed her like she was. Was it bad that she was enjoying it? That these two men—who were damn beautiful —thought she was sexy enough to capture and keep their attention? Even though from what Con had said, he hadn't seen much action in a while. That needed to change. He deserved happiness and love and someone to fall head over heels for him. *Maybe I should set him up... but with who? Who would be worthy of him? Who would treat him like their everything?*

The buildings grew taller, the traffic heavier as she directed Con into Broadbeach. As the afternoon began to fade into dusk, they pulled into the street where their favourite pizza place was. It was quieter during a weeknight, but the city was always vibrant. Tourists and locals alike wandered down the wide paths enjoying the eclectic mix of restaurants and cafes. After Con had pulled up and they stepped out, Katy took Levi's hand and waited for their friend to come around the car. Walking along, she hooked her arm through Con's and smiled at him. "We've been coming here for a few years now. They make the best food in town."

"You keep talking them up, and I'll have high expectations." Con grinned at her and Katy shook her head, rolling her eyes. He adjusted the strap of his guitar case on his shoulder and playfully poked out his tongue. The move had Katy snorting out a laugh.

"You just wait and see." Katy playfully elbowed him, before laughing again at his pout. She'd laughed a lot since Con had returned. Smiled too. In fact, she couldn't wipe the giddy grin off her face with the deliriously happy buzz she had happening. "Aww, boo, did that hurt?"

The smell of the pizza cooking in the wood fired ovens couldn't be beaten. Inhaling deeply, Katy filled her lungs and hummed. *Yeah, dinner.* "Hello, lovely Katy and Levi." After the usual chit chat with Tony, and introductions to Con, Tony instructed them to sit at a free booth.

"We're taking away today," Katy informed him, smiling.

It wasn't long before their order was ready and they were taking it down to the sand. A bottle of cheap wine and pizza straight out of the cardboard box was their dinner, but the view was a million bucks. The glitter strip's famous beachside towers at their backs, the three of them wandered down toward the water, white sand under their feet. The three-quarter moon sat high in the sky, illuminating their way as the ocean breeze caressed her skin. Both she and Levi loved this spot. They went there every chance they got. Stripping off their shirts, Levi and Connor spread them on the soft sand, using them as a blanket to place Connor's guitar case on and, on that, the food, bottle of wine, and plastic cups. As they sat on the still-warm sand, a lone jogger ran past them much closer to the water-line, lost in the rhythm of the beat pumping through his headphones.

"God, I've missed this. Sand is so different when there's an ocean to go with it, and no one's trying to kill you. Rob was right. I did need to come home."

"We're glad you're back, boo." Katy grasped his hand and squeezed tightly. "We've missed you, and the thought of you being in danger every day was terrifying. Since you walked in that door, I've been able to breathe again. Lee too."

"I'm sorry I worried you, Cupcake, but..." He hesitated. "...I needed to do it." Connor looked down, and Katy stroked her thumb over his hand. "I dunno if I achieved what I set out to do, but it's made me appreciate what we have here so much more. I don't wanna waste any more time. I wanna start living."

"Is that what your new tat's about? A new beginning?" Levi asked gently.

"No, it's a memorial piece."

"Can we see it? Or is it too personal?"

"No, s'all good. Here." He pointed to the back of his shoulder. "Peel back the plastic wrap and you'll be able to see it properly." It wasn't the only tattoo Connor had. There was another on his side in small script. She couldn't read the words in the dark, but she knew it was the code he lived by. The other, a full sleeve on his right arm, was an intricate Gaelic tribal tattoo celebrating his roots. Katy peered at his shoulder, and the image brought tears to her eyes. Heavy engineering boots, a rifle leaning against them, a combat helmet resting on the barrel, and a pair of dog tags hanging from the cartridge.

"Oh, boo." Katy covered her mouth and sniffed, tears dripping onto her cheeks as her heart broke for him. Levi's arm was instantly around her, but it wasn't until Con did the same, holding her tightly, that the sobs escaped her. Burying her head against Con's warm chest, Katy cried, mourning all their lost moments, their lost innocence, the life of the soldier Con was grieving for.

"Cupcake," Con murmured as he stroked her hair. "It's okay. Hush, baby."

"Dude, I know it's too painful to talk about now, but when you're ready, we'd like to listen to your story."

"Most of it's classified. I can't tell you much even if I wanted to relive it."

Katy felt the movement of his shoulders as he shrugged.

"We don't want mission details." Levi paused. She could just imagine him shaking his head. "Can you talk to someone though? Someone with clearance?"

Con gently pulled Katy's hair back off her shoulders, tucking a stray lock behind her ear. "I have been ever since it happened. But let's eat. Don't want it to get cold." As much as Katy wanted him to talk, wanted to hear his story and to help him recover from those past torments, she wouldn't push him into it before he was ready. There was no way she'd do that to him, so for now, she let the subject change drop. Hopefully, one day he'd open up to them.

Con reached down and snagged a slice from the box, passing it to her before reaching for another. Levi retold his story from his day on set, and as they ate, they laughed, relaxing together in the warm evening. Stories soon turned into reminiscing on the months they'd spent together before Con's first deployment, and Katy could almost pinpoint the exact moment they fell back into their groove, finding their equilibrium and themselves at the same time. Her relationship with Levi was super strong. She loved him like no one else in the world, and she knew he felt the same, but there was always a missing piece, part of their hearts that wasn't there. Now he was back. Now she could love her man, live without fear, without the possibility of death breathing down their necks. Con was safe—and damn, what a weight off their shoulders it was knowing that.

Pizza finished, Katy shifted, curling up against Levi's side. Con began strumming away on his guitar, singing softly with the tunes he played. She always loved the classics, and Con's rendition of Oasis' "Wonderwall" made her shiver. He had the most beautiful voice.

Levi rubbed the goosebumps that had formed on her skin. "Let's head home, sugar. You're cold."

"No, it's so nice down here." Katy shook her head and cuddled into Levi more, tugging Con to them. "Both of you just scoot closer and I'll be fine." The two men shifted, blanketing her in their warm bodies.

She couldn't help her sigh of contentment when Con started playing again. "This is the life, isn't it?"

"Fuck yeah," Con answered immediately.

A month later

The three of them walked through the wire gate of the lot. The machine Katy spied parked there, between two beat-up Fords, was sex on wheels. A beautiful gunmetal grey, the classic sports car was restored to perfection. Con had spent nearly all day every day over the last month at his father's old workshop, rebuilding it from the ground up. Katy smiled. He'd been doing okay—fewer nightmares and was somehow lighter, like he wasn't carrying the weight of his time overseas around with him. Counselling and his focus on building new memories in the garage that had meant so much to his father were helping him to rediscover himself. And now, seeing the results, she couldn't be happier that his hard work had paid off. It was... stunning.

He hadn't done it alone. He'd had loads of help—Kevin, his father's long-time business partner, was a master mechanic. The man loved American muscle cars as much as Con did. The beat-up old Shelby his father had imported was going to be their project car, but it'd never happened. Con's mother had been diagnosed with breast cancer and lost her battle with the disease mere months after it'd arrived at the workshop. His father hadn't coped well, drowning his grief in a bottle and prescription meds. Kevin had kept their business running while his father tried to drink himself into an early grave. It was only a matter of time after that that he'd disappeared into thin air. His body had shown up six months later floating down a river. He'd drowned, his body pumped full of the drugs and liquor he'd become addicted to. Con had mourned his loss once. Then, finding his body and knowing how he'd died had been even harder. Katy knew those demons still haunted him—he'd confided as much to her in one of their many emails to each other.

"Whatcha think?" Con asked them.

"Mate, she's beautiful. You've done such a fantastic job." The wide-eyed wonder in Levi's gaze radiated pride. And Con should be proud. His work was as good as any mechanic's in the shop, but he'd confessed to Katy that he couldn't work there. Temporarily, it was okay, but he'd confided that the thought of following in his father's footsteps made Connor's skin crawl.

"Thanks, Lee. We're really happy with it."

"I think I want to make love to this car. Or in it," Katy murmured absentmindedly, as she ran her fingertips over its sleek roofline. And she wasn't joking. It was sensual, downright erotic.

Katy looked over to Con and saw the heat bloom in his eyes, his nostrils flare as he watched her stroke the car. It was wrong, she knew it, but damn it turned her on to be the object of his desire. She followed his gaze as it tracked from her to Levi who was leaning in the open door, checking out the interior. The play of Levi's muscles under the white polo shirt had Katy licking her lips. Following the swell of his arse in the khaki shorts he wore —his rock-solid glutes flexing as he shifted—had Katy biting back a moan. She loved every inch of her man. And she wasn't the only one staring at him. Con had followed her line of sight and was watching, apparently riveted, by the way Levi moved. She shivered, feeling the heat in Con's gaze down to her bones as he took in Levi's form. God, that look, the sheer devotion Con had to him, was one of beauty. They were a team, so why had she agreed to set Con up with her friend? That night. What was she thinking?

Her friend had practically begged Katy to set her up with Con when she'd posted a picture of him and Levi on Insta. Miranda was totally sweet, a great catch for the right guy. How could Katy resist her when they'd been friends for years? But something didn't feel right. It was as if she was encouraging Con to leave them again. *I'm being ridiculous.*

Shopping with him and helping him pick clothes for his date made her head spin, getting her all mixed up. The place Miranda had suggested for dinner was so unlike Con that it made her cringe. He was a faded jeans and tee kinda guy—usually grey, but it varied between that and black or white—not the suave suit-wearing CEO lookalike that was standing before her modelling his outfit. She nodded her approval, albeit reluctantly.

His dark eyes flashed and he fingered the cuffs of his dark grey shirt, adjusting them under the black jacket he wore. "I'm nervous about this date, Katy," Con said quietly, keeping out of earshot from the people standing nearby. "It's been so damn long since I've done this, and I never do blind dates. How'd you even persuade me?"

"Boo, you need to get out there. Find your happiness." *But he's happy with us. He doesn't have to date to be happy.* Katy forced herself to end that line of thought. Again. It wasn't the first time she'd run through the argument in her own mind. Maybe that was why she was so messed up. He deserved so much more in life. Stopping him from dating would keep Con from the intimacy that went with being in a relationship. And that wasn't fair.

Just being friends with them wasn't enough. He deserved the world.

He sighed. "You're right. Maybe I should get back out there."

"Trust me. You're perfect for each other." The words sounded forced even to her own ears, and she was sure her smile was more of a grimace.

"Famous last words," he mumbled before letting the change room curtain fall back in place.

3

CONNOR

His date, Miranda, was nice. Cute and sweet, she was seemingly perfect for him. It was true, they had a lot in common —their interests in music and movies aligned, they loved the same food and were both runners, but truth be told, he was bored. Miranda seemed up for whatever he wanted and she wasn't shy with her affection, but it was almost too much. She'd had her hands on him all night, and Connor was suffocating. He wasn't wearing a tie, but he might as well have had one lynching him. She was right, but all wrong at the same time. Her perfume was too sweet, her lips too red, her hair too light. Not feisty enough, not... not the person he'd always wanted, but could never have. He had a healthy sex drive—not one that got satiated very often, but he was a dude. He had needs. And tonight? Nada. Flaccid as fuck. *What the hell is wrong with me?*

Katy had seemed out of sorts when they'd been shopping, and the tension had only gotten worse. Levi was walking on eggshells around her, not knowing what to say, but he had his nose out of joint too. He was pissed at something and had turned all surly. It wasn't a good look on him. But it was worse when his mask fell away and he looked like someone had killed his dog. He was miserable. Connor had to resist the temptation to blow off his date and try to put a smile back on his friends' faces, to make them laugh again. *Surely that's it. They're bringing me down, distracting me from a beautiful woman.*

Dinner was long and drawn out, but finally over, though Miranda wanted to move onto something else. Katy and Levi begged off a walk along the beach, and as much as it sucked to be on an awkward date, Connor was grateful for the chance to get away from his friends. Miranda slipped her hand into his and, hoping for some attraction to take hold, he didn't pull away. They walked together along the boardwalk down Surfers Paradise beach. He loved it there—the lights, the sounds. The rhythm of the waves crashing on the darkened sand and the cool breeze settled Connor in a way he hadn't experienced since leaving to join the army. The beach always did that to him though—gave him a sense of place, of peace, like nowhere else on earth.

"Connor, should we go down onto the sand?" she asked sweetly. He paused, looking at her closely. The innocent enough question had him pausing. Under the sweet smile, the doe eyes she flashed him, she looked like she wanted to eat him alive. *Does she wanna get lucky on the sand?*

"Um, Miranda," he began, but seeing her expression drop— the sides of her lips tilting down and the disappointment swirling in her baby blues as she looked up at him—had him backtracking. "I'm kinda tired. Could I perhaps take you home instead?"

Her eyes lit up and she flashed him a sweet smile again. But to Connor, that predatory gleam in her eyes—the one that told him she'd consume him whole—was back. And no doubt about it, there'd be teeth. He gave her a nervous smile, looking away when she stepped closer. *When did we stop walking?*

He motioned for them to move back to Connor's car and

when they reached it, he held her door open. The drive back to Miranda's house was quiet except for the directions she gave him, but her eyes never left him—it was obvious when she was turned on the seat, angling her body towards him.

He pulled into the drive and cut the engine. She lived around the corner from Katy and Levi, in a house much like theirs was before the renovations. There was no way he was staying with her, but he didn't want to head back to Katy and Levi's place either. They needed some time alone, to work out whatever it was that was eating away at them. Either that or have a good session to fuck the angst out of their systems, whatever its cause. Putting on a smile, Connor opened Miranda's door and walked her to the front step. He stepped back when she opened the screen.

"Home safe." She smiled at him and nodded her head towards the interior. "Wanna drink?"

"Not tonight, Miranda. I'd best be getting home." *I don't think I can let you down softly if I walk in your front door.*

"Maybe we can do this again?"

No. "Yeah, that sounds nice." *What am I doing?*

"Okay then, call me. I'm free next weekend."

"Great," Connor replied, forcing a smile. He didn't want to hurt her, lead her on—she was too nice for that. Maybe his wanting to protect her, albeit from himself, was because there was something more to his feelings.

He leaned down to kiss her cheek, but she turned her head at the last second and pressed their lips together, before licking his bottom lip with little swipes of her tongue. As much as Connor second guessed himself and whether he was attracted to her, he had to see where it could lead. He opened against her mouth and kissed her deeper, their tongues stroking together. It was... nice, but there weren't exactly any fireworks going off.

He broke the kiss and smiled at her. "I wouldn't be a gentleman if I didn't let you get inside now."

She ran her long nails down his chest, stopping at the button of his suit pants and grinned at him. "Being a gentleman is overrated."

"Not on a first date, it's not." He grasped her hand and squeezed it, stepping back again as he let go.

Confused and frustrated with himself for giving up a sure thing, he got behind the wheel and sped off. Three hours and all the back roads down to Byron Bay later, he stopped the car, cursing the situation as he got out. He breathed in the cool salty sea air and leaned against his car. Shaking his head at the stab of aggravation that hit him, Connor kicked at the grass, his shoe finding a stray rock and sending it flying in a high arc somewhere into the park. Taking a few deep breaths to calm himself, he looked out over the darkened beach, listening to the waves caress the shore. Instantly the weight lifted from his shoulders, freeing him.

Pulling his guitar from the back seat, he strummed it. He didn't have a song in mind when he started playing, instead letting the notes form into a melody, the melody into songs. He found himself humming Rag'n'Bone Man's "Skin." The poignant words drew him in and settled deep inside. Connor's eyes slid closed, and he played song after song.

The first rays of dawn kissed the sky warming his skin. Tilting his face up, he released a slow breath before blinking open his eyes and watching. Pinks and oranges splashed across the sky in ever brightening hues. The sun, a fiery yellow that morning, had breached the horizon sending shimmering rays across the water. The power of nature was captivating, and Connor stood transfixed as the sky changed from a pale predawn grey to a rich shade of blue he'd only ever seen above the Pacific.

A pelican waddled out onto the sand and spread its broad wings, flapping them and lifting into the air. Circling around ascending higher as it went, Connor realized that his life had returned to that state too. He was free to fly. He didn't have to go into the bowels of hell chasing terrorists, ending the life of someone, who with a split-second judgement was deemed to be an enemy rather than an ally. There were so many regrets, so many nights of vomiting up his dinner, of wishing day break would arrive so he didn't have to face the nightmares. But getting shot at and blown up was history for Connor, the horrors of war seemed faraway in his little patch of the world, even with the constant reminder from his PTSD. It killed him that his brothers and sisters in arms were still at it. He could never forget—he didn't want to anyway—but he might be able to move on and start to live again. Was Miranda the person to do it with? He didn't know, but he owed it to himself to see if a spark developed. And he deserved to be happy, didn't he? She was clearly into him. If he could get out of his head long enough, maybe he'd realize he was attracted to her too. At least if he was really present on their next date, it wouldn't be so damn awkward.

The early morning waves called to him, the perfect barrels beckoning. He stripped down to his boxer shorts and jogged down to the water. The surfers were already out—the waves pumping. The water hit his skin as he strode into the whitewash and he sucked in a breath. It was ice-cold. *Damn.* A wave began to peak and he dived under it. Rushing water surrounded him, cocooning him as he swam with powerful strokes. Still underwater, he opened his eyes, watching the wave curl into itself. Breaking through to its other side, Connor wiped the salt from his eyes and let the water swirl around him.

The issues he was working through—some small and others

not so small—were washed away, momentarily lifting the weight from his shoulders. Another wave broke and Connor duck-dived under it. Breaking the surface again, he relaxed, floating in the bobbing swell. In the warm early morning sun, the blue waters sparkled around him. He slipped under another wave, once again watching it curl over him. It was mesmerizing seeing the blue water change into the surging white foam as the wave was sucked up into a peak until it crested, crashing against the shore. Breaking the surface, he shook the water off his face before running his hands through his wavy hair. His buzz cut was growing out, the prickle of the short strands no longer as sharp under his palms.

Body surfing until the rumble in his stomach was too annoying to ignore, he got out and trudged up the sand to grab his towel from his gym bag. Drying himself off, Connor watched the surfers riding the waves. Seeing nature's power helped put everything into context for him. And it wasn't just dating either. It was everything, his entire life plan. Levi's birthday was coming up, and he'd been thinking about doing something for his oldest and closest friend that he'd never do himself. The problem was, it would push him into something he'd tried hard to avoid. He didn't want to be a mechanic like his old man—too many memories circled around him when he spent a lot of time in the space. Doing his car was bad enough, but a second rebuild? He knew that fixing up the old Harley which had been languishing in pieces in Lee's garage would be worth it. A plan began to form, and even though it wasn't where he pictured himself going, it was good to start seeing the forest from the trees. He smiled. He could do this; he would do it.

"Good waves out there?" Connor spun at the girl's husky voice. She was in a bikini carrying a longboard down towards the water.

"Yeah. Really clean but cold as a mother."

She grinned at his comment and kept walking, waving as she went past and he pulled a spare set of clothes from his gym bag.

Connor stretched his legs out, propping his bare feet on the timber railing. His thongs lay discarded under the table of the beachside pub he sat in. They served a killer breakfast there. Waiting for the waitress to make her way over to him and take his order, he strummed his guitar, playing random notes in a slow melody.

"Hi," the young waitress said, in a sweet melodic voice. Connor wondered why the owners had a child working there. "Can you really play that?" She pointed to his guitar.

"Yup, I can." He grinned.

"Can you play something for me?"

"Sure. But can I put my order in first? I'm starving." He jokingly clutched his belly, putting on a pained expression. She rolled her eyes, grinning, and looked at him expectantly, so Connor continued, "I just want the breakfast special with a black coffee and an OJ."

"No worries. I'll put it in now." As she walked away, she tossed a shy smile over her shoulder. "So can you play me a song?"

"Will do. Who do you like, doll?"

"Taylor Swift."

He thought about it for a moment and smiled. "'Back to December' it is." One of her earlier songs, it wasn't as big a hit as the others, but it had a beautiful melody, a great country vibe. Slow and sweet, the song told the story of regrets and doing things over, apologizing and growing up. Connor began strumming the opening chords and sung to the soulful tune. After carefully placing his coffee on the table, the waitress excitedly jumped up and down, letting out a quiet squeal.

"That's one of my favourites. Thank you."

Once he'd started playing, he didn't want to stop, and no one had told him to shut up yet, so he figured it was a win. He kept going and by the end of the fifth song, the café was packed, and people were gathered around listening to him as much as enjoying their food. He totally got a kick out of performing for them.

A middle-aged lady dressed in kaftans with flowing grey hair approached him. "Hi, I'm Tracey. You met my youngest, Stella." She pointed to her daughter waiting tables.

"Connor," he replied, shaking her proffered hand. "Nice to meet you. Your daughter's very sweet."

"I like you, Connor. You play beautifully. Do you have an agent?"

"Huh?" he asked, shaking his head. "No, no agent. I don't even play professionally. I'm just messing around."

"I own the café here in the pub and a couple of others on the Goldie. I need some entertainment a few days a week for all three of them. If you're interested—and if you can—I'd love for you to come and play there as a practice run." *Is she kidding?* That path, the one he thought he'd seen, suddenly had a fork in it, one that he'd never dreamed of exploring. Music had always been his passion, had always been a fundamental part of him, but it'd never been something he thought he could *do*.

"I'd love to." He beamed at the realization that he might not have to follow in his father's steps and become a mechanic. "Yeah, I'm interested. Definitely." They sat and spoke for half an hour, and she handed him a card.

"See you Thursday. I'm not promising anything permanent, but if you do well, then we'll look at having you play at all three."

"Thanks, Tracey. Can't wait."

Connor got on the road and headed straight home. He couldn't wait to tell Levi and Katy. Excitement and adrenaline coursed through his veins. His head still buzzed and he couldn't wipe the smile off his face even if he tried. He let himself in and jogged up the hallway, calling out, "Lee, Cupcake," as he went. He spotted his friend slouched on the couch, and Connor's grin left in a rush when Levi looked up at him. Sadness permeated the air between them.

"You haven't lost it, mate. First date, I'm impressed."

"It's not what you think," Connor replied. He didn't want to admit he hadn't sealed the deal with a girl who was so obviously wanting to, but he couldn't lie either. That wasn't him. Levi's derisive snort and the way he stood and walked away from Connor had him on the defensive. What did it matter even if he'd slept with Miranda? They were both consenting adults. Sex was sex. It wasn't a bad thing, something they should be ashamed of, even if they had slept together. Con's news went by the wayside as Levi slammed his mug down in the sink. Connor wasn't going there—Lee needed to cool off or they'd end up duking it out. Connor spun on his heel and walked back the way he came, heading straight for the bedroom he was staying in.

"Hi," Katy murmured from her doorway as he turned the knob to his room.

"Hi, Katy. I'm going to crash unless you need me urgently."

"No, go and catch up on some sleep, Casanova." The smile she flashed looked strained, something Connor could identify with after Levi's outburst. He gave her a weak smile back and closed the door, but a knock soon followed.

"I'm in jocks, but you can come in." He looked down at his boxer shorts making sure they weren't threadbare as Katy opened the door a crack.

"I know I said I didn't need you, but can we talk?"

"Sure, Cupcake, what's up? Apart from the ice-cold reception happening in the lounge room."

"He's upset. Give him time to cool off, and he'll be back to normal. He's just a little tense." She sat down on his bed and sighed, looking as defeated as her man in the other room.

Connor sat next to her and grasped her hand. It was small in his, soft and warm. He breathed in the scent of chocolate and vanilla that lingered around her—like it got under her skin at work and had become a part of her. "Katy, if this is about me staying here, it's no big deal, I'll just move out. I'm not gonna get offended if you guys need your space."

"No, boo. It's not you. You don't need to move out." Katy smiled at him, this one more genuine than the last.

"Are you guys okay? I'm worried about you."

"We're good. We've both been a little off. Things are changing for us, not in a bad way I don't think, but he's struggling a little with it."

"You wanna talk about it?"

"No, I'm okay. We're still happy."

"I'm always there for you guys. You know that, right?"

"I do. And don't worry, he'll come around when he's ready. I'll do the same one day." She elbowed Connor affectionately. "But, I need your advice. Lee's birthday's coming up soon. I've organized a party for him, but I wanted to give him something really special too. He's done so much for me, and I wanted to... I dunno, do something for him that he'll never forget, but I have no idea what to get him."

"I've been thinking about it too. I wanna do up the Harley he has in pieces in the garage. From what I could see, it looks like he has most of the bike in there. If you bought the rest of the parts, we could give it to him. He might not even notice the parts are gone if I can get some old boxes that we can stack up in their place. It could be a surprise, but it probably won't be finished in time for his birthday."

Katy's eyes lit up, and she threw her arms around him. "You'd do that for him?"

"I'll get help from Kevin at the shop." Connor shrugged. He wouldn't do the final assembly—he'd want Levi to do that with him—but he'd do what he could for his friend. "I've never worked on a bike before, but there's a guy in there who's a bike mechanic."

"So if we worked on that—well, you work on it and I supply any parts you're short—and I got him something else, do you think that'd be good?"

"I do. Whatcha gonna get?"

"What about... I dunno. I wanted something that he's never experienced before. Everything I think of, he's done for work."

"Why don't you do something just for the two of you to relax and, maybe reconnect? He's pretty bloody stressed, and you've been working crazy hours too. Go stay in a swanky hotel and get an in-room massage. Eat room service and drink some sparkly."

"Yeah." Katy nodded slowly. He could see the cogs turning in her mind. "But he loves our bed more than anything. Maybe I should do something like that here. I could cook him dinner and instead of buying him a massage, I could get someone out to teach me how to do it, then I could give him a happy ending too." She sighed. "Not like you can learn how to massage someone in fifteen minutes though. And what am I gonna do, give him a BJ when someone's standing there? Nah, that idea sucks."

He shook his head, smirking at the picture she'd painted. "You could be onto something though. Adelaide, a friend of mine from uni owns a mobile adult store. She'll come to you and you choose what you want. It's completely private." Connor smiled ruefully, scrubbing his hands over his hair. He didn't know whether to be jealous or whether to encourage it. The idea that someone else would help her choose a toy for them to use killed him, even if that person was a consummate professional. "Fuck, I can't believe I just said out loud that you should go buy some sex toys for you and your live-in boyfriend, my best mate. He'd better not take that the wrong way."

Katy grinned. "Nah, he'd be flattered that you wanna help him get off." The words were barely out of her mouth when she blushed and snorted out a laugh. "Oh God."

Heat flooded him, his dick hardening in his boxers. Hoping Katy didn't see, he leaned forward a little more, hiding the tenting that was happening down there. Covering his inner turmoil up with a grin, he tried to laugh off Katy's embarrassment. "You want me to get in contact with her? I don't have her number but I could IM her."

"Yeah. That sounds good. Thanks, boo," she said shyly, leaning into him as she did, and squeezing his hand. "Love you."

"Love you, too," he murmured back as she left the room. And that was his problem. He'd been in love with this woman for so long that persuading his heart to move on wasn't easy. That was why he'd left, why he couldn't stick around and watch his best friend love the woman he wanted with every fibre of his being. It killed him knowing he'd never be the one for her, but at the same time, she and Levi were perfect together. He couldn't begrudge them for finding their happiness. Now he needed to find his own.

Connor laid down, still above the covers, and adjusted himself. Thinking about Levi and Katy in bed together made him hard, but adding toys conjured up wicked visions that he didn't even want to try to banish. And what was worse—it wasn't Adelaide who he pictured helping them choose, but him. Him with them. Loving them. Between them. *Them.* And once the thought entered his head, he couldn't rid it from his mind. *I'm royally screwed.*

Levi

Connor had picked up his car and somehow instead of taking it for a drive up to the mountains, Katy had managed to wrangle them into shopping for half the day. As much as Levi hated to have spent the afternoon trying on suits, it was a good thing she'd insisted on it. Connor lived in jeans, so showing up to the restaurant for his first date with Miranda wearing them probably wouldn't have cut it. Especially in the restaurant they were in. One street back from the ocean in Main Beach, it was in yuppiesville—mansions and million-dollar apartments lined the streets, Lamborghinis and Ferraris were parked alongside. Levi's own Toyota was comically out of place.

Inside, the high-end restaurant was intimate. Candles flickered in the dim lights, the starched-white table cloths contrasting against the gleaming silver cutlery and sparkling wine goblets. It was renowned for its modern Australian-Italian cuisine, and after eating, Levi knew why. The prawn risotto and veal ravioli were mouth-watering.

Dinner should have been fun. Miranda was cute and sweet, and with Katy and her sass, they usually kept things interesting. Add in Connor and himself, and they should have been talking and laughing the whole night. That was why Katy insisted that they do the double date thing. But at best, it was strained. At worst, it was downright uncomfortable. Katy was miserable the whole night, and that put him on edge too. He didn't like seeing her upset and it grated on him to watch the attraction sparking between Miranda and Connor. From the moment they'd locked eyes, they'd gravitated towards one another until they'd eliminated the space between them. They hadn't taken their hands off each other since. It wasn't like they were making out at the table, but Levi could see from a mile away where the night was headed. He knew he should be happy for Connor—Miranda was perfect for him—but was he ready for a relationship? And would Miranda be patient with him while he readjusted back to being a civilian? Got a job? He was still attending group sessions and counselling three or four times a week, and probably would do so for years. Would Miranda support him when she eventually found out that he wasn't completely spared by the horrors he'd witnessed?

The restaurant had quietened down after a busy Saturday night, most of the guests having moved on.

"How has everything been tonight?" the waitress interrupted them.

"Great, thanks," Katy supplied.

"Can I get you anything else? We can't serve anything alcoholic after midnight so this will be your last chance to order drinks."

Levi shook his head and saw everyone else at the table murmuring the same thing. Their dinner conversation may have been awkward, but he was still surprised so much time had passed since they'd arrived at the beginning of the night. He hadn't realized their group and the four ladies apparently having a girls' night out would close the restaurant.

Miranda toyed with her empty wine glass, something she'd been doing whenever she wasn't all over Connor. Levi's jaw clenched. Why did he feel the need to physically remove her hand from where it perched on Connor's leg? Of course the tablecloth hid whatever the hell it was she was doing, and Levi was grateful for that. "Why don't we go do something fun?" Miranda suggested. "We could go dancing or head back to my place for a movie. I've got a new rom-com on Blu-ray, and my flatmate bought some war movie too. Connor, you were in the army, you'd like it."

He visibly shuddered and looked at Levi with what he could have sworn was dread in his eyes. Levi couldn't watch a movie like that—hadn't been able to since the day Connor enlisted. And Katy would walk out of a premiere if there was even a moment of violence in it. The vice grip Katy had on his hand told him everything he needed to know. "We might pass on the movie."

"Yeah, I'm not really up for it either," Connor murmured. A wave of relief washed over Levi. He was protective of his best friend—hell, he'd worried over him for years—and Miranda's insensitivity made his hackles rise, putting him even more on edge. He'd been tiptoeing around Katy, trying to lift her mood most of the night, but it wasn't working. And now, he'd had enough. He couldn't watch his friend fall in lust with this girl, or see them make love-heart eyes at each other again.

"Let's go to the beach then," Miranda pressed. She clearly didn't want the night to end, and who would with a man like Connor fawning over them? He wasn't ashamed to say that he was gorgeous, especially in the dark shirt and jacket he wore. Sleek and suave, with piercing dark eyes. But the parts that really made him, well... him, were covered or tamed down. The unruly waves his spikey hair was growing into were held in place by product and the intricate tattoos adorning his right arm from shoulder to wrist, his ribs and his shoulder were hidden from view. The script on his ribs was so detailed Levi had found himself wanting to trace it, to follow the curls and blunt lines along his side. But Levi's curiosity would remain unsated. Dudes didn't do that to each other.

Miranda's next comment dragged him out of his head and back into the conversation. "A walk would do us some good after this dessert." And it probably would, but there was no way he could go with them. A fierce streak of something ran through him when Connor turned to Miranda—surely he was just feeling protective of him. The desire, almost a desperate need for Connor to also say no gripped him. All he wanted was to end the night with the three of them together at home relaxing on the couch together. It made no sense for him to be jealous, but dammit, he was. He'd only just gotten his friend back, and now that Miranda had sunk her claws in, Levi was going to lose him again. He just knew it. The knowledge sent a sharp jolt through his heart, like a knife plunging in, the loss so intense his breath caught. He watched as Connor studied Miranda. His gaze held hers as if he was looking for something, searching. He thought the pain was acute, but instead, it overwhelmed him, like the knife was being twisted violently, when he saw Connor slowly nod, a small smile playing on his lips.

"Sure."

He was still holding Katy's hand. The extra pressure she applied, even though it was minute and for barely a second was enough to tell him he wasn't the only one it was killing. Or maybe it was wishful thinking on Levi's part—he shouldn't want his girlfriend to be jealous of her friend going on a date with his best mate, to share his confusion and the crushing blow to his heart.

"Sorry to be a downer, but I hurt my ankle this afternoon. I don't wanna aggravate it by walking. You two enjoy yourselves." Katy's words were a surprise to Levi. Was he so wrapped up in himself that he hadn't seen her limping? She hadn't said anything to him, but had he just missed it? He turned to her, concern for her blocking out the pain in his heart. He cupped her face with his free hand, wanting, wishing he could fix everything. She leaned into his touch and kissed his palm, and that simple gesture healed him, gave him the strength to put aside the clusterfuck in his heart and protect her.

"Let's get you home and get it strapped."

"Yeah." Katy squeezed his hand again. "Thank you," she mouthed.

The drive back to their house was quiet, Katy as lost in her own world as Levi was. The light he'd stopped at turned from red to green, and he moved automatically, following roads he'd travelled down more times than he could count, taking them home without conscious thought. He pulled into the drive and paused, looking at the now empty space next to his car where Connor had been parking.

"I should sell my bike. Make room for Con in the garage. He's worked too hard on his car to have it sitting outside overnight." He didn't want to, but he would. Connor deserved it, deserved to have a place of his own.

Katy jerked in her seat to face him, alarm written on her features. "No, you shouldn't." Katy's vehemence surprised him. He thought she'd appreciate getting rid of crates of unassembled bike parts and the frame which took up half the space in the garage. "That Harley is your baby. You can't get rid of it."

He sighed and shrugged, staring straight ahead. Cutting the engine, he sat back in the seat, dropping his hands to his lap. The need to make space in the garage would never have been an issue before, but now it was. Connor needed a place with them. He needed to know that their house was his home too. "I'm never gonna get around to fixing it. And let's face it, I'm no mechanic." The darkness in the car seemed to speak to him, whispering that his dream to fix the bike with Connor was dead. Was he overreacting? Probably, but he had to face reality. Connor was moving on. At the time Levi bought the Harley, it'd meant something to both of them. But things changed, and he had to as well. "I don't even know where to start with it, and it's not like I'll ever ride it." He ran his hand through his hair, sighing again. "I've got my car, so it's a waste of space. And money. It was probably ridiculous to get one in the first place."

Katy grabbed onto his arm, trying to twist him in the seat, but he couldn't bear to look at her. "It wasn't ridiculous, and there's no reason why you can't ride it if you get it put back together. You've always blamed your job, and I've let you, but it's not gonna happen anymore. You deserve it. Keep the bike."

He closed his eyes. Levi had never told her that he wanted to fix it up with Connor, kind of replacing the project Connor and his dad were supposed to work on together. He was embarrassed to admit that he'd wanted to give that experience to Connor, just as much as he wanted it for himself. "Yeah, but... I dunno. I s'pose I just need to wake up to the fact that it'll never happen."

Katy's warm hands on his face had him leaning into her touch, shifting his gaze to her eyes. She'd moved, sitting on the console between them to get closer to him. "I know you, Lee. You don't give up on anything that easily." She shook her head, her eyes imploring. "Don't start now. If you want it, reach out for it. You might be surprised."

"And if I'm disappointed?" he asked, knowing it was a loaded question. He sensed that Katy understood he was talking about more than the bike as they sat together in the darkness of their driveway, cocooned in the car together. What exactly he *was* talking about was still a mystery though. He was waiting for all the pieces to fall into place, to suddenly make sense, but it was all out of focus, a blur. He did know that he was changing. Or maybe not so much changing as realizing something about himself.

"Then you'll have tried." Those four little words that Katy uttered, with nothing but sincerity in her voice, were more comforting than anything else she could have said. It was as if she got it, that she could see what Levi couldn't yet. Like she was guiding him to where he needed to be to make sense of it.

He kissed her hand and pulled her close, burying his nose in her hair. She fit into his arms like she was made for him. And she was—Katy was his soulmate, the love of his life. Whatever the hell he was going through wouldn't ever change that.

Levi paced the lounge room. He'd been doing that—pacing and slumping down on the couch staring at the blank TV screen, then pacing again—for hours. The predawn light had begun to breach the darkness of the night sky, but the sun held little solace for him. Katy had long ago fallen asleep, but even though he'd laid with her wrapped around him, he couldn't do the same. And the more time he spent wearing a track into the hardwood flooring, the more frustrated and on-edge he became. *Where is he?* But he knew—Connor was with Miranda, probably in bed. There was nothing wrong with that, so why the hell did it feel like there was? It was irrational, sure, Levi would acknowledge that, but it didn't make what was going on in Levi's head any less real. Connor was out there enjoying himself with another woman. No, with *a* woman. They were both single and willing, so why was it grating on Levi? It wasn't like Connor was cheating, but apparently in the dark of night, Levi was beyond the point of reason and logic.

Weary and dejected, Levi sprawled out on the couch with a coffee in hand. His head hurt and he was in a shitty mood. He was glad Katy was giving him some space. She'd woken up earlier and put the coffee machine on, brewing a mug and handing it to him when it was ready. She hadn't even said anything to him before she went back to their room to get showered and dressed for the day. Guilt consumed him. He shouldn't be feeling sorry for himself on the couch. He should have been with Katy, loving her like she deserved.

The key turning in the front door had him swallowing hard. He was home. Finally. Levi looked up when Connor called out to him. He was so damn happy, like he was riding a high. The sight broke something in Levi and made him lash out. With venom in his voice that Connor didn't deserve, Levi stood and spat, "You haven't lost it, mate. First date, I'm impressed."

"It's not what you think," Connor replied. Levi huffed out a response and walked away. The angry mask he wore was slipping, his hurt bubbling just under the surface waiting to spill over. He couldn't let Connor see how upset he was. He knew why. He understood there was something more than being scared of losing a friend. But he wasn't going there. There was no way he'd let Katy think she wasn't enough for him. She was. Levi just had to get his head out of his arse long enough to shake this shit out once and for all. He slammed down his mug in the sink, taking a deep breath and closing his eyes as he rested his hands on the edge of the kitchen bench. Breathing out slowly, he stood there for a moment. *Get it together.*

Hours later and Levi was still too wired to do anything other than clean. He groaned. Tired and miserable, he couldn't stomach doing any more housework. He needed Katy; all he wanted was to hold her. She always managed to distract him when he got too stuck inside his head, but she was shopping with Emma for the day. It left Levi at home with Connor, not that he'd seen him. The other man had crashed almost as soon as he'd walked in, and hours later he was still asleep.

Pulling a bottle of water from the fridge, Levi downed half before leaning against the back of the couch. In the quiet of the house, he heard a door open and close, the shower turning on soon after. Knowing Connor was washing away the evidence of his activities the night before had Levi's blood boiling. All the insecurity, the stress and the self-doubt he'd been dealing with exploded. Levi was shaking. Betrayed and hurt, he stewed on it, glaring at the closed door while the shower ran. He wanted to blast through it and shake his best friend. Why did he do it? Why did he hurt Levi so fucking much?

Connor opened the door, and Levi found himself moving without conscious thought. His hands pressed against Connor's still damp skin, and he pushed him against the wall, stepping closer to him. "What the fuck, man?" Connor stuttered.

"Why'd you do it? Why?" Levi hissed.

"What?" Connor threw his hands in the air, before pushing back against Levi. "What the fuck did I do?"

"Stay with her." Sure, he'd thought it, but he'd never intended to say it out loud. Hearing his thoughts voiced surprised Levi. By the wide-eyed stare and his mouth popping open, Connor was just as shocked.

"I didn't," he replied quietly. Connor's hands were warm against his pecs through Levi's shirt, and it sent a spark of awareness through him. "I dropped her off then went for a drive. I ended up in Byron. Stayed down there for breakfast."

"Goddamn it," Levi muttered, slamming the heel of his hand against the wall. The pictures rattled, and Connor's grip on his hips tightened. His nostrils flared when Levi realized that he still had his hand on Connor's shoulder. Curling it, he massaged the firm muscles under his fingertips. "I'm sorry, I'm an arse."

Connor looked down, breaking their gaze. "Nothing happened between us. If it wasn't for her kissing me, I wouldn't have even done that. Is that fucked up? She wanted me, but I couldn't do it."

His friend was hurting and there he was wallowing in self-pity. "Why?"

He shook his head, sadness radiating from him. "Doesn't matter."

"Yeah, it does, mate. Talk to me."

"I couldn't do it, couldn't bring myself to go inside her house. I need to get laid. I'm as horny as fuck. But when she offered, I turned her down. I'm fucking confused."

Levi pulled him into a hug, needing to comfort him. "I'm sorry I was a jerk."

"Why *are* you being a jerk?" Connor asked quietly, still holding Levi tightly. He pulled back just enough to look at him. Levi sighed. He knew why. Jealousy would be a great explanation, but there was no way he was voicing that.

"I don't know," he replied, equally as quiet. "You're not the only one who's confused." Levi shivered and sucked in a breath when Connor ran his thumb down his side, following the line of his obliques. Shocked he'd liked it so much, Levi stepped back, breaking Connor's hold. What was he doing? What was he thinking? He couldn't touch Con, not like he'd been doing anyway. It was almost intimate. But Connor's smooth olive skin, his cut muscles, and the bulge standing to attention underneath his low-slung towel begged to be admired. Levi clenched his jaw and took a few deep breaths to get a hold of himself again. He wasn't attracted to his best friend. He couldn't be. But the images scrolling through his mind painted a very different picture.

"We'll work it out, mate." Levi flinched when Connor punched him lightly on the arm before stepping out of reach. Watching him walk away, he could only nod.

Katy

Her feet hurt from walking, her cheeks hurt from laughing and her credit card hurt from all the new clothes she'd bought. But, her outfit for Levi's birthday was sorted—a black lace jumpsuit with the tiniest little shorts and a plunging neckline paired with silver heels. She'd seen it and fallen immediately in love with it, and Emma had agreed.

"Okay, spit it out. I can tell something's wrong." Emma had stopped walking in the middle of the shopping centre. Arms full of bags, she looked ridiculous trying to cross them as she gave Katy a stern look. She couldn't help but laugh at her new friend. The funny thing was, they'd spent barely any time together, and yet they'd developed this crazy connection. She just knew that she and Emma would be friends for years to come. No wonder her cousin had fallen madly in love with her.

Katy sobered. "I don't even know where to start, to be honest."

"Tea and cake? Or cookies?" Emma grinned at Katy and linked arms with her, dragging her to the nearest coffee shop. They ordered and found a table for two in the corner of the cafe, hidden away among rows of indie books and artwork for sale.

Emma took her hand and squeezed. "You don't have to tell me anything, but if you want to talk about whatever it is that's going on, I'm here. Sometimes it helps to speak to a near stranger. Even though it feels like we've known each other forever."

"It does, doesn't it? And thanks for the offer. I'm just... I dunno... I'm not really ready to talk about things, mainly because everything is kinda swirling around in my head, and I can't make anything out. It's like being stuck in fog. I don't know how I feel about anything at the moment. I'm confused."

"Can you focus on the things that make you happy? Block out the rest?" Emma took a sip of her tea, setting down the giant mug after.

Katy stirred her coffee, watching the spoon swirl patters through the frothed milk. "I am, but something happened last night which is making me rethink things."

"Is it Levi?"

"I love him. More than anything." Katy smiled, thinking of her man.

"But?"

"No buts. I'll figure it out." Katy smiled again, this time knowing that she would do just that. The truth was, things had become clear the night before. Sitting down at dinner, she'd known. The protectiveness, the worry the platonic love she'd had for Con since the first day she'd met him was really something deeper. It wasn't the love between friends anymore. Perhaps it had never been. But she had Levi and never in a million years would she do anything to hurt him. He was far too important to her to do that to him. So as much as she loved Con, it'd only ever be friendship between them. "Lee and I are solid, and that's the only thing that matters. The rest will sort itself out."

"Do you have Levi's birthday present sorted?"

"Um, yeah, sort of. Con's helping me organize it." Katy grinned and leaned forward. "We're doing up his bike. Well, Con is anyway. I'm so damn excited about seeing him ride it when it's eventually finished." Dropping the spoon into her empty mug, she steeled her resolve. She had to get her runaway heart under control, and it needed to start right at that moment, especially because she was on her way home. He'd hooked up with Miranda the night before. And she and Levi were together. Katy had to remember that.

Arms weighed down with bags, Katy tried juggling her keys to unlock the front door, but it opened before she could grasp the right one. "Hi, Cupcake," Con greeted her as he swung the door open. It only took a second for him to relieve her of all her bags so she could step inside. "You did well today by the looks of it."

"I did." She nodded and smirked. "I picked up my outfit for Lee's party. And the shoes, oh my God, they're beautiful." Pointing to the smallest of the paper bags, a pink and black striped one, she added, "I picked up some cakes from work for you."

Con moaned, and she rolled her eyes, laughing at him as they walked down the hallway into the living room. "Place looks great, what have you guys been up to?"

Levi piped in, smiling at her as he met her in the middle of the room. "I tidied a bit this morning, and we just watched a replay of last night's footy match. I was just about to get dinner started."

Katy wrapped her arms around Levi and kissed him soundly. "That's so sweet, thank you."

"Anytime, sugar." Levi motioned to the bags Con dropped on the couch. "What's in there?"

"A few treats." She was being coy, but she didn't want to ruin the surprise.

"Urgh, fine." He pouted, letting her go. "Go relax. Con and I are cooking. Hope you feel like a barbie." With a finger under her chin, he tilted up her face and kissed her softly, his lips lingering on hers.

She cupped his face and leaned in close. "Love you, babe."

"Love you too. Now go. Outta my kitchen."

Katy laughed. It was anything but Levi's kitchen. He could cook two things—barbecued snags and toast—and usually both were burnt. She slapped his butt playfully and ducked out of his reach before he could tickle her. Picking up her bags from the couch she poked her tongue out at him and ran out of the room, avoiding Con's outstretched arm.

He followed her into her bedroom. Standing there, leaning on the doorframe he looked effortlessly sexy. Katy's heart flip-flopped and took a nosedive when she thought of him being with Miranda.

"I got a message back from Addy, my friend. She said she'd be happy to come over." At Katy's blank stare, he continued, looking sheepish, "Adelaide, the one with the toys."

"Oh, really?" Katy was stunned. "Okay, um... now what?"

"Call her up." He handed her a black business card with The Warehouse printed on one side of it in silver block lettering. On the other was a mobile number. "She's free on Saturday night. Give her your address and she'll come over." He shrugged. "Other than that, be honest about what you want to experience. Let her help you choose. It's what she does." She'd looked at Adelaide's website with the login details Connor had given her a few days earlier. Her range of toys on the public part of her website was only the tip of the iceberg. She held private tutorials on their use, which were perfect for inexperienced users like herself. Adelaide did couples coaching too—some with physical disabilities, others with relationship problems and some who just wanted to explore a kink in a safe environment. One of the kinks she'd found information on was threesomes. And by the looks of it, they were one of Adelaide's specialist areas. The images were graphic, but inspiring. Katy had spent hours analysing every one, imagining exactly how her, Levi, and Con could fit together like the trios in the pictures. Katy would love to speak with Adelaide about the possibility, but she was clue-less on how to raise it with her boyfriend.

At least she knew that Adelaide could help if they ever decided to explore that option. In nearly all of the images on her website, she was in the room, observing the couple or trio, guiding and praising them. She and Levi already had a pretty damn amazing sex life, but... what if?

"What about you?" she asked hesitantly. She wasn't really sure whether she was asking Con to go out or stay. She wanted him there, wanted him to be a part of them, but...

"What about me?" Con asked, confused. "I'll go out," he said as if it were a no-brainer. "I wouldn't want to cramp your style with me being in the other room."

The fact that he'd spoken to his friend suggested something so out of the box in the first place and had done it all for them, made Katy's heart expand. But there was a tinge of disappointment too, knowing it was another thing Con wouldn't be a part of. Not that Levi would go for that. She was sure that her growing feelings for Con were as transparent as glass to Levi. There was no way he hadn't figured out that she was falling in love with him. He had quickly become as dear to Katy as Levi was. Her love for Levi hadn't lessened—he was the love of her life and always would be, but she couldn't deny it anymore. If she was truthful, she'd always wanted him. Katy was attracted to both of them the minute she'd met them. Years ago, she'd thought it was mutual—she'd seen Con staring at her and had mistaken it for desire. It was so intense, so raw that his stare had taken her breath away. But then he'd looked at Levi the same way. And Con was as straight as an arrow. There was no way that look he'd cast their way was desire. It couldn't have been. And then he'd left, and her heart had broken. A piece of her soul went with him to the Middle East, but now that he was back, she couldn't help but hope. Of course, she had no idea what she was hopeful of, but as long as it involved Con in their lives, she'd be happy.

"I'll probably have a gig anyway," Con said jarring her back into the present.

"Wait, what? A gig?" He filled her in on his impromptu concert at breakfast that morning and how after speaking with the owner, he'd lined up a trial which, if he could pull it off, would possibly turn into a few gigs a week. Katy squealed and jumped forward, wrapping her arms around his waist. Levi jogged in with concern on his face.

"What's going on?"

"Connor's new job." She couldn't help the excitement in her voice.

"What new job?" He looked between them, confused.

"You didn't tell him?" she asked incredulously, squeezing Con tighter. She could smell his aftershave, feel the ripple of lean muscle along his chest as he tucked her under his arm, holding her close. She patted his stomach and added, "He's auditioning to play at a few pubs and cafes between here and Byron. Isn't that fantastic?"

"Dude, that's great." Levi stepped close and wrapped an arm around Con. The other one found her, pressing against the small of her back. Being enveloped in their arms, their strong embrace protective and loving, Katy was at home. All the pieces clicked into place. She wanted both of them. Would Levi be enough? Always. But with Con, that missing piece, the extra part of them which had been torn away when he'd left, leaving a gaping chasm in their hearts, slotted back into place. She pulled back, extracting herself from the midst of the hug to watch the two of them together, and *damn*.

Seeing them together, in something as simple as an embrace, had Katy wishing they were into each other—the three of them could be together then. Imagining Levi's familiar bulky shoulders and sculpted chest sliding against Con's leaner one, their bodies aligned and their tongues tangling as they kissed, they would be beautiful—like two caged wild animals, ferocious yet graceful in the most primal of ways. They could help each other too—Levi's passion would show Con how much he was loved, and Con would encourage Levi not to focus so much on living every second of life as the perfect Boy Scout. The morals clause in his contract with the studio had him second guessing so many of his actions that Katy wondered sometimes whether he needed the rush from the work he did to feel alive. But would they be happy? The two men had been friends since they were five. They'd grown up together. They'd shared everything. After Con's deadbeat dad had gone and got himself killed, Con had even lived with Levi's family. They were closer than brothers—best friends forever, minus the tackiness. If they found each other, if they fell in love, why would they need her? They wouldn't need or want her. She'd be in the way and would lose both of them. As the realization hit, Katy dropped her arms and stumbled back. She took a deep breath and let it out slowly. Their being together was a pipedream, one of those ridiculous notions that would never happen. She had to repeat the mantra to herself. The thought of losing the love of her life and her best friend to each other would be too painful to bear.

"When's your first gig?" Levi asked.

"Thursday night." He looked nervous. It was endearing when he shrugged his shoulder and flashed a sheepish smile her way. "Wanna come?"

"Are you kidding? We wouldn't miss it." Levi paused and asked quietly, "Will Miranda be there?"

"I dunno. Do you want her there?" The question was directed at both of them. She hated watching Miranda falling for Connor, but she couldn't—no wouldn't—stand in the way of his happiness. If he wanted her there, she had to encourage him.

"Sure, I don't mind." She was sure they'd pick up on the hollowness of her tone.

"Okay." Con nodded, but the look on his face—the resigned pull of his mouth, his lacklustre eyes—said it all. He wasn't happy. Would it be too much to hope for him not to invite her along? "I'll think about it. I dunno whether it's a good idea for her to be there when I'm tryin' to get the job."

4

LEVI

CONNOR'S FINGERS WORKED THE GUITAR AS IF HE WERE CARESSING a lover. His voice, like warm caramel, curled around them and created an intimate little bubble where it wasn't hard to imagine that he was singing just to him and Katy. Swaying to Connor's voice, Levi held Katy close on the dancefloor of the pub. It overlooked the river, a giant Bali hut with a bar at one end and a stage at the other. High tables surrounded this area, the picnic tables spread further out on the grassy slope went almost all the way down to the water. A breeze wafted through, the smell of rain in the air. Dim lighting in the gardens created shadows in the high palms, and the small spotlight on Connor had everyone's focus on him.

Levi closed his eyes and ran his fingers through Katy's long silky hair. She smelled of vanilla and chocolate, his favourite scent. Her warm skin was baby soft against his palm and her curves tempted him. He wanted to lay her down and make love to her right there on the stage next to Connor.

"This is my last song for the night. It's a smooth one so grab the hand of your guy or girl and love 'em." Connor smiled and began strumming the opening chords for Sam Smith and John

Legend's "Lay Me Down." Looking directly at them, Connor sang about missing a lover and being heartbroken. Part way through, he paused and reached out for Katy, pulling her up on stage with him. Levi let her go, but when Connor motioned for him to get up too, Levi smiled. Hardly missing a breath, Connor kept singing and shifted his gaze to Levi. His heart stuttered. *Is he singing to me too? It's a love song.* Part of him hoped so. But mates didn't sing each other love songs, did they? Confusion reigned supreme in his head, so Levi just let it go. It was easier not to think about it, easier to just live in the moment.

When Connor finished singing, he leaned in and kissed Katy softly on her lips. Seeing it was like a shot of lust-fuelled adrenaline straight to his bloodstream. He struggled to breathe through the instant haze of desire filling every pore in his body. Instead of pulling away, Con reached out, his firm touch on Levi's shoulder drawing him in. In Connor's embrace, Levi held him just as tight, the other man's breath tickling Levi's throat. He'd never had the urge to before, but he did then—he desperately wanted to kiss Connor. He wanted to haul the other man against his body and crush their lips together, to taste him, to caress him. *Goddamn it, I can't do this. What am I thinking? What the hell would Katy think if I did that? I can't hurt her like that.* Con kissing her is different—it's hot, but she'd probably think that he and Connor making out was a total turnoff.

Connor pulled into the drive and lifted Katy into his arms. Drunk, she'd fallen asleep curled around Levi in the back seat. He was going to hurt the next day—his head, his gut—Levi groaned already feeling it. He watched Katy wrap her arms around Con's neck, resting her head against his shoulder still asleep. Before he fell asleep himself, he dragged his arse from the back of the car and staggered after his friend. Levi fumbled the keys when he tried to open the front door; he was distracted. Katy had nuzzled her face into the crook of Connor's neck and was licking and kissing him there, sucking on the sensitive skin above his collarbone. He should have been jealous, annoyed that his girlfriend was kissing another man—logically he knew that—but he was glued to the sight of his best friend's eyes rolling back in his head. The gravelly moan that rumbled out of Con was doing things to Levi he didn't want to admit. His cock straining against the zipper of his jeans, salivating over the beautiful woman in his best friend's arms. Levi had to get Katy naked. Knowing she was the one making Connor moan like a man desperate for release had every possessive instinct rearing its head in him. But in the opposite way to what logic would have dictated he should react—he wasn't jealous, wasn't wanting her to stop. He wanted her to keep going, to give Connor what he needed. *How screwed up is that?*

By the time Levi stumbled into the bedroom, Con had already laid Katy down and taken off her four-inch heels. Still wearing her dark, low-cut skinny jeans and a silver top that was all tiny straps and low-cut necklines, she was stunning—all curvy and luscious. Levi licked his lips. Burying himself inside her until she was blissed out sounded perfect right about then.

Katy lifted her arm and covered her face blocking the light spilling in from the hall, rubbing her legs together as she did.

"What's up, sugar?" Levi asked. "You feeling okay?"

"No," she whined. "I'm fucking horny. I need you inside me, Lee. Con, tell him—he needs to."

"You heard the lady, Lee. Hope you're up for it." Connor turned away, and Levi reached out but let his hand fall away before he could grasp onto his friend. Instinct screamed at him to draw him close, to comfort him, to tell him... *what?* He wasn't sure. He'd seen something in Con's eyes—a momentary flash, but it was definitely there. Vulnerability? Loneliness? He wasn't sure.

Katy's frustrated growl made him laugh. "I can't get my damn pants off. My fingers aren't working anymore."

"I'll give you guys some privacy. Night." Con flashed a small smile that didn't reach his eyes, before leaving the room and closing the door behind him.

Torn between checking on his friend and looking after his girl, Levi stood there hesitating. His decision was made for him when Katy sat up and reached out for him, tugging him onto the bed.

"Levi," she breathed before she kissed him. Her lips soft against his, her tongue tracing the seam of his lips had him moaning. "Stay with me."

She needed him, and he'd never leave her hanging. Levi tugged the straps of Katy's top down, exposing her breasts to his hungry gaze. "Need you, Katy. Need to taste you now." He bent and captured her tight nipple in his mouth, tugging on the tender flesh with his teeth, making her cry out.

"Oh fuck, babe, yes," she hissed. "Please." Her begging sent a shiver through him. Levi moaned and ripped open the button fly of his jeans, palming his cock before tugging down her jeans. Burying his face in her pussy, he licked and nipped her sensitive skin. Her spicy-sweetness met his tongue, and he lapped it up, never getting enough of her taste. Levi lanced two fingers into her pussy and curled them, massaging Katy's G spot while he worked her clit between his lips. Over and over he thrust into her, working her up until she shuddered and went rigid, moaning her release as her inner muscles clenched around his digits. Levi knew exactly what it was like to have those muscles tensing around his shaft, pulling him into orgasm too. He couldn't wait anymore, couldn't stand the gap—although minimal—between their bodies. He crawled up and held himself over her, kissing her hard, their tongues tangling together as he ground against her.

Using her toes to push down his unbuttoned jeans, she ground out, "Fuck me, Lee. Hard and fast."

He loved her reactions, was addicted to the little sighs she made when he was hitting just the right spot, got off on seeing her eyes roll back into her head as he slid into her wet heat. Thrusting slowly, he prolonged his entry, teasing and tempting her with glimpses of what she'd asked for until he was eventually buried to the hilt. When Levi's balls were pressed up against her tight little arse, her legs wrapped tight around his hips, he withdrew and slammed back in, taking her in exactly the way she'd begged him. Kissing her, nipping her bottom lip, then soothing it with licks of his tongue as their lips melded together, Levi took her to the edge again, riding a fine line to hold off his own orgasm. The unstoppable tingle at the bottom of his spine had started. Levi clutched the sheets in an iron-fisted grip, desperately trying to hold off until Katy came again. Flutters in her pussy, quivers that quickly morphed into tight squeezes of her muscles around his cock, and her silent scream had Levi tumbling after her, coming so hard he saw stars behind his closed eyelids.

Connor

Connor lay on the living room couch drinking his first coffee of the morning when the message from the pub owner came in. He had to read it a few times before he believed it—he'd gotten the gig. Four nights a week, three different locations. He'd be making more than enough to support himself, even if he was renting a place on his own. He couldn't wipe the smile off his face. That was until the unmistakeable jingle of Katy's alarm on her phone sounded, followed shortly afterwards by Levi's phone ringing. He glanced at where they sat on the kitchen bench and winced. He didn't want to wake them up, especially with the killer hangover they'd probably both have.

He scrubbed a hand over his face and sighed. At least they'd had a few more hours sleep than him. After the ruckus the two of them made the night before, he guessed they'd passed out. But Connor had no hope of sleeping. Listening to the gasps and moans coming from the bedroom next door had him fisting the sheets to physically keep him connected to the bed; otherwise, he'd have been through their door in a shot, rolling around naked with them. Finally unable to resist it anymore, he'd given into temptation to relieve the iron rod tenting his boxer shorts. But jacking off hadn't taken the edge off. Instead, having his hand on his cock while letting his mind conjure up pictures to match Levi and Katy's gasps and moans had Connor imagining exactly what it would be like to be between them. He tugged on the piercing at the base of his balls before letting his fingers drift lower to rub his hole, while he worked the other lubed up hand over his aching dick.

His inevitable orgasm had barrelled towards him in record time when he'd lifted his legs and pressed a finger inside the tight pucker of his arse. He'd never had a cock up there—not a real one anyway. Connor's last hookup had begged him to try it. He'd always been curious, had heard about the magic bundle of nerves that could shoot a man into orbit. She'd found it, and he'd come so hard, he'd passed out. The memory of the fullness, the stretch and burn were almost enough. He'd breached himself with two of his fingers, pumping in and out while he'd gripped his dick. The overload of sensations pushed him past the edge, the tingle at the base of his spine gathering momentum quickly and spreading outward until Connor shot his load. Breathing hard, his fingers still stretching his ass, the cum cooling on his chest and chin, Connor had let his eyes drift closed. God, he'd wished, wished so hard, but it was absolutely pointless. And didn't that knowledge suck.

On the fourth ring of Levi's phone, he gave in, answering it. "G'day, Levi's phone. Connor speaking."

"Hey, Connor, I'm DJ. I work with Levi. Is he there?"

"He's, ah... in the bathroom." Connor winced. He hoped that was the right answer to give DJ, rather than he's already left.

"He's supposed to be coming in this morning to train with the Titans, but the director is having a fit because he's not here yet. Can you get him to call me urgently? I need to know when he'll be arriving so I can fend him off."

"No worries. I'll give him the hurry up and get him to call." *Fuck.* He disabled the alarm on Katy's phone while he was in the kitchen, and scratched the two-day old growth on his face, grimacing at the thought of their hangovers. *I need a plan.* When he remembered Katy's fix for a headache—*Lush*—he grinned. She loved the place, would come home with bags full of bath bombs and soaps. He ran the water, dropping in one of her favourite bombs before pouring another couple of mugs of coffee, setting one on the tray straddling the bath and taking the other with him.

Connor knocked on the door and opened it a crack. All he could hear was deep breathing. He tiptoed into the room and, without looking at them, set the coffee down next to Levi. *How the hell do I wake them without looking at them? Man up, Connor.* He stole a glance and stopped in his tracks. Both were completely naked, the sheet discarded at the bottom of the bed. Levi lay on his back, his legs spread open while Katy was wrapped around him. *Fuck me.* Perfect—that was the only way to describe them.

Levi didn't have an ounce of fat on him—which Connor already knew—but he'd underestimated the beauty of the other man's physique. Levi could have been one of the models in those Greek statues, and the morning wood he sported was nothing short of impressive. Connor licked his lips, wishing he could get his hands, his mouth, on the other man.

Connor's gaze moved to Katy, and he took in her curves, the swell of her breast pressed against Levi's chest, the flare of her hips and the contour of her arse. Right down to her cute purple sparkly-painted toes, she was perfect. He wanted her with a fierceness that hadn't dampened during the years they'd been apart. Connor knew he was staring, but he couldn't help it. Hell, he couldn't do anything else.

"Gorgeous, isn't he?" Katy rasped in a sexy morning voice. Connor nodded before he even knew what he was doing. There was no use trying to hide the tenting of his loose track pants from her, so he pushed on.

"How ya feelin', Cupcake?"

"Like shit. My head's gonna explode."

"Your alarm was going off. Something about Australian Bride flashed up."

"Fuck." Katy closed her eyes and groaned.

"I've run a bath, and there's coffee in the bathroom already."

"You're a lifesaver, thank you." Holding her head as she sat up, Katy moved to the edge of the bed. He looked away, giving her a little privacy, but his eyes were drawn to the man before him. The little voice in his head—the one chanting "you don't like dudes"—was getting drowned out by the reality of his body's almost visceral reaction to both Katy and Levi. Pushing it aside, he shook his head.

"Lee, mate, you've gotta get up. You've gotta go to work." He didn't budge, didn't even flinch when Connor called out to him. He reached down to shake him awake, but the other man's warm skin under his palm, firm muscles relaxed against his touch, had Connor sliding his hand down his chest. Touching him in a way he'd never been able to do before, Connor yearned for the chance to show him—both of them, really—what was in his heart. He ran his fingertips over the sprinkling of chest hair to his abs, feeling the ridges of his six-pack as he moved. He shook Levi and repeated himself, his voice an almost unrecognisable rasp. Lee stirred and moaned, covering his eyes with his arm. Connor watched every muscle in his upper body shift as Levi moved, and Connor's gut clenched with want.

"Why do I feel like shit?"

"Hangover, man, and you need to go to work. DJ called, said something about training with the Titans."

"You're shitting me. That's today?"

"Sorry, mate, you've gotta get there now." Connor picked up the mug and held it out to his friend. "Here, I brought coffee."

"Ta." Levi sat up and clutched his head. "I feel like crap. And why's the room spinning?" He moaned. "I'm gonna puke."

"I'll help you up when you're ready." Levi downed half his coffee and swung his legs off the bed, swaying as he did. "You gonna be okay for work?"

Levi grunted his response and held out his hand for Connor to pull him up. Slinging the other man's arm over his shoulder, Connor guided him into the bathroom and turned on the shower. Stumbling forward, Levi stuck his head under the water.

"I think I'm gonna pass out." Levi swayed in the shower, his skin turning pallid. It had Connor moving, stripping off his track pants and stepping in the cubicle with his friend. He pushed him gently against the tiles to steady Levi and directed the spray onto him, wetting his hair before shampooing it up. The strands were silky under his touch, the shorter parts on the back and sides softer than he'd imagined. Connor kept his movements quick, trying not to let himself enjoy the contact with his best friend too much. He'd gone from jealousy to longing in what seemed like a heartbeat, but in reality, it'd been a long time coming. Connor was man enough to admit to himself that his sexuality wasn't as straight as he'd once thought it to be. It wasn't like anything would ever come of it though. As long as he kept reminding himself of that fact, he'd be fine.

"How're you doin' now?" Connor asked, keeping his voice low.

"Really? You're standing starkers in a shower with me, washing my hair because I drank too much. I only had like three JD and Cokes. I shouldn't be that wrecked."

"When was the last time you drank anything? I bet you haven't touched a single drink in years—at least since you've been on the show." Connor shook his head and huffed out a laugh. "No wonder you feel like shit."

Levi groaned and held his stomach, flattening his palm against his six-pack.

"Don't worry, we'll get some food in you and you'll be right."

Levi shook his head. "No food."

Connor put down the shower gel he'd just picked up. "Bud, you can't train with a professional footy team without eating anything. Bacon and eggs'll do ya good."

Levi moaned, what little colour he had in his face, draining fast. "Why does it have to be today? God, I don't wanna go in."

Connor smiled. The poor guy was miserable, but it was totally self-inflicted. He didn't have that much sympathy. "Think you can wash yourself?" Levi nodded, and Connor handed him the gel. Squirting some on his hands, and rubbing it over his belly, Levi paused and leaned back against the glass again, closing his eyes and taking a deep breath.

"Breathe through it, mate. You'll be right." Connor took the body wash from Levi and ran his hands over Levi's shoulders, soaping him up. Slicked up muscle glided under his palms.

Smooth, warm skin against his own had Connor biting his lip to hold in a moan. Levi had his eyes closed, his head leaning back against the tiled wall. Connor was grateful for it. He was hard, but he didn't want to be. There was no hiding it or denying it. How would he explain himself if Levi saw? The dude was not only straight but totally in a relationship. And there Connor was, naked in the shower with him, hard as a freaking telegraph pole and washing him. He looked away, unable to meet Levi's gaze if he opened his eyes.

He tried desperately to ignore the body of the man in front of him, but his gaze kept snapping back to Levi's hard planes, warm golden skin, and blond hair. He drank in the sight before him, knowing he'd never again be in that position. Lower still and Connor's hands stuttered. Levi was hard too, his cock thick, rivulets of water dancing along his skin. Connor sucked in a sharp breath and washed down to Levi's waist, forcing himself to keep going, or maybe he was making himself stop.

Levi's words broke him out of his spell. "I'm okay, mate. Don't worry. I won't ask you to wash my junk." He huffed out a laugh that sounded as uncomfortable as he probably felt standing naked in the shower with his friend.

Connor cleared his throat and handed him the gel, stepping back and out of the shower. He didn't know whether to be disappointed or relieved. Either way, he was grateful that both of them were in the same predicament—at least his friend wouldn't call him a perv if they were both walking around with boners. Connor shook his head as he towelled off. He needed to get laid—being unintentionally celibate sucked donkey dick. He needed to hook up with a nice girl somewhere that he could enjoy the hell out of so that his ridiculous infatuation with his best mate and his girl would disappear. *I know it will... I think. Maybe.*

He made a quick exit after that, wrapping the towel around

his waist as he left Levi's bedroom and knocked on the other bathroom door to check on Katy. "Cupcake, how're you doin'?"

"I'm hungry and late. Think you can be a prince and make some toast for me?"

"Yeah, no problems." He paused. "Hey, what can I make for Lee? He's pretty green."

"Weet-bix, full cream milk and a banana cut up on it. It'll be the only thing he can keep down."

Connor grimaced. How could that possibly cure Levi's hangover? But Katy knew him best, so he'd do it.

Katy rushed out, still buttoning up a pristine white chef's jacket as he placed the Vegemite toast on the bench for her. She didn't normally wear much make-up, but this time she was done up like she had been for their double date over the weekend. Seeing his surprise, she kissed him on the cheek, squeezed his arse and grinned. "Thanks, boo. This photo shoot's important. Australian Bride is doing a two-page spread on the shop— photos of my work and everything. I dunno whether they'll want me in any of them, but figure I'd be better off looking a little prepared."

He smiled. "You look gorgeous. You'll knock 'em dead."

Looking at her watch, she swore under her breath. "I gotta go."

"I want details when you get home." Leaning in, Connor stole another kiss on her soft cheek.

"Good luck, sugar. Love you," Levi called from the doorway.

"You too, babe." Katy broke away from Connor and moved into Levi's arms. He turned away, trying not to watch as they kissed goodbye, but was unable to stop himself. Seriously, he was a masochist. Watching Levi pull her into his arms and nuzzle their noses together, his lips lingering against hers was a new kind of torture. Sweet and sensual, it was exactly how Connor wanted to kiss her, kiss both of them.

The door clicked closed, and Connor realized he was staring at the sizzling bacon in the pan, without actually seeing anything. Shaking himself out of his funk, he flipped it and went back to staring.

"Dude, you rock. Thanks," Levi spoke from behind him, his voice muffled by the food he was shovelling in. "Whatcha doin' today?"

"Got a few bits and pieces I need to take care of. Nothing much, but I'll be busy most of the day."

"Hey, you were great last night. I don't think I've seen a guy on an acoustic guitar get people dancing before."

"You and Katy were the only ones most of the night, and you were slow dancing. Doesn't exactly count as rocking the crowd, but Tracey must've liked it. I got the gig."

"That's awesome." Levi clapped him on the back, his hand lingering and squeezing his shoulder. He stood much closer than he normally did and Connor's eyes slid closed, a craving for the other man coursing through him. Levi's murmured words sent a prickle of awareness through him. "Told you you're good. Don't talk yourself out of it."

"Thanks, man." Connor's voice was husky, raw from all the feels ripping him apart.

Dropping his hand, Levi stepped back and Connor could breathe again. "Can I ask you a personal question?" When Connor nodded, he continued. "Did your Prince Albert—that's your piercing, yeah?—did it hurt?"

"Not as much as you'd think. The other ones were worse—not pain wise, but they took longer to heal."

"I've thought about nipple rings but, you know—work." He shrugged.

Connor turned to face him, his brows knitted in confusion.

Levi held himself back so much because of his damn job—tattoos, piercings, bike—anything he wanted to express himself with was a no-go. "Do they have your balls in a vice? Why are they so uppity about what you can and can't do?"

"I've got a morals clause in my contract. If I so much as think about doing the wrong thing, they'll fire me. None of the stuff I want is worth my job."

He nodded, finally understanding. "That sucks."

"A bit, but it's a trade-off." Looking at his watch, he groaned. "I'm late. Gotta go." Grinning at Connor, Levi's face transformed, and Con's breath caught. Levi's radiant smile had his heart stuttering. "See you tonight, honey." Connor lunged for him as Levi snatched a piece of crispy bacon from the pan and bit down on it. Laughing, Lee winked at him and jogged out the door, Connor grumbling good naturedly under his breath.

Connor was still wiping his hands on the rag he kept in the back pocket of his coveralls as he walked to the shop for lunch. Sweat beaded on his brow and ran down between his shoulder blades. He'd unbuttoned the coveralls and wore the arms tied around his waist. He hoped no one minded him not wearing a shirt, but it was as hot as the devil's arse crack walking down the street. He was picking up the orders for everyone—it was the least he could do to say thank you to his father's old partner when he was using their tools, their time and their space to rebuild Levi's bike. It still wasn't even close to being finished, but at least he'd started it. He'd sent the fuel tank away to be primed for painting, and some other parts were still on order, but there was plenty of wiring and reassembly of engine parts that he could do in the meantime. He didn't notice Miranda until she stepped directly in his path. "Hi, gorgeous. How are you?"

"Hey, Miranda. I'm good. How're you?"

"Great now that I've seen you. You have plans tonight? I'm stopping to get a drink before I go home. Maybe you could join me. Or you could come over for a nightcap." She smiled sweetly at him, but he wasn't fooled. Connor unsuccessfully tried to bite back his laughter. Underneath the sweet exterior, she had the mind of a vixen. Maybe she was exactly who he needed to spend time with rather than fixating on his impossible-to-get best friends. Seeing his hesitation, she added, "Or we could hang at Levi's party tomorrow?"

"That'd work better. I've been in the workshop all day so I probably won't be great company tonight, but tomorrow night's great."

"Fine," she sighed, rolling her eyes but grinning at him. "Pick me up tomorrow night."

"Will do." Connor smiled but stepped back when she went to kiss him. "I'm all sweaty and greasy. You don't want to get dirty."

5

KATY

Katy sipped her juice and looked out across the dancefloor of the sports bar. They were in a converted warehouse overlooking the river. The deck outside had a spectacular view of the Surfers Paradise skyline to the east. They were in the quieter end of town, but the bar had a great vibe. All distressed timber and deep red bricks with heavy steel beams and walls of glass, the place was modern, yet had the charm of a restored building.

Leaning against a high table made of heavy railway sleepers, she watched as the DJ spun records on the turntable, old school style, and moved to the beat of the heavy dance music pumping out of the speakers. Their friends were gathered around them laughing and drinking, quite a few dancing too. Katy should have been happy—everyone was enjoying themselves—but her heart was heavy. She'd had fun the night before—probably too much.

It was late when she'd walked in the door to find Levi and Con, feet propped up on the coffee table, drinking ginger beer and watching a rerun of a championship boxing match. Empty bottles littered the table and she'd raised an eyebrow at them until Lee had cracked open another one and held it up for her, while Con patted the couch between them. Pizza had arrived a few minutes later, and with the boys clearing the table and answering the front door, Katy had flipped the channel to *The Big Bang Theory*, hid the remote and pulled the table closer so she could put her feet up. There wasn't even a murmur of dissent when they'd re-joined her on the couch. Instead, the boys had gotten comfortable, handed her a slice, and made a marathon of the old reruns.

The wait-staff placed Levi's cake on the biggest table in their sectioned-off area and waved at her. Katy nodded and smiled as she walked over to them. She liked how it turned out —totally different to what she was used to making, but that was half the fun. A football field complete with plastic Maroons and Blues players, painted on sponsors' logos and a scoreboard reflecting Queensland's last win in the State of Origin, was a nice change to what she was used to working with. She'd applied the finishing touches the night before, while she was still riding the high from the interview she'd rocked with *Australian Bride*. Katy smiled as she pressed the sparklers into the cake, ready to light them when Levi eventually made his way back to her.

She scanned the dancefloor checking where he was. Her eyes landed on Con and Miranda. Drink in hand, Con had his other wrapped tight around her waist as they moved as one on the floor. Miranda straddled his leg, her hands in his back pockets while they danced, the same way they had been all night. And Katy hadn't been able to take her eyes off him. Between he and Levi—who was avoiding the dancefloor like the plague—her attention had been split. Annoyed at herself for not enjoying the night she'd worked so hard to plan, Katy dragged her eyes away and searched the rest of the area.

An arm getting thrown around her shoulder and the flash of a camera startled Katy. Sarah, her friend, stood next to her taking a selfie. Katy pushed away from her and pursed her lips, irritated at herself for her reaction to her friend.

"What's up, Katy?"

"Nothing." Even she could hear how sullen she sounded.

"You're being shitty." Sarah hiked up her eyebrows daring Katy to respond and when she didn't, Sarah continued. "You've been shooting daggers at Connor all night. Sick of him in your space?"

"What? No." Katy shook her head. "He's great...." She didn't know how to put into words what was going on in her head, wasn't sure if she'd share it with Sarah anyway. "He's not imposing on us at all. He's smart and sweet, and we love having him with us."

"So what's the problem then?"

Katy bit down on her knuckle. "It's nothing. I'm being stupid."

"If you're not happy, it's *not* nothing." Sarah looked her over, assessing her. Katy was no good at hiding her emotions at the best of times, but that night she was raw, exposed. She wasn't surprised when Sarah asked, "Are you falling in love with him?"

"No, I mean, he's Lee's best friend. They're like brothers—"

"That doesn't mean you can't fall for him."

Katy shook her head more vehemently this time. "We've been friends forever. I love him like a brother." Katy winced. She didn't love him like a brother—not even close to it. And there was no doubt that Con was ogling Levi the day before. After that, she wouldn't even classify their relationship as brotherly; especially not after Levi had told her that they'd showered together. She closed her eyes, fear overtaking her. *If they're in love, they won't need me. I want them happy, but where would it leave me? It'd tear me apart—I'd lose the love of my life and both my best friends.*

"Well?" Sarah prompted.

"Well what?" Katy asked, unaware of Sarah having even asked her a question.

"Are you and Levi okay?"

"Yeah." Katy paused and nodded, smiling. "Yeah, he's great. We're great. I love him."

"I'm always here if you want to talk, you know that."

"Thanks, Sarah." Katy gave her a small smile, her attention shifting to Levi when he wrapped his arms around her, kissing her temple. Katy snuggled into him, needing his strength.

"You okay, sugar? You've been quiet tonight."

"Having a bit of a rough night, but I'll be okay."

"Yeah, me too." He squeezed her tighter and Katy breathed him in, never wanting to let him go.

She sliced a piece of cake and plated it, handing it to her man, before kissing him softly. "Happy birthday, babe." He winked at her and took a bite, his eyes rolling back in his head at the dense black forest cherry cake she'd made. Grinning, she cut another piece and held it out to Con. Her insides knotted when Miranda snatched it out of her hand before he could grip it. He pursed his lips together, stifling a grin when Miranda held out a forkful, trying to feed him. The fact that he saw the humour in what she was doing made it a little easier to stomach, but it still cut like a knife when Con turned his attention to Miranda and took the bite she offered. She loved her friend, but *God* what was she thinking setting them up? She wanted him happy, but it was tearing her apart watching Con with her. And the guilt at being so selfish was eating Katy alive.

Con was drunk, and Levi was taking Miranda back to her place, no doubt dropping Con off there too, before Levi headed home.

Ironic that it was his birthday and he was the designated driver, but it wasn't surprising. Katy couldn't handle another headache like the one she'd struggled with the day before—there was no way she was doing it again. She kicked the front door closed and dropped her shoes on the floor. She'd abandoned them in the club, dancing in bare feet toward the end of the night, and her feet were killing her. The damn jumpsuit she wore wasn't comfortable either. It looked super cute on—short shorts with a low V-shaped neckline that sat just above her bellybutton, and long sleeves—and totally worth wearing, but her skin was starting to get irritated by all the taping she had to wear to keep her boobs in place. A hot shower would do her a world of good.

She stripped as she walked to their attached bathroom, dropping the jumpsuit halfway down the hall. Her nude under-wear went next, the G-string falling by the bed and, finally, the damn tape. Dumping it in the bin beside the toilet, Katy turned on the water and waited for it to heat before stepping under. Streaming down on her, Katy held her breath under the spray. Tired muscles relaxed in the pounding heat and she sighed in relief when, one by one, she held the soles of her feet in the stream. Resting her hands on the tiled wall, Katy closed her eyes and tried to quiet her mind. She didn't wish for much, just the impossible. Fucking irony. She shook her head. She was being greedy and forgetting how wonderful her life was. She had an amazing man who would do anything for her. Levi loved fiercely and was loyal to a fault. She adored him with every fibre of her being. Katy wouldn't give Levi up for the world, so Con being happy and falling for someone was a good thing—it meant that the three of them would be happy. They didn't need to be together for that—who the hell had a three-way relationship anyway? No, she was exactly where she was supposed to be.

Flipping off the water after washing herself, Katy dried and brushed out her hair before pulling on one of Levi's oversized T-shirts. Some guys thought lingerie was sexy, but not Levi. He loved it when she wore his clothes—and she loved being wrapped in something that smelled of him, that told him how she craved his strong arms around her. And with Con staying at Miranda's house, he was sure to do just that.

The door crashing open startled her, making her move towards it to check on Levi. As she did, Con yelled, "Honey, we're home."

"Shh," Levi hissed as another crash sounded, a set of keys falling onto the floor when Con stumbled.

"It's okay babe, I'm up," Katy reassured him as she leaned against the wall, smiling at the sight before her. Levi was trying to manhandle a drunk Con into his bedroom, but Con had other ideas, grasping onto the doorframe.

"Damn," Con breathed, perusing her from head to toe. His gaze was like warm honey, making tingles erupt all over her as he openly appreciated her. "I love you, you know." He was slurring, the shots he'd downed earlier in the night still affecting him. "And you, Lee. Love both of you." Katy couldn't help but grin. He was an adorable drunk.

"Come on, boo. Let's get you into bed." Katy moved to stand on Con's other side and wrapped her arm around his waist, helping Levi guide him into his room.

"I'm hard again," he moaned, rubbing the bulge in his jeans.

Turning to Levi, Katy nodded to the bed. "Let's get him lying down, and we'll be able to get his clothes off."

"Fuck, yeah. I'll look after you, Cupcake."

"Not tonight, boo," she replied gently. Levi unzipped his jeans as Katy pulled off his shoes and socks, tossing them onto the floor.

"Lift your arse up, Con," Lee ordered quietly, tugging down his jeans once he did. Katy reached out and helped guide them off. She moved back up his body and unbuttoned his shirt.

Smoothing her palms over his muscled chest, Katy pushed the soft material off his shoulders. Con smiled a lazy, contented grin. But there was heat lurking behind the liquor-induced haze. Levi took his hand and pulled Con up so he was sitting on the bed, then straddled one of Con's thighs to hold him in place. While Levi did that, Katy knelt behind Con and pulled his shirt away.

Running her hands over his smooth skin, Katy caught the hitch in Con's breath and the subtle way he swayed between her touch and Levi's. Sitting there, legs spread, wearing only a pair of tight black boxer shorts, Con pushed his hand down, adjusting the erection tenting them. A moan, that was almost illicit with the need tainting it, had Katy shifting, moving to the side so she could help Con lie down. The two of them were barely wearing anything—Katy only a T-shirt and Con in his underwear—and she found herself wishing that Levi would hurry the hell up and get undressed too.

Con ran his callused hand up her leg, tracing the curve of her ass, as he fisted Lee's shirt and pulled them toward him when he laid back. Katy pitched forward and fell on top of him, her breasts pushing against the hard planes of his chest. Levi hovered over them, holding himself up with one strong arm, the other hand on Con's chest, his strong fingers flexing into the lean muscle there. Katy couldn't tear her eyes away from the sight of them together. Levi's knee was pressed between Con's legs, and Con rocked his hips, grinding against the thick muscle with smooth, sensual movements.

She couldn't resist touching him, a shiver racing through her body as she trailed her fingertips over his rippling abs. Con nuzzled into her hair, the puff of warm breath against her temple making her sigh. Levi moaned quietly before going rigid next to her. Whatever spell was winding itself around them was broken, the growing intimacy between them instantly evaporating.

"Ah, I... we... I've gotta go." Levi stumbled off the bed backward and hit the wall, his chest heaving with the breaths he sucked in.

"Me too," Katy whispered, inexplicably close to tears. Shame pulsed through her as she jumped off the bed and raced out the door. She was pushing them into something neither wanted. Desire clouded her better judgement, and it was going to destroy their relationship. She just knew it. What the hell was she thinking, undressing Con and touching him like she had a right to?

Alone and instantly missing the warmth of the two men she'd been so close to a second ago, Katy cried.

Levi

It would have been so easy to let go, to kiss the plump lips of the man in front of him, to give into temptation. But it wasn't easy, and he couldn't give in. Connor's touch—so different to Katy's—held him pinned to the spot as Connor rutted on his leg. The thing was, Levi had no idea whether it was visions of Katy almost naked and looking as hot as hell in his T-shirt, the shots his friend had downed, or whatever the heck it was growing between the three of them—assuming Levi wasn't totally off his rocker and imagining things—that had Connor so turned on. But whichever the reason, Levi's dick didn't seem to mind. He was hard as stone in a pair of jeans which were, at that moment, far too tight.

Levi was starting to admit to himself that it wasn't just his girlfriend who turned him inside out, who had him hard in an instant. It was Connor too. The dream he'd been having over and over of the three of them together, sweaty and sated, had him waking up every morning with a boner which demanded satisfaction. The fact that he now had memories of Connor's soapy hands running over his skin, of his lean body aroused as much as he'd been, made him swing back and forth between blindingly horny and terrified. What did it mean? He'd always classed himself as straight, but maybe he'd just been oblivious. Maybe he hadn't wanted to acknowledge whatever it was that he was struggling with now. He may not have been sure of his sexuality, but he could no longer deny that Connor did something to him. The other man's strength, the knowledge that Connor could and did pull him down, knocking him completely off balance—metaphorically as much as physically—had Levi so damn close to giving in that he was wobbling on a tightrope, only a misstep away from a long drop with a very hard landing. And yet, he was tempted, so tempted to jump, to freefall into his best friend. It was only Katy, sexy in his tee and lying next to him, on top of Connor, and the knowledge that he'd break her heart that stopped him from leaning in to kiss Connor. And wasn't knowing that—realizing that maybe he'd denied another side of himself—a total mind fuck?

Hovering above Connor after he'd pulled him down, Levi tentatively pressed his leg between Connor's a little harder, giving the other man a touch more friction against his cock. The punch of Con's hips up had Levi imagining diving off that tightrope and showing exactly how far he could fall. He never intended the moan that escaped his lips to break free, but when it came out at the same time as Katy's sigh, Levi went rigid. What in the hell was he doing? He couldn't do that to Katy, couldn't hurt her by taking that step.

Wouldn't.

The force of his thoughts slammed into him like a freight train, and he stumbled back off the bed, connecting with the wall before he could fall. Hands pressed against the cool surface, Levi's heart pounded in his chest, beating hard enough that he could hear the rushing of blood through his veins. Katy rushed from the room, tears in her eyes. She could tell what was going through his mind. He knew it. When he turned back to Connor, what he saw broke him, crushed his heart like it was in a vice. Where a moment ago he was playful, sensual, his face had paled and he held a pillow in front of him, shielding himself with it. Scrambling up the bed so he was in the far corner, Connor looked like he'd been slapped. Levi was torn, literally being ripped in two. Who the hell did he choose? His girlfriend—the love of his life—or his lifelong best friend? He'd hurt both of them, all because of his selfishness. All because he thought he might, one day, be ready to accept that he had another side to himself he'd hidden from.

Levi dropped his gaze and, with the weight of the world on his shoulders, slunk away from Connor. Hands in his pockets, he stood outside his own bedroom and looked to the closed door. The physical barrier between them spoke volumes. He turned away and headed for the couch in the living room.

"Catch ya later. I'll be back tomorrow," Connor muttered. They'd barely seen him in the week since the clusterfuck that was the aftermath of Levi's birthday party, but when they had, he'd been distant. Connor wasn't the only one though. Things had been strained between all of them, and the guilt of it ate Levi alive. Every time he looked at Katy without her smile, he wanted the ground to swallow him. He'd put that misery on her face by playing with fire. He'd taken her happiness, and Levi didn't even know where to begin to get it back.

Connor stood before him, waiting for a response. On the

surface, he looked good in his jeans and Henley, but the dark circles under his eyes told Levi he also lay awake at night. Not that he'd needed the hint—he'd heard Connor's pained moans from the room next door. The nightmares he'd been plagued with had broken Levi's heart. He'd wanted so much to go to him, but he hadn't. He couldn't risk hurting Katy more.

"You planning on staying at Miranda's?" Not that it was any of his business to know, but something in Levi's screwed up brain made him ask.

"Yeah, probably." He shrugged. "Maybe. I dunno yet."

"Well, have fun." Levi couldn't look him in the eye anymore, couldn't see the judgement in his gaze.

"You too, mate." His response was quiet, withdrawn, much like he'd been for the better part of the week. Levi sighed and scrubbed a hand across his forehead. He had a headache.

Katy's hands on his shoulders, massaging them had him leaning into her touch. She murmured to him, "Dinner'll be ready in a few. Why don't you go shower? You'll feel better."

"Yeah, sugar, thanks." He gave her a small smile and stood up. He hated breaking the contact between them—the first for days—but she was right, he needed a shower.

It was unlike Katy to keep her mobile with her at the dinner table, but when it dinged with a message, she practically jumped for it. If he didn't know better, he'd think she was nervous. But over what? Taking a deep breath and blowing it out slowly, Katy looked over at him and opened her mouth as if to say something. Hesitating, she stopped and shook her head. "Gimme a minute. I'll be back."

Levi watched, confused and more than a little worried, while Katy pushed back her chair and walked to the front of the house. When he heard the door, Levi stood and followed the path she'd taken, calling out, "Katy, you okay?"

Standing before him with Katy was a familiar face. He'd seen her before—her style was unmistakeable—but he couldn't place where.

"Lee, do you remember Adelaide?"

Hearing her name, jogged his memory. He knew exactly where he'd met her before. "I do." Levi smiled and held out his hand. The woman before him looked like a more daring version of Sandra Dee with her hot pink hair and sweet yet sexy styling—she pulled off the black corporate looking dress with just a hint of cleavage, pale pink cardigan with the top button done up, fishnets and killer heels really well. Even the suitcase she wheeled around with her matched her style. "Good to see you again. You're Con's friend, aren't you?"

"I am." Adelaide smiled and shook his hand.

"Let's head into the lounge room." Katy led them to the room he'd just come from and sat awkwardly at one end of the couch. "Sit here, Lee." She patted the middle seat—her usual spot.

"Not that I mind visitors, because Adelaide you're always welcome here, but what's going on, sugar? You're kinda freaking me out."

"I wanted to get you something special for your birthday. I'm not sure whether it's a good idea anymore... this week has kinda sucked, but well...." She trailed off, looking awkwardly between the two of them.

Levi sat down heavily and held his head low. "I'm sorry, Katy. It's my fault—"

"It's not. It's mine—" Katy stopped talking when Levi reached out and squeezed her hand.

"It's not your fault. Never think that." When Katy wrapped her arms around his waist, Levi kissed her temple and held her tightly. He looked over when he heard Adelaide lay down the case she was rolling in and sat down on the armchair next to Katy.

Katy pulled back and looked him in the eye. "Okay, so Adelaide owns a mobile adult store. She's come here because I asked her to help us choose some toys that we might have some fun with. I thought you'd appreciate being discreet about it rather than going into a store somewhere. And given we've got no idea what we're doing, she can instruct us on how to use them properly, rather than just buying something random online." She was rambling adorably and the relief of knowing he hadn't screwed up their relationship too badly filled him. That was until thoughts of *that* movie filled his brain and made him cringe.

"Um, okay," Levi hesitated. "What sort of toys are we talking about?"

"I have everything available that you'd find in an adult store. Obviously, I've only got a few samples here and some new products that I can leave with you tonight, but if you find something specialized that I don't have on me, I'll order it in and deliver it to you. My most popular products are vibrators, plugs, cock rings, lube, and cleaners for the toys."

Okay, this doesn't sound half bad. Hella good actually. Levi nodded, smiling when with a hint of excitement in her voice, Katy asked, "What would you recommend for beginners?"

Adelaide's friendly smile had him at ease. He was comfortable with her already. When she unzipped the bag, flipping open the lid, Levi couldn't deny he was curious. Peeking inside he saw that it was packed full of neatly stacked boxes, satin bags, and bottles of all sizes. She moved a few of them around and lifted some out. "Okay, so if you haven't played with toys before I'd recommend a starter pack of sorts; something for each of you." She took out a smooth purple vibrator. "This is one of my favourites." After describing all the features, she handed it and a few others to Katy who turned them on, playing with the different speeds.

"I like that." Katy put the purple one down then reached out for it again, before pulling back.

"It's okay," Adelaide encouraged. "Play around with them, get to know them and how they feel. The more you check the products out now, the more likely it is you'll be happy with your decision." Seeing Katy handle the vibes of all different shapes and sizes made Levi want to toss her over his shoulder caveman style and carry her into bed, not leaving until she'd come so many times she couldn't see straight. He discreetly adjusted himself while the ladies were absorbed in the different vibrators, pulling his hand away just as Adelaide turned her attention to him.

She smiled, this one knowingly. "Don't worry, I haven't forgotten about you. I'd recommend one of these for you." She pulled out what looked like a silicone ring with a bullet in it. "It's a vibrating cock ring. Safe to wear with or without a condom, depending on whether you two use them or not. As long as you're using lube, there's no pain getting it on or off. It can be used during masturbation, oral sex, vaginal, or anal sex." *Anal sex. With Connor.* Heat flared in him, desire roiling low in his gut. Never mind the semi, he was at full-mast now. She handed it to him and he turned it over in his hands. *What would it feel like to use it with them?* "It's intended to be snug. It'll delay orgasm but not prevent it..." Adelaide kept talking but Levi's thoughts had drifted. The what-ifs circled around his head just out of reach, taunting him. The thought of losing Katy almost killed him. He wouldn't hurt her, but his absolute visceral reaction to even the thought of what sex with Connor would be like, had him sucking in a breath staving off the light-headedness.

When there was silence, Levi looked up at both of them. "Levi, are you okay?" Adelaide asked, her head tilted to the side. It was as if she had him under a microscope. The room suddenly became too hot and he wanted to flap his collar just to get some damn air flowing. He could hammer nails with his boner, and he was sure she could see straight into his head and the dirty fantasy highlights reel he had spinning around in his psyche.

"Yeah, um," he stalled. "I like this one." He picked one of the random cock rings and thrust it at her.

She took it and looked around the room, her gaze snagging on the pictures hanging on the wall. She studied them intently before doing a casual perusal of the rest of the open area. She again paused at the back door. He knew what was there; Katy had complained more times than he could count about his and Connor's thongs being left near the door. "You've got a beautiful place. Did you renovate it yourselves?" The random subject change away from sex toys had Levi reeling, but it hadn't fazed Katy. She filled Adelaide in on what they'd done, finishing with the wall in front of them.

"You know how a place suddenly feels like home when you've got all your stuff unpacked and in the right spot. That's what it was like when we put our photos up."

"Yeah. Yeah, I can see." Adelaide nodded and her gaze bounced between the two of them. Pausing, she picked up another box and flipped open the lid. "Okay, the final toy that you might want to consider tonight is an anal plug." Lifting it, she showed them the array of five different sized plugs, the largest one easily the size of his fist. She selected that one and held it up, Levi's eyes going wide. With a grin, she added "This is for experts, not you guys. In fact, the only one that would be appropriate for you is this small one." She set it aside and picked up a plug that was a little thicker than his thumb. Neither he nor Katy spoke. Levi dared not look at her either. He couldn't bear it if she was horrified. Adelaide launched into a description of why they might want to explore anal sex and how to prepare for it. With every word she spoke, Levi's breath quickened and his heart pounded. Closing his eyes, he tried to get his over-eager dick under control, but instead couldn't help but imagine Connor spread before him, Levi's fingers—or better yet, his cock —sinking into his depths.

"If one of you wears it while having sex, it will simulate a threesome." You could have heard a pin drop in the room. He couldn't even breathe, but unable to stop himself, Levi swept his gaze over to Katy, staring at her wide-eyed as she flushed but turned away. Guilt hit him with the force of the five-thirty express from the city. Here he was imagining being with Connor when his beautiful girl was sitting next to him. Self-doubt and disgust in himself and his lack of consideration for Katy gnawed at Levi, deflating his tenting erection quickly.

"I'll go get my purse," Katy said, suddenly breaking the silence and racing out of the room. She had him scrambling to compose himself. Scrubbing his hands over his face, he could feel Adelaide's eyes on him. He knew she was watching them, her gaze assessing him. Adelaide placed a gentle hand on his arm, stilling his movements. In a quiet but confident voice, she murmured, "You know, Levi, there's nothing wrong with what you're feeling. There's nothing wrong with taking some time to figure out something that's got your head spinning."

"Yeah, I...." He didn't even know how to respond. She was clearly good at reading people—she'd managed to latch onto his secret desires pretty damn quickly. He knew if he tried making up some bullshit excuse for his reaction to the butt plugs, and how the idea of a threesome tempted him like nothing else, she'd see straight through him.

She continued, "Being in here with the two of you, it's obvious. Looking around the room, I can tell. Look, Levi. Really look at who is in front of you. Reach out and grab hold or you won't find your happiness. None of you will."

"Katy and I are solid. We've had a rocky week, but we're

strong enough to survive a few bad days." Levi wasn't sure if he was explaining it to Adelaide or trying to reassure himself. A bit of both, perhaps.

"Yeah, I know you two are." She gave him a small smile. "But there's more to you than that. Don't be afraid to be honest with yourselves." She leaned in and squeezed his arm before dropping her hand, whispering, "Bye, Levi," before moving over to where Katy stood in the doorway. He watched in stunned silence as they spoke in hushed tones and she hugged his girlfriend and made her way to the door, letting herself out.

When the door clicked shut, Katy asked quietly, "Was that okay? That was fun, wasn't it?" The uncertainty in her tone wrecked Levi, utterly gutted him. She was usually so confident, but not then. He'd been so self-absorbed, so selfish that he'd been blinded to Katy second guessing herself, and he hated himself for it. Levi couldn't keep the distance between them anymore. Taking her into his arms, he nuzzled her hair, breathing her in. His uncertainty, his inability to get his head in the right place melted away, and he held her tighter, wanting— no needing—the connection with her.

Levi whispered, his voice rough, "You did good, sugar. I love you."

"So, you wanna head out and grab a late movie?"

"You don't want to try what we bought?" he asked, confused.

The grin she threw his way was wicked. "My toy needs charging. Few hours and we'll be sweet." She nodded towards the door. "Come on, let's go."

The stars in the night sky were bright. They always were in that quiet stretch of white sandy beach on the Broadwater. Levi shifted the take-home packs of ice cream, the remnants long since melted, and stretched out his leg. They'd ended up skipping the movie in favour of dessert on the beach. They'd walked the length of the kilometres' long path, finishing the decadent mango and double chocolate tubs.

Now, wrapped in a blanket, holding Katy in front of him, Levi looked across the smooth waters. On the other side of the inlet lay The Spit, a long peninsular protecting the Broadwater from the pounding waves of the Pacific. Beyond that to the south, the towers of Surfers Paradise lit the night sky. To the north was South Straddie, a giant sand island covered in lush forest that lay dark in the pre-dawn. Katy shifted, having long since fallen asleep in his arms and Levi leaned down to kiss her, breathing in the sweetness of her skin. As he sat there, watching the tide change and the water lap against the sand, Adelaide's words replayed over and over in his head. *"Look, Levi. Really look at who is in front of you."* She wasn't fooled when he'd tried to play off her comment. It scared him knowing she could read him so easily. Was he really that transparent? *"Reach out and grab hold or you won't find your happiness. None of you will."* That's what scared him. Wanting the impossible didn't make for a happy life —that much he was certain of. All he had to do was look back on the last week, and it was obvious. But what was he supposed to do?

6

CONNOR

NERVES SKITTERED THROUGH CONNOR AS HE STOOD AT MIRANDA'S front door. He couldn't decide if he wanted to be there or not. No, that wasn't quite right. He liked Miranda. She was sweet and funny, a great girl, but he wasn't sure how far to take things between them. They'd only been on a few dates, so it wasn't like they were in a relationship and they certainly hadn't talked about being exclusive. But it still didn't sit right with Connor to start anything physical between them when he was unsure of how in to her he was. And knowing how fucked up he was about what'd gone down after Levi's party and the strain it'd put them under was doing his head in. He couldn't focus long enough to make a decision. Was he happy to go out, leaving Katy and Levi to indulge in their shopping expedition? Or did he want to crawl into a hole? *God, what if they ask for a tutorial? What was I thinking?* It didn't matter though. There was no way his crush on his best mate was reciprocated—Levi had made it clear enough when he'd stumbled back off the bed and looked at him horrified—and as if it would have been anyway. Connor had to suck it up and move on.

He raised his hand to knock, but before he connected with

the dark timber front door, it swung open. "Hi," Miranda greeted him. "Were you planning on standing out there all night or were you gonna knock? I don't bite you know." Her smile turned wicked, and she wiggled her eyebrows. "Most of the time." Connor couldn't help but laugh.

"Hey, Miranda. Thanks for the invitation." He held up a bottle of wine. "Wasn't sure what we were ordering for dinner, but this is a good one."

"I've cooked. We're not ordering." She smiled and rolled her eyes. "Come on in, and you can pour me some while I finish dinner." He followed her through the living room into the kitchen, and she pointed out the cupboard where the glasses were to him. Connor poured two while Miranda finished cooking on the stovetop, then dished up two plates of grilled chicken, salad, and crusty bread. The crisp white he'd brought over was a pretty decent match to their meal.

Conversation flowed easily while they ate and long after they'd finished the cherry chocolate mousse, they still sat at the table talking. He was having a good time, and that surprised him more than it should have. Miranda was great; he liked being around her. He could definitely see them being good friends, especially with so much in common—music, food, movies, and she was a runner too.

"Want another glass? You don't have to drive home tonight, do you?" Miranda went to the fridge and pulled out another bottle, and Connor stood as she left the table.

"You want me to stay the night?" he asked, uncertain of how he should answer. His feelings were still up in the air, and the last thing he wanted was to hurt her.

Returning to the table with the bottle, she looked up at him. "Hey, I like you. I think you like me. I'd be lying if I said I didn't want to hook up. I'm good with casual for the moment, but if it turns into more, I'm fine with that too."

Connor smiled, relief coursing through him. He might not be ready to hand her his heart, but a night with her certainly wouldn't be a hardship. Reaching out, he took her hand and squeezed. "I've had fun, Miranda." He'd barely uttered the words before she was stepping forward, wrapping her arms around his neck and pressing her mouth to his. Connor swiped his tongue across her bottom lip, and she opened to him. Deepening the kiss, Connor surrendered and enjoyed the touch of the first woman he'd been with in far too long. He directed Miranda to the couch and guided her down onto the soft cushions. Propping himself up so his weight didn't crush her, Connor looked at her and found himself wishing he was with Katy. He closed his eyes and forced the thought from his head. He couldn't go there—it wasn't fair to Miranda, and he had to face the fact that Katy would never be his, that Levi wouldn't be either.

Connor leaned in again and nipped Miranda's throat before kissing a line down to her collarbone and back up to her mouth. He let out an "oomph" when Miranda pushed him off her and straddled him, tugging off his Henley and tossing it aside. Chest to chest, arousal flared inside him. Kisses and teasing licks against his throat had him shifting, rocking his hips to get some friction against his painfully rigid length.

Miranda hopped off him and slid to her knees before him. After pulling open his button fly, she curled her fingers around him. Her hand on his dick, even with the thin barrier of his boxers between them, had Connor thrusting into her grip. He hissed when cool air hit his heated skin as she yanked down his underwear exposing his cock. Her startled, "oh," had him cracking open his eyes. She was eyeing his piercing thoughtfully, biting her bottom lip. He was beyond the point of caring whether she liked them or not—if she wanted his Prince Albert gone, he'd take it out. He'd do almost anything as long as she put her hands back on him.

Connor arched into her grip as she curled her hand around the base of his cock and stroked him, leaning down to tentatively lick along his length. A strangled moan left his lips when hers closed around the head of his shaft, and her tongue flicked the ring protruding from it. Soft fingertips trailing down under his sack, brushing up against the barbell piercing, had Connor shuddering. He involuntarily punched his hips forward as Miranda massaged his balls, forcing himself deeper into her mouth. Connor balled his hands into fists and fought off the orgasm threatening to erupt from him, and the raw need to pump into the hot, wet cavern engulfing him while he chased his orgasm. He had to be gentle, logically he knew that—his piercing could easily chip a tooth—but *goddamn* he was so close. So. Fucking. Close.

Picturing the old lady from *There's Something About Mary* pulled him back from the edge—the dog licking into her mouth was enough to make him gag, to pull him back from teetering on the precipice. A memory of Katy's reaction when he'd told her and Levi how he stopped himself from coming popped into his head. Connor gasped, an electric shock pulsing through his body with the thoughts of the beautiful woman he'd been lusting over for years and her hot-as-sin boyfriend. Images of them filled his mind's eye, flashing before him. Katy's smile. Levi's laugh. Katy dancing as she cooked. Levi lifting weights. Katy sleep ruffled and in need of coffee. Levi sprawled out, naked on his bed, fast asleep. Connor moaned, the pictures of them turning erotic: Katy kneeling between his legs sucking his cock and palming his balls; his lips on her pussy, licking and spearing inside her with his tongue until she came, while Levi pressed into him from behind, sliding his cock deep inside, anchoring Connor with strong arms against his broad chest. *"Fuck, Lee. Gonna come."* His balls drew up tight, the tingling heat at the base of his spine unstoppable as his cock throbbed, cum erupting from him in thick white ribbons across his abs. The waves of Connor's orgasm crashed over him and he cried out.

"Lee, Katy."

Where a second before there were warm bodies pressed against him, cold air filled the space. Boneless and still humming from his epic orgasm, Connor cracked his eyes open and tried to figure out where they went. But Miranda standing rigid and shaking had him scrambling to sit up. She looked fucking furious—her jaw was clenched, and anger flashed in her eyes.

"Get out of my house you piece o'shit."

"What?" He blinked, totally surprised at her outburst. What had he done wrong?

"I won't be some ruse for you to hide behind." She pointed to the door and in a deathly calm voice added, "Get the fuck outta my house."

"Huh? Ruse? What're you goin' on about?"

"You didn't even feel me stop touching you, did you?" she spat. "You were so damn wrapped up in your fantasy that you didn't feel me let go and get up. You yelled out Levi and Katy's names for fuck's sake." Her voice shook with anger as she glared at him, disgusted. "You wanna fuck *both* of them. You can't even make up your mind on who you want. I won't be the girl you're with for show while you're lookin' to fuck more than one person on the side, especially not my friends. Get outta my house."

Stunned, he sat on the couch, his mind furiously ticking over everything that had just happened. *What the fuck?* He'd heard their names. No, he'd *said* their names. Confusion and shame welled up inside him like a lead balloon. Seeing her shaking with fury, her face red, eyes sparking with anger, made Connor's gut flip sickeningly. "Fuck," he cursed, shaking his head in self-disgust. He hadn't meant to hurt her. *Why the fuck did I start something with her when I knew I was so fucked up inside?* He scrubbed a hand over his hair.

"Miranda, I'm sorry. I... I'm so sorry," Connor said quietly. He picked up his clothes and turned to her, ready to apologize again. He didn't want her to change her mind—he didn't deserve that. But he did want to try to set things right, to tell her he was an arse.

"Don't, Connor. Just go." She sounded tired, resigned. He nodded and, head hung low, walked out. Palming his keys, he considered driving home, but he promised Levi he wouldn't go back there until the morning. There was no way he would risk walking in on them testing out what they'd bought. No fucking way would he be able to hold himself back.

Driving, he pulled into a car park at the beach. He hadn't had a destination in mind while he drove; he just found himself there. Just north of Surfers Paradise it was quiet. The place drew him in, helped him think, helped him make sense of the mess his heart had become. He looked out over the glass-like surface shimmering in the light of the three-quarter moon. Connor sat down on the sand, his arms wrapped around his legs. One thing was obvious to him—he didn't have a crush on his best friends; it was a whole lot more than that. So what were his options? Did he try to ignore it, keep living with them like the third wheel he was? It'd destroy any chance of him ever finding happiness. There was no way he could let himself become intimate with another person after treating Miranda so badly. And where would that leave him? He was resigning himself to becoming a cat lady if he pulled away from everyone. He could move out, get his own place, and put some distance between them. But even that would only work until he saw them again, until the craving reignited within him, leaving him shaking and desperate for a fix. Like a damn addict, he'd keep going back for more until he was a shell of himself. He deserved better than that—he'd done his time in hell, and he wasn't going to live it again if he could help it. If he left, started afresh, could he be happy? Could he walk away, once again leaving the two people who meant the world to him?

Connor squinted, pulling down his shades to block the sun's morning rays as his limited options rolled through his mind on an endless loop. The warmth of the dawn sun hit his skin and Connor stretched his aching muscles. He'd been there for hours, mesmerized by the lapping water, working through the thoughts bouncing around in his head and warring with his heart. He still didn't know what to do, and the uncertainty was like an anvil on his shoulders.

Connor went back to his car to get his sneakers from his gym bag and change into a pair of shorts. Setting out, he jogged along the boardwalk, dodging the early morning crowd of people. Dog walkers, surfers carrying boards and personal trainers working out with their clients dotted the paths. But Connor ignored the lot, trying to get some clarity.

He was lost in his own world until, "Yo, Con, wait up," broke through into his thoughts. He recognized that voice. Spinning around, he saw Katy's cousin Nick, and his best mate, Mike, catching up to him.

"Hey, guys. How's it hangin'?"

"Good, mate, you?" Nick answered.

"Fuckin' dandy." Connor scowled, kicking himself for being a dick.

Nick huffed out a laugh. "Wanna talk about it?"

"Nope." He didn't mean to sound so churlish, but the last thing he wanted to do was pour his heart out to Nick and a man he'd only met for the first time at Levi's birthday the week before.

"Good. We can pick up the pace then," Mike replied, saving him from deflecting the conversation any more. They ran together, feet pounding the path. On their left was the ocean, the morning swell picking up, the waves glittering in the bright sunlight. Surfers rode them into shore, carving and cutting along them. Dogs and their owners ran along the shoreline. On the right were the towers—hotels and apartments, office buildings—and older beach huts, the surf club and oceanfront mansions.

Clear blue skies and a warm breeze should have made for a beautiful run—flawless like the day was—but Connor blocked it all out. Seeing the happy people around him, living and loving life made the knife in his chest plunge deeper. Why had he gone and let his heart run away with him? Why couldn't he love someone like Miranda? Someone uncomplicated? Available even? But no, as if it wasn't bad enough that he was in love with one person already in a relationship, he'd gone and fallen for two. And better yet, they were together, and talk about perfect for each other. This was why he'd left in the first place, why he'd run. It'd held off the yearning for the woman he couldn't have but had never obliterated the desire. Coming home was a bad idea. He'd known it, but like a blind fool, he'd tried to fulfil Rob's dying wish.

Connor picked up the pace, pushing himself and trying to outrun the pain until sweat soaked his skin. Kilometres passed under the steady beat of his running shoes, his two silent companions matching him step for step until finally, he couldn't run anymore. Out of breath and desperate for water, Connor followed Mike and Nick into the beachside park, collapsing against a tall palm, the smooth bark pressing against his back.

Exhaustion coursed through him, the lactic acid in his muscles making his limbs unbearably heavy.

"Fuck me, haven't done a workout like that since I've been home." Sweat dripped off his brow as he bent over, resting his hands on his knees, trying to drag air into his lungs. "Burns like a mother."

Nick stretched his legs, leaning against the same palm Connor was. "What are you running from, mate?" he gasped.

"Fuck," Connor groaned, frustrated.

"You can talk to me, to us, if you need to, bud. We'll always listen."

Connor huffed out a humourless laugh. "Yeah, you guys'll be so understanding of my fucked up life."

Mike's eyes flashed with annoyance. "Don't be a prick or so fuckin' judgemental of us."

"That's the fucking problem though isn't it—the judgement." Connor threw his hands up in the air and paced. "Knowing that the one thing I want is wrong. Goddammit," he shouted, kicking at a stone and sending it flying. Hands in his hair, he tugged on the curls that'd grown since he'd returned home. "I can't handle it anymore. I just can't do it."

"What can't you do, Con?" Nick asked gently.

"No, it's what I'm gonna do. I've gotta leave the Coast, and not come back. Cut all contact, maybe." He shook his head. There was no way he'd do that. He couldn't even if he wanted to —Katy would never stand for it. "I can't see any other way to move on. I can't get 'em outta my head, ya know?"

"Don't do anything rash, Con. Can you open up more to Katy and Lee? Maybe work through whatever it is you're dealing with, with them?" When Connor shook his head, his shoulders sagging, Nick continued, "Get away if you need to but don't just leave. You three have been friends forever. It'll break their hearts if you walk," Nick counselled him.

"I know, but I can't...." He trailed off, raking his fingers through his hair and wiping the sweat from his brow.

"Look, I know we don't really know each other, but maybe that's what you need—someone independent, detached. Come hang at my place for a while," Mike offered.

"Nah, mate. I don't wanna get in your way." Connor shook his head and pressed his lips into a sad smile. "Didn't you say last weekend that your girl was flying in today? I'm not gonna let her come all the way across the damn country and have me sittin' there like an idiot while you want some alone time. And don't you have kids? They'll probably be there too. Nah, you don't want me around. I'll just check into a cheap hotel somewhere."

Nick rested his hand on Connor's shoulder and squeezed gently, getting his attention. The other man had this way about him which commanded attention. Connor shouldn't have been surprised—Nick was a lawyer and a damn good one at that. He exuded confidence without being arrogant, strength without being overbearing. "Come to my place. It's big enough. You won't even know we're there most of the time and you can spend as long as you need to figure things out. There's no way I'm letting you stay in a hotel when we live down the beach from them. And you aren't gonna make the decision to leave your friends, your home while you're alone. I'll give you my spare key when we get back to the cars." *A good ten kilometres away.* Connor groaned and scrubbed a hand across his forehead.

"Are you sure? I don't wanna put you out, but I could do with somewhere to hide out and think for a few days. Get my head on right."

"You won't be in the way, and Em would love to have you too." Nick smiled at him encouragingly.

"It would be kinda nice having someone independent to talk to. But don't worry, I won't get in the way and like I said, it'll only be for a few days." Connor sighed, looking out over the ocean he loved. It was the first time he'd ever been sad seeing it. "Just until I figure out where to move to."

"That's our Uber." Mike pointed to the bright green hatch pulling up at the curb driven by the cute blonde. "How about we head on back to the cars and you two can work out the deets? "

Connor smiled gratefully at his friend, before falling into step between them.

Four days. Four days had passed since he'd seen Katy and Levi. He was like a recovering addict counting the number of day's he'd been clean. It was probably as torturous too. Between the two of them, the messages had been constant. He'd deflected most of them, answering with just enough detail that they wouldn't worry, but at the same time letting them assume he was still at Miranda's house. It was the coward's way out, but he didn't think he'd be able to explain why he couldn't see them anymore.

Now, sitting in his therapist's office, he showed her Levi's last message. **We're glad ur happy with M. Guess ur living there now.** The first time he'd read it, he'd sucked in a breath and swallowed around the lump in his throat. Seeing it again didn't make it any easier. The pain in his chest still so fucking raw. The text was innocent, yet filled with assumptions that were entirely wrong. The misunderstanding didn't surprise him, but now they thought he'd moved out. *Are they happy I'm not there anymore? That they've got their lives back, without me in it*? The thought broke him. Loneliness as vast as the Sahara Desert swallowed him whole and sucked the life out of him. He'd been staying with friends, and had gone to group sessions every day, but he was so alone. He couldn't shake the dark storm cloud that hung over him. He was barely eating, he drank far too much and was lethargic.

"Is M for Miranda? You didn't tell me that you two were serious."

"We aren't anything."

"Why not?" she asked, sitting back in the armchair and crossing her legs. She was laid back and he liked that about her, but she had a sharp mind like a steel trap. She didn't forget anything; it was unnerving at times. "Last time you spoke about her, you were going to see where things led." Yeah, he'd told her that. At the time he was trying to persuade himself it was the right thing to do.

"Because I fucked up. I called out another person's name when she was giving me a blow job. Didn't even know I'd done it until she yelled at me."

"When we're at our most vulnerable, our most raw, sometimes our true selves come out. I know you were struggling with whether you were into her. Maybe your subconscious answered the question for you?" Pausing, she added, "What prompted Levi's message? You live with them."

"I called out their names," he whispered. "I haven't been able to face them. I haven't gone home since it happened." Connor sighed, scrubbing a hand over his face.

"Where are you staying?"

"With Katy's cousin and his wife."

"That's a lot of upheaval and stress. Have you had any more episodes?"

"Yeah," he nodded. "At the garage. One of the boys knocked a toolbox off the bench. The noise set me off."

She sat quietly and assessed him in the way she did sometimes, waiting to see if he'd fill in any more of the details, but he couldn't. The flashback he'd had was a bad one. It'd freaked out most of the guys, but Kevin's father was a Vietnam vet. He'd seen his fair share of episodes, so he'd known what to do. "Connor, you need your family. And Katy and Levi, they're it for you."

"No," he rasped, shaking his head. What was he doing? He couldn't live like this anymore. He couldn't stay so close, yet so far. The yearning to see them, to be with them—and not even sexually, although that was definitely part of it—was slowly killing him. Every day he stayed at Nick and Emma's was a day he was delaying the inevitable. But he was living with a dead dream and clutching its rotting corpse, unwilling to let it go so he could live. And wasn't that the promise he'd made to Rob? To himself when he'd been discharged from that shithole he'd been stationed in for far too long?

Tears sprang to his eyes, and the remaining pieces of his heart crumbled into dust. Clutching his chest, Connor curled up on the couch and sobbed. He was mourning for himself, the lifetime friendship he'd once had, that was now destined to end if he wanted to survive into the future, even crying a little for the hope that he'd be able to have a normal relationship with someone like Miranda. He'd managed to fuck that up spectacularly. Connor hated being alone, but that's how it looked like his future would pan out. The vast void stretched beyond him, bleakness wrapping its tendrils around his heart. The screen on his phone blurred more as the tears ran down his cheeks and his chest heaved with sobs.

Leslie, his counsellor, moved to sit next to him, rubbing his back with warm hands. He turned away from her, not able to face her anymore. "Shh, it's okay." she murmured, over and over.

Tears fell down his cheeks as he rested his head against the scratchy material of the deep blue couch. He had nothing left, physically or mentally. Exhaustion overwhelmed him. Nightmares had plagued the nocturnal hours, but now they'd morphed into some sick and twisted mind-fuck. It wasn't just Rob who he was reliving losing in that desert, it wasn't just his bloodied body he cradled as the life left him, but Lee and Katy too. Watching their eyes dull and them take their last breath had him jolting awake, drenched in sweat and shaking so hard he had trouble unscrewing the cap off a bottle of water.

"I have to go." Connor tried to sit up, but after not having eaten for two days, his body didn't even have the strength to do that.

"Your attacks, and I'm guessing your nightmares, are getting worse because of the stress you're putting yourself under. Talk to me. Let me help you get through this."

Connor wrenched himself off the couch. Standing on shaky legs and lightheaded, he threw his hands up in the air. He didn't shout, but it wasn't far off. "You wanna know what's wrong? Fine. I'm in love with them, okay? Both of them. And they don't feel anything like what I do. It's killing me watching them, but I can't help it. I can't stop loving them. And I can't watch it anymore. Every time I see them, it's like my guts are being carved out with a rusty fucking blade, and I'm slowly bleeding out on the floor."

"Have you talked to them about it?"

His laugh held no humour. "Yeah, because I can tell my best mate and his girl that I wanna be between them when they fuck. That's gonna go down real well." It was torturing him, but the only way he could think to fix the mess he'd got himself in, was to extract himself entirely. Airlift himself out of the quagmire that his life had become and start afresh in a place where no one knew him, where he could carve out a future for himself away from the two people who meant the most, but who he could never keep. The thing was, they'd never been his to begin with.

Katy

Cold. So, so cold. A shudder wracked her body, rattling her bones. Her muscles seized and Katy groaned. When had she been hit by a freight train? Pain radiated from her very pores and the hacking cough she was suffering from only made things worse. Like a kick to the ribs every time her lungs spasmed, she sounded like a sixty-year smoking veteran. Katy tried to lift her head from her makeshift bed on the couch, needing another blanket from the hall cupboard, but fell back instantly. The daggers shooting through her temples made her vision swim.

The TV was on, but she just wanted quiet. She did her best to keep her head still when she looked around for the remote, but it was a few feet away on the coffee table. Without getting up, she had no hope of reaching it. Whatever exercise equipment they were advertising was just noise, and it hurt her head even more listening to it. Katy bit back tears, slowly lifting a heavy hand to wipe the errant ones that had slipped free. It matched the ones she'd shed since Con disappeared, leaving them as soon as he'd jumped into bed with Miranda.

She hadn't been well for a few days, but that morning it was far worse. She was only at the shop for twenty minutes when Dylan had insisted she go home. The throb of her four-day headache had turned blinding, the bright sunlight outside her shop acting like a lance to her eyes, spearing right through her. Katy had barely made it home, staggering in the door. She should have fallen into bed, but instead, she'd gone over to the couch, shoved the half-folded clothes out of the way and laid down, watching TV instead of sleeping like she should have.

But the blankets she had folded on the armrest weren't enough to keep her warm. Desperately trying to reach for another of Levi's polo shirts in the pile of folded laundry on the floor, Katy let out a frustrated cry when she couldn't get it. The move sent another jolt of pain through her head, radiating through every inch of her body. She curled in on herself and let the tears fall. She needed painkillers, but she couldn't get up to get them. And another blanket. She needed her man, but her phone was sitting in her backpack near the front door.

The bang of the screen door closing had Katy letting out a shuddering breath, thanking the stars for answering her pleading. "Lee, babe, I need you." Her voice was husky, damaged from the barking cough that had slammed her.

"No, Cupcake, it's me. What's wrong?" Con asked, the thump of his footsteps quickly announcing his approach.

Katy steeled herself against the agony of moving and wiped her eyes. Con didn't need to worry about her. He had his own girl to care for; there was no way Katy was going to be a burden on him. She'd manage herself. Hell, she'd been sick before—this was no different. "Never mind, I'm fine."

Another shudder rocked her, and Katy clamped down her groan, biting down on her tongue to stop it escaping.

"Katy, you're sick." Con lay his cool hand across her forehead, and she sighed. She wanted to melt into his touch, let him soothe her. *No, no I can't. He's got his own priorities. And he left us. He doesn't need us anymore. I shouldn't need him.* Unreasonable as it was, it hurt that he hadn't even made time to call and let them know he was staying at Miranda's for a while. He'd barely even bothered answering their texts. It wasn't like they were his keepers, but Katy had thought they were friends. And friends didn't just disappear.

"I'm fine, don't worry about me," Katy croaked, forcing the words past her throat. Every swallow was like knives shredding her oesophagus. Talking only made it worse. "Get what you came for and go back to Miranda's."

"Shut up, Katy," he chastised her. "You're burning up. You need to get this fever down or you'll do some damage."

Katy moaned, the ache intensifying to screaming pain when she tried to push his hand off her and sit up. "I'll be okay, Connor."

Con gently removed the tie from her hair, his hands caressing her face. His lips pressed against her forehead in a gentle kiss had Katy breathing him in, all spice and man. She relaxed back onto the cushions, no longer fighting him. His murmured words were quiet, just like the rest of the room had become, as he soothed her. His slow movements kept her from jerking too much, even as he peeled away the blankets she'd wrapped around herself. "You're so damn beautiful," he whispered, before kissing her temple softly. Katy closed her eyes and sighed, wishing just for a minute that he was hers to love.

"Does Lee know you're sick?"

"No," she croaked. "He's filming all day."

"You're too sick to be by yourself, Cupcake. Why didn't you call me?" Con ran his fingers through her hair, his gaze holding so much warmth, but at the same time, sadness.

"You left." Katy closed her eyes, trying to hide the tears welling in them. "I didn't think you wanted to see us anymore." It'd hurt when he'd moved out, especially because of the way he did it. She was pissed with him, but mostly he'd broken her heart. Knowing that he didn't want them anymore had flayed her. But she'd forced herself to put up a strong front—Levi was hurting too and he needed her.

"I'm sorry," he murmured, leaning down to press his lips to her forehead once more, kissing across to her temple. "I'm here now. Let me help you."

Katy was too weak to argue with him, to question why he was being almost intimate with her when he'd been with Miranda. She started shaking violently. "Shit, you need something to get rid of this fever."

He laid her down gently, moving ever so slowly until she was stretched out again. Katy let her eyes drift closed as Con stepped away. She heard rummaging around, water running and then two tablets were dropped into her palm. The crack of the lid from a bottle sounded, and Katy forced her eyes open. Struggling to swallow the pills down, she winced, a pained groan escaping her lips.

"Give it a few minutes. They'll kick in soon." He placed a cool, wet cloth on her forehead, and it was like heaven. The headache sending stabbing pain through her temples immediately lessened. A shudder tore through her and Con set to work on her clothes, unbuttoning her chef's jacket and pulling her white pants down her legs. "Sit up, Katy. I need to get this uniform off you. You need to cool down."

She wanted to cry. She already was. Swiping angrily at the tears tracking down her cheeks, Katy struggled to sit upright. But Con wrapped strong arms around her and pulled her into his embrace. Burying her face in the crook of his neck, Katy cried. Yes, she was sick and hurting, but that wasn't the worst part. He'd left her, left them, and she missed him. He didn't know it, but he'd broken her heart, and she wanted her friend back. Lee hadn't said anything, but she knew he wanted Con with them too. He belonged with them, dammit. They could make him happy.

"Have you eaten anything?"

"No," she mumbled into his chest, not wanting to let him go. He was warm and solid, and there. God, she'd missed him.

"I'll make you something. Lee's mum used to make the best chicken soup. You think you're up for that?" Katy hummed her agreement before yawning, and Con replied, "Lie down and rest. I'll get started."

He held her hair back as she rested her head on the armrest. Dressed only in a tee and her underwear, Katy curled into a ball, wrapping her arms around her chest to keep warm. She was cold, but the thin cotton blanket Con laid over her moments later helped. The medicine she'd taken must have started to take the edge off her fever. Katy sighed as the cool material hit her skin, warming her up, and she snuggled into the couch. The sounds of Con working in the kitchen faded as sleep began to take over. Eyelids heavy, exhaustion coaxed her into relaxation, pulling her towards slumber.

Katy startled, every muscle in her body tensing as a loud bang tore through the quiet of the room. The breeze flowing through the open doors at either end of the house was warm on her face, the only part of her uncovered.

"Sugar, baby, are you okay?"

Katy didn't have the chance to respond to Levi's question as Con shushed him as he raced down the hall. "Mate! She's asleep."

She managed to croak out a response, sounding more like a hoarse whisper than the volume she'd intended. "I'm awake."

"Why didn't you call me?" Levi knelt before her and ran his fingers gently through her hair. Katy turned into his touch, nuzzling against his hand. Featherlight kisses rained down on her temple as he caressed her.

"You were filming. I didn't want to interrupt."

"Next time, interrupt. You're more important than filming. If you needed me, I would have been here." Levi rested his forehead against hers and whispered, "I can't lose you, too."

"You won't. Ever." Katy closed her hands around Levi's shirt and held him close. She didn't realize how much she'd needed the reassurance that they were solid until Levi had voiced his own worries. He had nothing to fear—she loved Levi. Needed him like the earth needed the sun to sustain life.

"Rest, sugar. I've got you." The couch shifted, and the heat from Levi's solid body moved away. Katy didn't want him to leave, but she knew he needed to speak with Con. She hated intruding on their conversation, but her head still pounded every time she moved. They'd be picking her arse off the floor if she tried to give them some space.

"So?" Levi asked, almost petulantly. Katy opened her eyes again, craning her neck to see into the kitchen. Levi was crowding him into the corner. He may have been a few inches shorter than Con, but their height difference didn't matter then. Levi was using his bulk. "What's goin' on?"

"I, um...." Con looked away, his shoulders dropping.

"What? You're moving in with her?"

"Yeah, um, something like that," Con muttered, still not meeting Levi's eyes. Levi was defensive, hurt. Chest to chest with his best friend, his fists clenched, his body language screamed aggression, but Katy knew him better. He was all bluster, and once the wind went out of his sails, he'd be broken inside unless Con treaded carefully. "I'm here to pick up some stuff."

Levi grasped Con's shirt in his fists and shook him. "What?" The shock and incredulity were obvious in his tone. "Last week you didn't even want to get serious with her, and now you're movin' in together?"

Con pushed Levi's hands away. They fell easily when he sidestepped Levi's grip. "It isn't really your problem though, is it?"

"No, of course not." Levi leaned against the kitchen cupboards looking defeated. He wore his heart on his sleeve and Con was breaking it all over again. "But mates look out for each other, don't they?"

"Yeah. Yeah, they do." Con nodded, running his hand through his hair. "Sorry, man, I've been a bit stressed out about this. It's a big decision."

Levi reached out, this time gripping Con's arm, spinning the other man away from Katy. "Why don't you take things a little slower if it's worrying you?"

Con shrugged out of Levi's grip but reached up to squeeze his shoulder. "Soup's ready, mate. Don't leave Katy waiting. She hasn't eaten anything all day." He spun and walked to the front of the house, but even Katy could see the unshed tears in his eyes. Con was hurting too. She just didn't understand why.

"Suit yourself then. Don't talk," Levi snapped. Slamming down a bowl, Katy was surprised it didn't shatter. Fists resting on the benchtop, he stood there, breathing hard. Katy moved, tentatively standing up and walking towards him. Lightheaded, she gripped onto the furniture as she silently padded over, the timber floors warm under her bare feet.

Katy reached out for Levi, but as she did, Con came back in. He wasn't carrying anything, but that didn't mean anything—he probably had his bags stacked at the front door.

"Guys, I'm gonna go."

"Con," she pleaded, "please think about this. We don't want to see you get hurt. We love you."

"I love you, too. But I need to do this. Please understand," he replied, cupping her face in his hands.

"We'll stand by you, whatever you decide. And our door is always open for you to come home. Just don't shut us out, please." Katy's eyes welled with tears. She didn't want to lose him again, but Con was slipping from her grasp. Levi's strong arms wrapped around her, his big body behind her. Her man gave her strength, but knowing Con was going to walk away tore her heart out.

"Don't worry about me, Cupcake. Don't get upset. I need to do this. I'm not ready to talk about it yet, but I need to do it."

"I'll call you soon." Katy slipped her arms around his waist. Levi still had a hold of her. It was like he couldn't let her go either. "Thanks for looking after me."

"Anytime, Cupcake."

Con flashed a weak smile at Levi. His eyes were expressive, often revealing much more than Con thought he did. This time she saw so much emotion in them, none of it good. If he was moving in with Miranda and he was happy about it, why did he look so damn sad? Resignation, misery, and heartbreak were written all over Con's face. The dark rings under his eyes suddenly looked more like sleeplessness rather than nights being in a lover's arms. Watching him turn away, hands in his pockets, his gaze focussed on the floor, Con looked broken. Why was he doing this? Why was he leaving again?

"Babe," she gasped, her tears falling freely. Levi sheltered her in his arms while she cried, tucking her against his body and holding her close. His shuddering breaths left her in no doubt he was struggling too. Watching Con walk away the second time was easily as bad as the first.

"Hi Miranda," Katy greeted her friend when she picked up her mobile. "How are you, sweetie?" She'd been as quiet as Con over the last week, and now that Katy was feeling better, she was determined she was going to catch up with her friends again. She and Levi needed to get back the balance they had in their friendship with Con, and now, with his girlfriend. As much as it pained Katy, seeing him with Miranda was better than not having him in her life at all.

"Fine," Miranda responded sharply. Katy's eyebrows hiked up, and she pulled the phone away from her ear looking at it as if it would shed some light on her friend's murderous tone.

"Is Con there?" Katy asked tentatively. "I told him I'd call him, but he's not answering his mobile. I thought maybe we could catch up."

Miranda huffed out a laugh but it didn't sound happy. "He didn't tell you, did he? Fucking coward."

"Tell me what?" Confusion laced her tone, and she frowned. What in the hell was her friend talking about?

"Ask the arsehole yourself," she growled before adding, "He hasn't been here since I kicked him out." When there was no further explanation, Katy pulled the phone away from her ear again. Miranda had hung up, the line between them dead. *What the hell just happened? Tell me what?*

Katy dialled Con's phone again and left yet another message. Then she waited. And waited. She had a partially decorated cake sitting in the cool room waiting for her, but there was no way she could concentrate on it with her current mood. Stripping out of her chef's whites, she hung the jacket on the hook behind her office door and sat in front of her computer, attempting to get her mind around the mountain of paperwork sitting in her in-tray. An hour later she was pacing, walking back and forth across the length of her small office. It was quiet, so still that she could hear the ticking of her watch as the seconds crawled by.

The shrill ring of her mobile cut through the air and startled her so much that Katy fumbled, dropping it despite the death grip she'd had on it. Skittering under the desk, Katy was down on her knees in a flash, reaching for it.

"Hi, Con," she said, sitting up and smashing her head on the desk. Rubbing the spot at the back of her crown, she complained, "Ow, shit that hurt."

"You okay, Cupcake?" he asked, concerned.

"Yeah, I smashed my head on the desk. Why haven't you been answering?"

"Cut to the chase next time." He laughed nervously.

Katy was confused and downright frustrated at his evasiveness. Her tone was cutting. "Don't change the subject."

"Okay, okay. I'm on a lunchbreak at the moment. I have to finish off this part of Lee's bike I'm working on. Why don't I come over tonight and we can talk?"

"Or we could come over to wherever you're staying." From Con's intake of breath, Katy knew she'd hit a sore spot. "Where is that by the way?"

The extended pause on the line had Katy wondering whether he'd answer, but his quiet response shocked her. "Nick and Emma's."

Nick and Emma's? Katy blinked, her jaw slack before the indignation set in. Far louder than she should have for her business, she accused, "You're staying at my cousin's house and you didn't even bother to fucking tell me. What the hell, Connor?"

"I needed some time to think. I'm sorry. For everything. I'll come over tonight and explain."

Clenching her teeth together to stop herself from saying something she'd regret, Katy ground out, "I'll be home by six tonight. Make sure your arse is there."

"Okay," he responded quietly before hanging up. Fury and devastation warred for the top spot in her psyche. *Why did he go to Nick's rather than come home to us? What did we do to drive him away?* All the ups and downs she and Levi had been through over the past week, going back to that place they were in—that limbo—when he was enlisted, was for nothing. A part of her heart had been missing, and Levi had spent the whole week on edge, constantly checking his phone for a missed call or text and hovering over his email account. And for what? So Con could enjoy a beach holiday rather than coming home to them?

Katy shot off a text to Levi. Six o'clock couldn't come soon enough.

7
___

LEVI

SOMETHING WAS UP, BUT WHATEVER IT WAS, KATY WASN'T
talking. She'd sent him a cryptic message about making sure he
was home by six because Connor would be there. Like he was a
damn teenaged girl at a One Direction concert—or whoever the
teeny boppers were listening too now that they'd split up (and
Levi wouldn't admit to liking any of Louis, Harry, Zayne, Niall or
Liam's songs)—giddy excitement had filled him at the news. But
for some reason, Katy wasn't happy.

The knock on the door had his girlfriend stomping down the
hall to answer it. "Hey," he heard Connor greet her. He couldn't
hear Katy's response, but from her mood, he could just imagine
her standing at the door, arms crossed with a scowl on her face
and motioning with a tilt of her head for Connor to come in.
Levi grinned. His girl was a firecracker.

"How are you feeling?" Connor asked tentatively as they
entered the room. Sure enough, Katy wore a scowl and still
had her arms crossed over her chest, but his eyes were drawn
to the man behind her. The shackles around his heart loos-

ened a little. Seeing him, being in the same room as Connor had Levi desperate to go to him. Relief and something a lot stronger flooded through him, the butterflies in his belly taking flight. Levi had the crazy urge to trace his fingertips along the beard his friend had grown, to smell his scent again, to just be close to him. He'd never wanted to touch another man so much.

Katy sighed and answered. "I'm fine." She gave him a small smile. "It didn't take long to feel better once I got rid of the fever."

"Good, I'm glad." Their conversation was strained, and Levi was clueless as to why. He hated being on the outside, but considering the tension, he was glad he was.

"Hey, mate," Levi greeted him. Trying desperately to come across as casual, he pulled two beers out the fridge. "We missed you around here."

"Thanks." Connor held up the bottle in a toast when Levi passed it to him and turned to Katy when she started speaking.

"Listen, about today, I'm sorry. It wasn't right for me to yell at you. You don't have to answer to me, but I was hurt."

Connor nodded and reached for her hand. Levi took in the sight of them together, and his heart stuttered. The two most important people in his world stood before him. Sure, Levi would kick Connor's arse for whatever he'd done to hurt Katy later, but at present, he wanted his two people to fix whatever it was between them. He needed them to.

"I haven't handled things well at all. I should have told you, talked to you about what happened between Miranda and me. I didn't mean for you to worry. I just needed some space."

"You can talk to us." Levi reached out and punched Connor lightly on the arm. It was either that or hug him tightly, and Levi's emotions were riding far too close to the surface for him to do that. "You know that, don't you?"

"Yeah, I do." Connor sighed and leaned against the back of the couch. "It just hurts."

"What did that bitch do to you?" Katy demanded. Levi bit back a grin. He could just imagine the *dah, dah, daaah* sound effect as the plot thickened.

"No, it's entirely my fault. Miranda didn't do anything wrong—"

"She kicked you out, Connor." *She what?*

"Miranda was great. Things were great, right up until I yelled out the wrong name when we were... getting intimate."

"Whose name?" Levi asked, a sick desire coiling in his gut for it to have been Katy's. An even quieter voice in the back of his head wanted it to be him.

"That doesn't matter, but I hurt her. She was justified in kicking me out and calling me whatever the hell names she's called me."

"Why didn't you come home?" Levi asked, curious to know the answer, but trepidatious at the same time.

"You two were busy. I didn't want to interrupt." With Connor unable to look at either one of them in the eye, it didn't take a genius to know he was bullshitting.

Katy called him out on it. "Connor, this is your home too. There wasn't anything that would have been important enough to stop us being there for you."

"Even a session with your new toys?"

"You knew about that?" Levi stuttered, embarrassment racing through his veins. "Wait, she kicked you out last weekend? Where the hell have you been?"

"Nick and Em's," Katy supplied. Shock had Levi staggering back to lean against the back of the kitchen table chair in their open-plan living room.

"I didn't want to interrupt your night with my latest fuck up."

"You wouldn't have interrupted much," Levi admitted sheepishly.

"What, you didn't find anything you liked?" he asked Katy. "From what Addy told me, she has a great range in that suitcase she carries around with her."

"We got a few things." Levi shrugged. It was an eye-opening experience and Levi hadn't been able to get the butt plug out of his mind since he'd bought it, but what it meant scared him more than he thought possible. How could he admit to Katy that he hadn't fantasized about pressing it between her curvalicious ass, but into Connor's tight hole.

"That's good. Isn't it?"

"Never mind us," Katy shot him a worried look. She was right, there were other things they needed to be concerned about other than the butt plug burning a hole in his bedside table drawer. "Con you said you needed some space. Talk to us. We wanna help."

"I can't stay here anymore. I need to move away."

"Okay, so find a place." Levi shrugged, feigning how simple the solution was. But his heart told him it was something far more than that. "We'll help you get settled wherever you wanna go."

Connor sighed and shook his head. Levi's heart stopped. *Oh God, no.* "I'm thinking of moving away from the Coast. Maybe Melbourne, but I haven't decided."

"What? No," Katy breathed, clamping a hand over her mouth and Levi instantly moved towards her, needing her comfort. He was operating on autopilot, as if he was having an out-of-body experience. He couldn't bear the thought that his best mate would be on the opposite side of the country to him, too far away to really hang with.

"I can't stay here," Connor pleaded for his understanding. The broken-hearted look on his face tore at Levi's heart. Devastated him. The dark circles under Connor's eyes made him look tired, the bloodshot whites giving away the rough time he'd had. *Is it the nightmares? Or something more?* He didn't have his ramrod straight posture anymore either. Levi had seen it in his stance the last few times they'd been together. His shoulders were slumped and his hair, longer than usual curls, was a mess, like he'd been running his fingers through it in frustration.

"Why?" Levi asked, hoping he was doing a better job of masking his pain than both Connor and Katy were doing. He needed to be strong for them, to pick up the pieces when their lives turned to shit. Whatever was about to go down had the power to destroy them. Levi just hoped that he could hold it together long enough to keep them intact.

"Because my insides feel like they're being eviscerated. I can't live with my heart being broken anymore. I need to move on, to forget."

Katy pulled out of his embrace and went to Connor, wrapping her arms around his waist and burying her head in his chest. The knife through Levi's heart twisted. He couldn't lose Connor again. It'd slay him. But Connor was hurting so bad. Every protective instinct in Levi reared its head. He needed to fix things for all of them, to give him something only he and Katy could give to Connor, even if it was only for one night.

He stepped up behind Katy and kissed the side of her throat before wrapping a hand around the nape of Connor's neck, bringing him close. Enveloping his two people in his arms, a sense of rightness swept through Levi. "Please don't leave, Con," he begged, his voice cracking on his friend's name.

Levi and Katy moved as one, Katy tugging on Connor's snug black tee until he bent and Levi squeezing his shoulder, massaging the lean muscle there. When Katy brushed her lips against Connor's, electricity arced between the three of them. Levi sucked in a breath, balling his hand into a fist at Connor's nape to stop the instinct screaming at him to pull him in for a kiss like the one he was watching.

"Katy," Connor groaned, his voice almost breaking on the word. A haunted look settled on his face as he pushed back with visible effort, before shoving a hand through his hair. His dark eyes were troubled, his next words coming out as an anguished whisper. "I can't."

Levi's heart broke for what his best mate was going through, yet at the same time, determination settled through him. He could help. Both of them could. "It's okay, Con. Take what she's willing to give."

"What?" Con snapped his bewildered eyes up, meeting Levi's gaze.

Conviction spurred Levi on. This was right—the three of them together—and he wasn't going to sit back and hope anymore. Levi was taking the bull by the horns. "Katy needs you." *I need you.*

Katy had a white knuckled grip on Connor's shirt, clutching desperately to him. Levi was doing a little of it himself—holding tight to his best friend. "Kiss her," Levi barely whispered. He bit back a moan when Connor slid his arm around Levi's waist, bringing him into a three-way embrace. Their gazes locked and Levi found himself fighting his instincts again. He couldn't do it. *Could he? No.* Fear and arousal coursed through him, creating this crazy cacophony of noise in his head—every thought, all the uncertainty about what his attraction meant for them circled through him like a vortex. Connor could usually read him like an open book; Levi hoped he couldn't this time because he was sure Connor would be ashamed of how scared he was. Instead, Connor leaned down and touched his lips to Katy's, tentative at first, barely meeting them for small tender pecks until Katy swiped her tongue along Connor's bottom lip and he opened to her.

Levi's heart warmed. Knowing he'd helped them find each other could have brought him to his knees, but instead, he loved his girl even more. She was so damn brave, so full of love and life—she was who Connor needed. Levi needed to be closer to them, needed to be connected in the only way he knew how. He trailed his lips along Katy's throat in a whisper-soft kiss. The scent of chocolate and vanilla filled his senses, mixed with something spicier—Connor—and his need turned ravenous. Licking and sucking on the column of Katy's neck, Levi walked his fingers under the waistband of her tank and slipped it up. Connor's hand brushed his own, and the other man pulled away from Katy, their gazes colliding once more. Whatever Connor read in his eyes this time had all hesitation evaporating, and he let go of his grip on Levi to whip off Katy's shirt. Standing topless between them, Katy's tanned skin against the black of Connor's shirt had Levi growling. *Oh fuck yes.*

"Bedroom. Now," Levi ordered, palming Katy's firm breast and Connor's even firmer ass. The other man groaned, punching his hips forward. The denim of his well-worn jeans was soft under Levi's touch, but the muscle underneath it was anything but. Levi shuddered, marvelling at the difference between the two people before him—so soft, so curvy and strong and hard. It flipped a switch in him and had him growling commands at them, something he'd never done with Katy. But Connor responded to it, lifting Katy effortlessly without breaking their kiss. With her legs wrapped around his waist, Connor carried Katy to the front of the house, leaving Levi to follow behind. He stared at their form together, committing every inch of their bodies to his memory.

"Con, put her down so I can undress you both." Katy's moan had Levi smirking, and Connor's hum had him adjusting himself. His cock was so damn hard, it could hammer nails. But the spark between them that was finally being given oxygen to feed the flame wasn't about pleasing Levi, and he'd seek no relief from the two people before him. They needed to focus on each other.

As Katy slipped her legs down Connor's waist, Levi grasped the other man's tee and drew it up over his body. He couldn't help letting the backs of his fingers brush against Connor's lean muscle. But as much as he yearned to go further, to touch and caress, to kiss and love on the other man, fear stopped him cold. *Focus on Katy and Connor, not me.*

Katy dropped kisses down Connor's sternum and Levi moved behind the other man. The scars that marred his shoulder drew Levi in. He touched them, running his fingertips over the angry red lines. He remembered the taste of that skin, knew without a doubt that the hazy dream he'd had of rubbing against Connor and biting him had been real. Trailing his fingers down to his waist Levi reached for Connor's fly. Leaning in close Levi found the button and bit down on his lip to stop himself from nipping Connor's shoulder again. Levi sucked in a deep breath filled with the other man's scent. *Ah God.* Eyes sliding closed, Levi prayed to whatever deity that might be listening, to stop him from blowing his load in the next thirty seconds.

Levi fell to his knees and unlaced Connor's black Chucks, yanking them off and tossing them aside before reaching up to Connor's hips. Long, strong legs and an arse that begged to be kissed and nibbled on before him, Levi ground his teeth together and curled his fingers under the waistband, slipping his jeans down. He drank in Connor's bright blue boxer shorts curving around *that* arse. Unable to tear his gaze away, he revealed inch after inch of tanned skin and dark hair. Connor was so different to Katy, but Levi was enraptured. Muscles flexed before him, and after sending Connor's jeans the same way as his shoes, Levi reached up for his boxer shorts. There was no slow reveal this time. Levi didn't even watch as they came off—he couldn't bear the torture of being so close yet having to hold himself back. Leaving Connor's underwear around his ankles, he stood and returned to his position behind Katy. He had to get back to safe ground—something, anything—or he'd be bending Connor over and sliding in deep. And wouldn't that be the end of their friendship! Connor would knock him on his arse and Katy would probably give him his marching orders.

Shaking the idea from his head, Levi concentrated once again on Katy. She was pressed tightly against Connor, her arms wound around his waist. His friend had one of his hands tangled in Katy's hair, cupping the back of her head as he made love to her mouth with his own. The other caressed her breast, worshipping her tenderly. Levi pressed his lips to Katy's shoulder and snuck his tongue out to taste her. He could never get enough of her sweet skin. Moaning quietly, Levi ran his calloused hands down her sides, following the dip of her waist down to the flare of her hips and to her low-slung shorts. God, he loved every inch of her, every perfect piece of her inside and out. Pushing her shorts off her hips, they dropped to the floor, but the sight didn't capture his attention. No, that was snagged by Katy's hips undulating slowly as she rocked her pussy—still covered in the sexiest black satin scrap of material that he'd ever seen—against Connor's rigid length. *Fuck me sideways, his piercing is so damn hot.* The glint of the silver ring had Levi's concentration riveted. Peering over Katy's shoulder, staring at his best friend's junk, Levi was abso-freaking-lutely salivating. His cock pulsing and ready to blow with just the sight of the two of them near nude together had Levi grinding his hips against Katy, instinctively trying to relieve the pressure in his balls. He had to get her underwear off. He grasped the material at her hips, but Connor's hand on his stopped him short.

"Let me do that. Please, Lee," Con begged. Levi released his hands and dropped an open-mouthed kiss on Katy's shoulder before pointing to the bed.

"Get on it. I wanna watch you make love to her." Levi's command, the best attempt he could muster at holding himself back, came out as a growl. He went to lean against the wall, distancing himself from them. If he got any closer, there was no way he'd be able to stop.

"No." Katy halted him in his tracks. "I want you with us." She held out her hand to him, but he shook his head.

"No, babe, not this time. You're all Connor's tonight. Next time we'll share you."

"Fuuuck," his friend groaned as he grasped the base of his cock and squeezed, closing his eyes and looking every bit as pained as Levi. Katy moved back onto the bed and stretched out, parting her legs as her head hit the pillow. Connor crawled over her and hovered, gazing at Katy with a look so full of love it stole Levi's breath. Lowering until his body blanketed hers, Connor kissed her. For long moments he sipped from her mouth, urgent yet tender, his hands mapping every inch of her like he was memorizing her curves.

Connor moved his mouth to her throat and caressed her, licking and nibbling, worshipping her. Levi moaned and stroked himself through his workout shorts. He was painfully hard and so damn close already it wasn't funny. He was seriously going to embarrass himself before he even pulled his dick out. Watching Connor draw Katy's fingertips into his mouth sucking and biting on each of the pads, then giving her a wicked smile and burying his face in her breasts had Levi shuddering.

"You're perfect, every inch of you, Cupcake," he murmured, before latching onto one of her nipples, teasing it with his tongue and teeth. Watching the fluid thrusts of Connor's hips as he stroked himself against Katy's leg, had Levi wishing it were him. And when Katy gasped and arched her back, grinding against the leg he had pressed between hers, Levi moaned too. Katy cried out, and Levi had to curl his fingers around the base of his cock, squeezing hard, desperately trying to stop himself from busting a nut too early.

Connor had slid down her body, running the tip of his nose along the line of her G-string, sneaking his tongue out to lick her through the satiny material. Katy looked over at him, their eyes locking for a moment before his gaze was drawn to Connor again. Watching the two of them together was the hottest thing he'd ever seen. Beauty and strength in both of them, they were a perfect fit. "She's so wet, so ready for me, Lee," Connor murmured, wonder in his tone as he turned to watch Levi slowly jacking off. Levi's cock pulsed when he saw Connor's nostrils flare, the gravelly tone when he spoke to Katy turning him on even more. "Lee's over there all by himself, stroking his cock. You want him on the bed with us? You wanna touch him too?"

"Yes," she cried out, and Levi couldn't resist her. He used one hand to strip off his shorts and underwear, kicking them off in one hit, while he reached behind his head with the other and tugged at the neckline of his tee. Completely naked, he climbed onto the bed and glued himself to Katy's side, getting as close to them as possible without going a step too far. Connor was already pulling her underwear down her legs, tossing them haphazardly to the side.

Connor dropped his mouth onto her and Katy visibly shuddered. With a talented tongue and deft fingers, he took her to the edge fast, hitting every hot button Katy had. It was enthralling, so damn sexy to watch the other man with his girl. Did that make him twisted? Probably. Anyone else and there'd be hell to pay, but with Connor, it was right, almost inevitable that they'd end up there together.

When Katy's hand closed around Levi's cock, jacking him slowly, Levi was done for, barrelling towards an orgasm that he so desperately wanted to hold off from. "Oh damn, I'm too close," he moaned, shifting his hips back and out of Katy's reach.

"I can feel your pussy fluttering around my tongue," Connor rasped on a moan. The raw need in his voice had Levi's dick pulsing. He sounded just as overcome, just as drunk on desire as Levi was. "Ride me, Cupcake. Come on my face so I can love you." The dirty words coming out of that sexy-as-fuck mouth had Levi shuddering, the tingle in his spine growing.

"Lee," Katy called out reaching blindly for him. "I want your cock in my mouth."

Levi hissed, clamping his fingers around his cock like a vice. Grinding his teeth together, he growled, "Let Con hear you scream his name when you come."

"Nghunhn," Con grunted as Katy went rigid. Levi knew the feeling, had experienced the tight clench of her inner muscles clamping down on him as she came. Her keening cry as she thrust her hips, riding out her orgasm had Levi tipping over the edge. Two passes over his cock with his precum-slicked fist and he shot his load, emptying himself onto her flat stomach. Sensation whited out, enveloping him in a tingling rush from head to toe that blinded him with its ferocity. Levi's grunts mixed with Katy's higher-pitched moans and Connor's groans to create a symphony that made his orgasm linger, lasting longer than ever before. When Levi peeled his eyes away from the ecstasy written on Katy's face, he looked over at Connor, to see him watching them with an intensity that had Levi itching to reach over and drag him on top of them. Instead, Connor shifted off the bed, moving to his jeans and getting the condom out of his wallet.

Sheepishly, he explained while rolling it down his length, "It's been in here for a while. It's still good though." After taking a deep breath and blowing out, he added, "There's always a risk of it tearing with my piercing."

"Get up here, Connor," Katy growled, making Connor tilt one side of his mouth up in a smirk.

"So fuckin' sassy," Levi murmured with a smile.

Connor settled between her legs and kissed her slowly again, mashing the evidence of Levi's orgasm between them. Levi reached out and grasped Katy's hand. It was about the only movement he could make after coming as hard as he did.

"Please, Con. I need you," she whispered.

"Me too, Cupcake." Connor lined up and pressed inside her silky folds, causing Katy to gasp and Levi's cock to twitch. They were perfect together, so damn beautiful that Levi stared at the point they joined, wanting to remember every minute detail. There was no way he and Katy would ever be the same together again. Levi prayed that Connor would stick around—losing him might mean the end of everything he held dear.

He rocked slowly in her. There was no animalistic fucking going on; it was all fluid grace. Connor made love to her, fusing them together so completely it left Levi in no doubt that Connor had loved Katy for years. His whispered sweet nothings were meant for her ears alone—something just for the two of them. And that was more than fine with Levi. His heart swelled knowing the bond he'd seen grow had finally morphed into the one thing they'd both wanted, but had never taken.

"Cupcake, I'm close. Come with me." She didn't answer; instead, she tightened her hold on him, gasping as she went rigid again. His glides into her turned choppy, his breath stuttering as he cried out and rode the bliss of his orgasm. Watching them come together was by far the most beautiful, sensual thing he'd ever seen. The only thing better was watching the two of them fall asleep together, Connor the big spoon as Katy used his shoulder as a pillow.

He woke spooning Katy, sharing the pillow with her, while Connor lay on her other side holding her close as he ran his fingers through her hair. Levi could see the remnants of their midnight snack sitting on the side table behind his friend, their wine glasses with the empty bottle no doubt still on the floor.

"Hey," he whispered.

"Morning." Connor's smile was relaxed, content for the first time in a long time. The lines on his forehead were gone; instead, he wore a sleepy, happy smile.

"You okay?"

"Yeah." He nodded. "You?"

Levi closed his eyes and laid there quietly thinking about what the change the night before would mean to his and Katy's relationship, to the bond that each of them had with Connor, and he smiled. Wanting Connor to be a part of them, for Levi to be able to express what he'd ached for, was something he'd struggled to admit to himself, but their night together was better than he'd ever dared hope for. It was everything he'd ever wanted. Well, almost everything. But he wasn't quite ready to take that step—he might not ever be. "I'm good too."

Connor raking his fingers through Katy's hair didn't stop, except now his fingers lingered, brushing them against Levi's chest before starting again at the top of her head. Each touch sent a jolt of lightning through Levi. He really did want this, but he couldn't help think of how Connor had left them before, and how he was just about to do it to them again.

"Why'd you run?" Levi asked softly.

"What? I didn't run." At Connor's defensive response, Levi opened his eyes and raised one eyebrow. "Yeah, okay. But it's not like I went far. I just needed some time."

"You disappeared for six years. You had leave but only came back once, and you didn't tell us when you were taking it the other times so we could meet you. You ran."

"You're right." He sighed. "I was in love with someone, and it hurt too much to see her happy with another man. And it wasn't like I had anyone special in my life to miss me." His shrug infuriated Levi.

"Are you kidding me?" he spat in a much too loud whisper. "That's what you thought?" He jabbed his friend in the shoulder and blew out a frustrated breath. Tempering his voice back to a level that wouldn't wake Katy, he added, "Mate, you were special to Katy. And you're my best mate. You're special to both of us."

Connor shook his head, the lines on his forehead appearing again. The light dimmed from his eyes before Connor looked away. "You two are special to each other. I've always been the tag along."

The memory of a young, scared Connor resurfaced. Those days when he didn't know what'd happened to his dad, when Child Services were trying to take him away and Levi's parents had fought to keep him. Alone and unknowingly rejected by his aunt and uncle in the UK—Dr Stratford and his wife were apparently far too good to have their orphan nephew living with them—Levi had begged his parents to let his friend stay. He'd never forget his mum's words, *"He's our family, Levi. Maybe not by blood, but that doesn't matter. Family doesn't give up on each other, and we aren't letting him go. Hold tight to him, okay, baby."* Levi wanted to reach out and caress Connor's shoulder, but he didn't. Holding tight hadn't worked before, maybe this time Connor needed to *want* to stay. "Is that what you think now? After last night?"

Connor shook his head, his gaze imploring. "You two'll always have each other and I'll still be jackin' off in the spare room if I stay."

Knowing he couldn't say anything to keep Connor there was like a dagger piercing his heart. "You're still leaving."

"I don't see any other choice. What happened last night..."

He scrubbed a hand over his face and blew out a breath. "It's not like we can keep going. You've got your job, and you guys are meant to be together." Frustration laced his words, but he knew Connor well enough to know that there was no changing the man's mind once he'd made it up. And whatever the result, Connor would follow it through. A longing as deep and fathomless as the oceans filled Levi. He wanted his friend close, needed him there. *But my job—it wouldn't be around for long if news of our threesome ever saw the light of day... yeah, there is that.*

"It was her all those years ago, wasn't it? You fell in love with Katy."

Connor started to shake his head in denial, but the fight left him when he could no longer meet Levi's gaze. Raising his eyes back up, he asked, "What gave it away?"

Levi huffed out a quiet laugh. "Your eyes follow her around the room like a freakin' puppy dog. And instead of wild monkey sex, you made love to her last night."

Connor flicked his gaze down to Katy and the adoration pouring off him made Levi want to wrap him in a hug and never let go. Connor's whispered words struck a chord with Levi. "She's easy to love."

Levi grasped Connor's wrist, stopping his motion through her hair. "Is that why you're running again? Because you think you can't have her?"

"Like I said, you two are the couple here. I'm the third wheel. You aren't gonna want me here forever—you'll wanna get married and have kids and, what... I'll be the pathetic, creepy mate the kids call uncle who lives in the spare room and is in love with their mum?"

"You're an idiot sometimes, you know that? She loves you too." The silence lingered between them, their gazes colliding. Levi could see Connor wanted to add something more. Hell, there was something he wanted to say too—*what about me? Are you in love with me? Do you want me like I want you?* But the words remained unspoken. He wasn't brave enough to admit them out loud. Levi laid there for long minutes, just looking, taking in his fill of Connor and Katy, watching as Connor gently kissed her forehead, as the lazy smile once again appeared.

"Mmm," Katy sighed, reaching out to Connor as she snuggled back against Levi, connecting them from chest to knee. "Last night wasn't a dream, was it?"

"No, Cupcake," Connor murmured. "It wasn't. Are you okay with what happened?"

"Hell yeah." Katy laughed a husky, sleepy laugh before Connor tilted her face up to him and captured her lips in a slow kiss. "I'm happy, but I'm also late for work. Again. I need to get my arse outta bed." Wrapping a hand around the back of his neck, she pulled Connor's face to hers again and kissed him hard and fast. That sense of longing filled Levi again, pulsing through his body.

Levi then watched with amusement as she rolled over to him, climbing him like a cat. He went willingly onto his back, snaking his arms around her body to hold her close while she teased his lips with a barely-there kiss.

"I probably reek of sex, but I'm so late." Katy slipped off him and, naked, she dashed out the room. Her chef's whites, together with most of their other clothes were sitting in the laundry room. Five minutes later, she was ready and running out the door, slamming it in her wake.

"Damn, she's like a hurricane when she's late." Connor grinned and raised his arms above his head, arching his back as he stretched out.

"You can say that again," Levi's laugh got caught in his throat as he swallowed his tongue, and stared at the rippling lean muscles of Connor's abs and that delicious vee which led to a patch of dark hair nestling his package. Before his semi gave him away, he swung his legs off the bed and onto the hardwood floor. Connor climbed over to his side and stepped off the bed at the same time as Levi, but stumbled, falling straight into his arms. Reflexively, Levi hugged Connor close, holding the other man to his body.

"Ow shit, pins and needles." Connor shook out his foot, and they looked up together, their gazes locking. So close and both completely naked, the air seemed to get sucked out of the room. The other man's lips were barely a couple of inches away, begging him to sample them. But that was the problem. Once he'd had a taste, Levi wasn't sure he'd be able to stop. As much as Levi wanted that, he wasn't sure if he was ready for it, wasn't sure if he'd *ever* be ready. And where did that leave Katy? He'd never—absolutely no question, ever—leave her feeling like she wasn't enough for him. So Levi did what he did best—he deflected.

"Thanks, Con. For making her happy, I mean." He smiled at his friend and resisted the temptation to stroke his hand down Connor's face. "I'm stoked it's you she fell for. Anyone else and I'd have to walk away. That'd kill me."

Connor leaned his forehead against Levi's and squeezed his hips. "You really think she's fallen for me?" The vulnerability in his tone wrecked Levi.

"Yeah, she's loved you forever. I didn't understand it while you were gone, but seeing her now—with you around—I know it."

Connor exhaled, the stress visibly leaving his body as his shoulders relaxed. He nestled his head against Levi's shoulder, hugging him tighter. The soft stubble on Connor's cheek had Levi pulling him closer, while the heady mixture of Connor's spicy aftershave and sex filled him with want. Levi breathed him in, savouring his unique smell. He had to give him this—the reassurance that he wasn't alone, that Katy needed him too. *That*

I need him. If only I wasn't such a pussy. Their nudity, the contact between the two of them wasn't about sex, it was comfort. It was love.

Levi kissed his forehead and whispered, "Please stay." He ran his hands down his friend's bare back and snaking his arms around Connor's waist, he hugged him close in exactly the way he'd wanted to do in bed.

Connor closed his eyes and returned his head to Levi's shoulder. His breaths were ragged, his voice breaking on the last of his whispered words. "I don't wanna go."

Connor

Connor stepped out of the steaming shower he'd escaped to after whatever the hell had gone down between him and Levi earlier. One minute he'd been trying to stand and the next he'd been in Levi's arms. And hearing Levi beg him to stay, tell him that Katy loved him had pushed him to the edge. He'd wanted it, damn well craved it. He'd wished desperately that it could be a reality, but could it really? He'd been worried about everyone's judgement, had told himself that it'd never work. How had anything changed? It hadn't. Instead, he'd given into temptation. He was scared—terrified that their affair would leave him broken beyond repair. But like a sucker for pain, a total masochist, he couldn't keep away.

"Hey, Con, what time's your gig tonight?" Levi yelled from the other room. "If I can move after today's filming, I'd like to be there."

"Eight," he called out, scrubbing the fluffy white towel over his hair, before wrapping it around his waist. Steam coated the mirror, but it didn't matter. It wasn't like he was going to shave; he was finally at the point of almost having a proper beard. "Whatcha filmin'?" he asked, walking into his bedroom and pulling a pair of shorts out of his cupboard.

"I'm doin' a few specials on preparing for *Tough Mudder*," Levi said as he came to stand in the open doorway of Connor's bedroom. "DJ, our location manager, set up some exercises with the army, training at the barracks in the mountains. Should be fun."

"Cool." Connor hesitated before pulling off the towel and getting dressed. He had planned on heading to the mechanic's shop to see if any of the parts he'd sent away for rust proofing had been returned, but one day wouldn't make a difference. Levi's bike was as close to being finished as it was going to get— another day or two and it'd be ready for painting. That bit and the assembly, Connor wanted them to do together. "Hey, I can come if you like. I was gonna do a few bits and pieces, but it can wait. I might be able to give you some pointers."

"Yeah, great." Levi's smile lit up his face and Connor's heart skipped a beat. With an excited grin, Levi asked, "Can we take your car up the mountain?"

Connor chuckled. "Yeah, I've been itchin' to let her loose on the winding roads up there." Deciding against the shorts and shirt, Connor retrieved his heavy-duty combat boots and camos from his cupboard. If he was going to help Levi, it would be from by his side.

Closing his eyes, Connor tried to breathe deeply. Tried being the appropriate word. He could barely get a breath in, but even still, the smell of eucalypts and the damp mossy undergrowth wafted to him on the cool breeze. The light sprinkling of rain they'd had on the way up the mountain had given a chill to the wind and left everything smelling fresh.

The beauty of the surrounding scenery did nothing to ease him; Connor's chest was tight. He fought to gasp in another breath. It was as if an elephant was sitting on him making him struggle to get air into his lungs with each inhale. *Damnit. Fuck.* Frustrated, he ground his teeth together as he tried in vain to steady his shaking hands. His heart beat hard, each pump vibrating through him.

"Lee," he wheezed, unsure whether his friend would have even heard. They hadn't even started the run yet. No, they were getting the grand tour, the director insisting they see the training village even though both the army and the location manager had already ruled it out for possible filming. He shouldn't be struggling, but his mind teetered on the edge of a ravine into hell, and knowing exactly what was down there in its depths— the memories, the grief and powerlessness—scared Connor more than the war ever had.

He was already trailing behind the group, leaving Levi to his thing, when the memories crashed into him. Alert, panning his gaze, he looked through the windows of the empty squat building, to see another opening on the opposite side. Through the windows was an alleyway, the flash of movement there catching his eye. Connor reached for his gun, but it wasn't there. *Why not?* Instinctively, he felt for his sidearm, but he wasn't wearing his holster either. Or his body armour. *Jesus fucking Christ.* His heartbeat thundering in his veins, panic seizing him, every muscle in his body turning to jelly. *Hide.* Dizzy, he reached out trying to steady himself, but he went down on his knees. He was a sitting duck. Fucking target practice.

Gravel crunched underfoot and Connor raised his fist—the sign for freeze—as he tried desperately to get a handle on where the enemy was, but his unit didn't stop—they kept talking... they kept walking. Frantic, he looked up scanning the rooftops, waiting for the inevitable moment he'd see it—the wink of metal in the sunlight. The gun that would end him.

"Fire at will." His commanding officer's voice rang through the quiet village. Connor's muscles wouldn't work. Everything in him screamed to take cover, but he couldn't move. Like sinking down into a pool of quicksand, he was rooted to the spot. When would it happen? When would the lance of fire-like pain from the bullet tearing his body apart come?

"Connor, *Connor*." The voice was familiar. *Rob. No! Take cover. You die too. You can't die. Molly doesn't deserve to lose you, you don't deserve to die. Please.* Strong hands on his biceps shook him and instinct had him fighting back, warding off the enemy. He struck out, connecting with a hard body but a grunt was the only indication he'd even affected the insurgent.

"Con, you're home. You're safe." The hands left his arms and cupped his face and Connor recoiled, shying from the blows that would come. They did that—the enemy would beat him to a pulp if they got their hands on him. But they couldn't, could they? He was there, in the middle of his unit. They protected each other. Connor looked around wildly. Why wasn't he protected? Bodies were everywhere. Blood stains seeping into the dirt, the pools of red flooding outward and turning a deep brown as the dust settled. All of them, gone. Mangled piles of limbs twisted into barely recognizable forms. A tortured cry ripped itself from his throat as he twisted, trying to reach his brothers and sisters.

"No," he gasped, his lungs on fire. He needed to breathe, but he couldn't. Why couldn't he? He fought, trying to push the wall of muscle away. Like he was underwater, the sounds around him became muted, his vision swimming. Blackness started to close in on him.

"Look at me, Connor. Focus on me. Breathe." *Levi? No, he can't be here.* "You're back on the Goldie. Remember? Your first day back we went and laid out on the beach. You were listening to the waves, relaxing. Katy was there too. You were singing with your guitar." He remembered that. The inner calm, the peace he got from being with his best friends washed over him. "That's it. Take another breath." He did and the dark shadows colouring his vision lifted.

"Con, I need you to look at me. I need you to see me." Connor followed Levi's soothing voice and finally focussed on him. Right in front of him, their faces close together, he was all Connor could see. His gut sank, confusion and horror washing over him. "Just look at me. Don't worry about anything else. You're safe. You're home. No one's gonna hurt you. Ever. Okay?" Connor found himself nodding, wanting to do anything to keep the strength of those hands on him. They were the only thing keeping him upright.

"I'm gonna give you a tablet. It's the one you normally take to help calm you down. Can I do that? Can you open your mouth for me?" Connor's movements were slow, but he managed a nod. When he did, he felt Levi reaching into his pocket, getting the pill bottle out and Connor opened his mouth. The acrid taste of the medicine under his tongue filled his mouth after a moment and he began floating, the pain drifting away. Levi's strong hands stayed on him, comforting him.

His head throbbing, he slumped forward, falling into Levi's arms and resting his head on his friend's shoulder. He breathed deeply, smelling no cordite, no blood. There was only cedar and orange, only Levi. The tablets always made him drowsy—he hated taking them, but he was finally going numb, finally getting blessed relief from nerves that were too raw, from memories that were so terrifying, they'd broken and scarred him for life.

"I'm sorry," Connor whispered. "I ruined everything."

"Nah, you haven't ruined anything. Not at all," Levi responded, lulling Connor to sleep as he ran his fingers through Connor's hair. "But this position is hell on my knees. Let's get you up and into the medical centre so you can sleep. The doc's right here."

"No," he breathed, his muscles clenching tight. "Not the infirmary, please." Connor was ashamed at the weakness, the vulnerability in his voice, but he couldn't handle another flashback, and that's exactly what would happen if he went in there. The harsh antiseptics, the beds, and nurse's scrubs would send him back to those early days after Rob's death when mending his body had been the army's main concern. Call him bitter, but the damage to his mind didn't ever seem to have been as big a worry until his treating doctor's deployment ended and he was replaced by another one who'd done part of her residency in the psych ward. She'd diagnosed Connor with PTSD and a few other things with complicated names when his nightmares bled into waking hours. Yeah, there was no way he was going back into a hospital unless he was dying. "I'll go back to the car and stay there."

Levi squeezed him tighter. "Yeah, okay. I'll come and check on you."

When Connor woke, he knew he'd slept for hours. The sun was low in the sky and the heat of the day had passed. He got out and stretched, needing to take a leak and get a drink. He was hazy, like he was seeing the world through cotton wool. The meds always did that to him. Looking around as he walked over to the exercise yard, he followed the breathing and exercises his therapist had given him. He counted out of order too, keeping his mind as occupied as he could. He didn't want a repeat of that morning, but he was not going to let this beat him. He was going to function, and right at that moment, it meant going to find Levi.

When he saw his friend, he was soaked through and covered in mud jogging towards a collection of cameras. Connor guessed it was the finish line, but he wasn't exactly the expert on how they filmed segments of the show.

Levi looked high on life, a broad smile lighting up his already gorgeous features. Connor looked around, trying to figure out who Levi had done the course with. Two men in olive camos ran behind him, covered in as much mud as Levi. They'd taken his place. He should have been running with his best friend, but his damn disability had stopped him short. Connor sighed, but he hated that he'd just proved the doctors right—his medical discharge was warranted. He didn't want to get angry, hated the pity party for one he'd had when he was first diagnosed, but he couldn't help being pissed. *No, dude, that ain't happenin'. Suck it up, sunshine, and appreciate what you have.* That was it, the key—Connor wasn't sure what the future held for him. He could end up that weird, lonely uncle sleeping in Levi and Katy's spare room, but whatever life had in store for him, he was going to live every moment like it was his last.

The production crew clapped and cheered as Levi slowed his run to a walk. Visibly out of breath, he paced it out, shaking off the lactic acid in his legs as his breathing slowed, before dropping onto the ground, sitting cross-legged in the grass. He waved off the director as Connor walked over to him. "You okay, mate?" Connor asked. He smiled, proud of his friend's effort in finishing the course.

"Yeah," Levi replied, flashing him a grin in return. Turning to the man hovering close by he added, "Just gimme a minute to catch my breath then I'll do the close." When they were alone again, Levi groused at him playfully, "Don't just stand there." He held out his hand for Connor to help him up. "Lemme get this over with then I can have a shower and get in your car clean. Otherwise you'll be carrying me home."

"Like fuck." He laughed, feeling lighter just being with Levi. "I'll leave you here before I let you dirty up my brand-new interior."

"Whatever. Tonight, I'm on the bottom." And like that, Connor's biggest problem was the erection tenting his camos. And what a great look that would be for a children's program— *Look here, kids, I've got a boner over fucking my best mate's girl. In a threesome. With my best mate. Who I'm also hot for.* Thank God, he wasn't in front of the cameras.

"You're on the bottom of what, Levi?" DJ, the location manager, asked, pointing out where they had the last of the cameras set up.

"Nothin', mate," Levi replied, barely missing a beat. Damn, they needed to be more careful in public. Levi was so worried about his job that he wouldn't even repair his bike. He'd wanted piercings forever and tatts too, but had held off knowing that it didn't suit his image for the show. And now he was potentially putting it on the line so Connor could jump into bed with them? *What am I thinking letting him risk everything he's worked for?* Connor closed his eyes and slowly exhaled. How could he stay when he might be forcing Levi's hand to risk something he loved? Especially when he was so damaged.

———

"You sure you're up to coming tonight? If you'd rather have some alone time with Katy, it's cool. I don't have to stay at your place either. I still have Nick and Em's key," Connor added as he pulled into the off-street parking just outside Katy's shop. He cut the engine and willed himself to smile at Levi. It probably looked fake as hell, but after Connor had realized how much risk he was putting Levi in by being with them, he'd had a hard time putting on a genuine one.

"Yeah." Levi nodded. He took a breath like he was nervous, and blurted out, "I know this is new and you were probably shocked as shit yesterday, and, yeah, we do need to have a sit down to figure out boundaries and all that other stuff, but can we maybe just go with the flow or whatever? I don't want it to be a one-night thing, especially not when you and Katy feel the way you do about each other."

Connor studied Levi, wanting to laugh at his nerves, but so grateful for the fact that he'd just laid it out there, giving him the opening Connor had dreamed of. "I'm happy to go with the flow. I'd kinda love it if last night wasn't a one-off." He flushed, embarrassed that his sex life outside of the night before had been virtually non-existent for a long time. "I know you two are exclusive. I'm happy to do the same if...." Connor shrugged, leaving the rest unsaid.

Levi nodded quickly. "I'd like that. We should talk to Katy too. Maybe if she wants to keep this thing between us going, you could watch us together." Levi lifted his shoulder in a half shrug, his uncertainty showing through. Connor would never say it out loud—Levi might kick his arse—but he found it adorable. "Or I could watch again." Levi shot him a shy smile and Connor's heart warmed.

"Did it feel weird to you? Watching me with Katy, I mean?"

"Nah, not weird. It turned me on. I kinda want to see her give you a BJ. She gets so into it." Levi pressed down on the bulge between his legs and Connor stifled a moan. *I'd get into giving you a BJ too.* "What about you? You okay with this? With us?"

"Yeah." Connor nodded, before shrugging his shoulders and adding, "I never thought I'd even be lucky enough to kiss her, never mind love her like I did yesterday. And you being there made it even better."

Levi smiled at him and clapped a hand on Connor's thigh, quickly removing it. "Come on, let's go in and get our girl."

The chime on the door tinkled behind them as it opened and Levi stepped through. "G'day, Dylan, is Katy out back?"

"Sure is, sexy." The dude looked up and flashed a smile to Levi, making jealousy churn in Connor's gut and a low growl escape him. As soon as it did, the other man's gaze flicked over to Connor and he did a slow perusal, checking him out. Heat bloomed in Connor's cheeks and with a chuckle, the dude Levi had called Dylan asked, "You gonna introduce me to this hot piece of sex on a stick, Lee?"

Levi's eyes widened momentarily, his mouth popping open as he froze like a deer in headlights. Yeah, Dylan had stunned him, and Connor couldn't help but bite back a laugh. "Ah, Con, this is Dylan, Katy's other pastry chef. He looks after all the stuff you see in the counter and does some of the decorating for Katy. Dylan, Connor, my best mate."

"Nice to meet you, Connor." Dylan held up his flour-coated hands giving him an apologetic look. "I'd shake, but it's easier not to. Anyway, I've heard lots about you from Katy. Welcome back and thanks for your service."

Connor swallowed, his throat suddenly dry. He appreciated the sentiment but his emotions were a little too close to the surface, too raw, for him to respond with much more than a "Thanks." Connor was grateful he didn't have to continue the conversation when Levi wrapped a hand around his bicep and tugged him across the room.

"Sugar?" Levi called out as he poked his head through the security-coded door to the rear work area.

"Hi, babe. I'm in the storeroom. Come and take a look at the cake I just finished."

They walked through into the cooled room, and Connor's mouth dropped open. Damn the talent this girl had was off the charts. He couldn't believe what he was seeing. The three-foot-high replica of Cinderella's castle came complete with a horse-drawn pumpkin chariot, Cinderella in her white ball gown and Prince Charming waiting at the top of the stairs. Every minute detail stood out—the individual leaves on the bushes, petals on the flowers, every shingle on the roof and curl of fabric in the dress. It was magnificent. *Katy* was magnificent.

"Holy crap, that's amazing," Levi breathed. Connor was speechless. But unable to resist touching her anymore, Connor reached out and took the camera she was holding, handing it to Levi.

Clasping her hand in his, he listened as Katy explained, "It's a one-off design for a customer. I've been working on it for nine days. The chariot alone took me four hours to make." Turning to him, she smiled tentatively, her blue eyes seeking out his approval. "What do you think, Con?"

The memories from the night before careened into him—Katy writhing in pleasure beneath him, the tight clasp of her pussy as she cradled him while they came together, the love in her gaze when he rolled them to the side and held her—and he fell deeper under the spell she wove. "Fuck me," he stuttered. "It's—"

"Yes please." Dylan laughed from the doorway. Instinctively Connor dropped Katy's hand and put some distance between them. He may have been in her bed, in her the night before, but whatever they had would never be public. Especially not with Levi having to guard his job.

Connor feigned a chuckle, but it sounded strained even to his own ears. "It's fuckin' amazing. But how could someone eat it? It's a work of art."

"Yeah, I couldn't bear to cut into it." Katy smiled and shrugged. "But that's the reason they bought it."

Connor's phone chimed with an incoming message. He was

going to ignore it until Katy motioned him to get it. When he saw who'd sent it, he grinned. His cousin, Ford, was bringing his partner to the Gold Coast for a holiday. After close to a decade, he was going to see his only living relative—Ford's parents didn't count. They weren't Connor's favourite people in the world. Stuck up and with major superiority complexes, Connor steered clear of his father's sister and her doctor husband wherever possible. It wasn't hard when they were in the UK, and he was on the other side of the world. How his cousin ended up being such a great guy was beyond Connor, and even though there was nearly a ten-year age gap between them, they'd always been mates.

Katy linked arms with him and added, "Come on, let's head home. You can tell me all about why you're suddenly as excited as a puppy dog on the way."

8

CONNOR

Two weeks later

A THUD SOUNDED IN THE DARK AND KATY SWORE. THEN, SOME rustling and the closing of a door.

"What's up, Cupcake?" Connor mumbled into the pillow. He missed her naked body pressed against him already. After his gig the night before, he'd spent hours tasting and worshipping her body, taking turns with Levi to pump into her. Sandwiched between them, her leg hooked over Levi's waist, they'd made love for hours, he and Levi staving off their own orgasms to see how many they could give to Katy. He'd counted four before he'd lost it when Levi was driving into her and Connor shifted, inadvertently coming into contact with the other man's dick. Both slicked up with Katy's essence, they'd ground against each other momentarily, sliding in an erotic dance. Katy's tight, hot centre, her cries and the shudder she'd let loose when they'd both connected and prodded her opening had Connor gritting his teeth and caving into sensation. Rutting against them both for only a moment, Connor's orgasm swept through him like a hurricane, making him spill his seed into the condom sheathing him. Hearing Levi's moans joined with Katy's higher pitched cries had another pulse erupting from Connor. His choked cry added to the guttural groan Levi let loose, and he watched as Levi fisted his cock and pumped, painting them with his come as he hurtled off the edge, riding out his release with heaving breaths.

Another dull thud and Connor's sleep-hazed mind turned back to what had woken him. Katy.

"I just tripped. This room is too small for all our stuff. If I can find my sneakers, I'm goin' for a run with a few of the girls, and then I have to duck into work for a while. I'll be back in a few hours. You two stay right where you are so I can join you when I get back."

"Mmmhmm," he mumbled, leaning into Katy's kiss as she hovered over him, before snuggling back into the soft pillow again. With one eye open, Connor watched as she walked around the bed and kissed Levi's temple.

Running her fingertips down his cheek, she whispered, "He's still wiped out too."

"Mmm," Connor half responded, unable to resist the pull of sleep.

A light breath fanned his face, and soft lips brushed against his own. Warm, wet glides of his open mouth against Katy's, their tongues touched, stroked. But this kiss was different somehow. Then it hit him. *Oh fuck.* The scratch of stubble teased his cheek, and Connor moaned softly, pulling Levi closer. As every hard inch of the other man's body pressed against his own, Connor deepened the kiss, going from zero to sixty in a heartbeat. Fire burned through him, and Connor gasped, Levi nipping his lip. Running his hands over Levi's chest, he mapped every ripple of muscle under his palms. He flicked his fingertips over Levi's erect nipples, causing the other man to buck his hips and moan. Knowing he could do that to him—damn, what a turn on. Warm skin, he knew from endless months of staring, bore a natural golden tan, and taut muscle had Connor diving in for more. He'd dreamed of this—of being able to touch Levi too, to kiss him and love him. Of there being no barriers between them.

Connor ran his hand down Levi's back, and over a sensitive spot. Levi shivered and Connor hummed, insanely pleased with himself. Sliding lower to the other man's ass, Connor grabbed a handful of the perfect globe and pulled him closer, rocking against him. Like Levi, he was steely hard. Levi's name on his tongue was more a moan, animalistic in its sound as it was ripped from Connor's chest when he ground against his best friend.

But Lee's reaction—his hard shove—had Connor nearly falling off the bed. He was stunned. Utterly floored. One minute he was in his arms making out, and the next he was frantically grasping the sheet trying to stop himself landing on his arse on the floor. Levi staggered backwards off the mattress and, fell over his own feet, hitting the wall. He plastered himself against it like a spooked animal about to rear.

"Connor, what the hell? I'm asleep and you're kissin' me?" he yelled, wiping his mouth with the back of his hand. That one action—the one where Levi wiped away the only evidence that Connor had been connected with him—shattered him. A moment before, the heat that'd bloomed in Connor was bright, but now it was devastating, like a wildfire that left everything in its wake charred beyond recognition. Dead. Rejection seared him, a cruel twist of fate that killed off any hope of continuing not only his friendship with Levi, but what he had with Katy too.

It was over.

Done.

"I'm sorry," he mumbled, blinking back tears. Shifting off the bed, Connor backed out towards the door. Searching for his clothes, which—*fuck my life*—were at the opposite end of the room, Connor motioned to them. "Go back to bed. I'll get my stuff and leave, give you some space."

"Wait." Levi held his hand up. "Gimme a minute." Connor shook his head and turned, about to walk out the room. Absolutely gutted, and angry at being so fucking stupid as to fall for his best mate, he swiped at the tear drop that fell to his cheek.

"You moaned my name like you want me. Do you?" His tone was harsh, and as much as Connor wished it wasn't accusatory, it was. Humiliated, Connor wanted to crawl into a hole and hope the world forgot him. Instead, he leaned his shoulder against the door jamb, still facing away from Levi. "Forget it. I should have pulled away as soon as I realized it was you. I'm sorry."

Footsteps on the hardwood flooring told Connor that his friend was pacing. With every pass, the cool breeze Levi left in his wake, tormented Connor's naked body. Levi was close enough to touch, but as much as he yearned to comfort him, Connor knew from the pacing that he was riled up. And there was no way Levi would let him anyway. Connor knew in his gut he'd never touch his best friend again. They were forever past that point.

"I don't think I can do it." Levi's words echoed through the room like the crack of a gunshot, piercing the remaining shreds of Connor's heart. His legs nearly buckled underneath him. He knew it was coming, but it didn't make it easier to hear. That was it, the end of everything he'd held dear. He was about to be tossed away again, like every other time someone was supposed to love him. First, his mum—not that she'd wanted to leave, but the cancer hadn't exactly given her a choice—then his dad, who hadn't even had the courage to fight for him, drowning himself in a bottle, and then drugs to numb the pain, all the while letting Connor mourn alone for not one, but two, parents. Levi's parents had taken him in, but only because they were too good to let him go into a system that would have spat him out a few years later. And then, when he'd finally found a home with his brothers- and sisters-in-arms in a hellhole, Rob had upped and died. The only two people left in the world who gave a shit about him were Katy and Levi. And his stupidity had just destroyed that. *I'm a fucking idiot.*

The crushing pain in his chest had Connor struggling to breathe. *Oh God*, he'd just lost everything. A choked sob left him, but he bit it back just as quick. Nodding his response to Levi's comment, Connor cleared his throat in a futile attempt to hide the devastation in his tone. "I get it. Tell Katy I'm sorry. I'll talk to her later today. Explain, you know, so she understands that it was my fault."

Levi's hand on his arm had Connor trying to shrug away, but it was no use. Connor found himself spinning to face the other man. Exposed, vulnerable and raw, he silently begged Levi not to hurt him even more. "No, that's not what I meant."

Connor's silence at Levi's words wasn't because he didn't want to talk. He couldn't. If he had any hope of not breaking down into a sobbing mess, he had to keep his mouth shut.

"I feel it too. Whatever it is between us. I always have, and I dunno how much longer I can keep denying it." He sighed like the weight of the world was on his shoulders. "But I'm terrified." The raw honesty in Levi's gaze, in his words, stripped Connor bare. He reached out, but when Levi jumped back like he'd been stung, Connor let his hand drop. The sharp stab of pain that accompanied Levi's move had Connor lowering his gaze—Lee's admission didn't mean he'd ever act on it; moving out of his reach was to be expected. He had so much to lose with Connor just being in the same room as them; it wasn't like he was just going to flip the bird to his responsibilities. Not the Levi he knew. As much as it killed him, he wouldn't want Levi to change.

Levi sat down on the bed, his knees spread and elbows resting on them. A slightly different pose and he could have been *The Thinker*. He was certainly perfect enough to be immortalized in a sculpture.

"I'm scared I'll lose Katy." He looked up at Connor, fear and desperation written on his features. "I can't live without her. She's the most important thing in my life. But I can't... you...." He scrubbed his hands over his face, keeping them there while he mumbled, "I want the same thing with you that I have with her, but what if she's disgusted with me, with us?"

Hope, fierce and bright, like a ray of sunshine breaking through summer storm clouds bloomed in Connor. "She won't be."

"How can you be so sure of that, Con?"

"You said she loved me, and I know she loves you." He shrugged his shoulder. "She gets it. She gets whatever this is between the three of us."

"I feel like I'm cheating on her."

Yeah, he'd thought the same the first time it was just the two of them, even after they'd agreed to have one-on-one time with each other. Katy had insisted on it, saying there were three two-way relationships which needed to blossom and stand on their own, as well as the one that involved all of them.

Connor moved over to his bag and pulled out a pair of clean briefs, sliding them up his legs. This wasn't a conversation to have naked. Emotions were raw enough—they didn't need to be starkers too. "Has it worried you in the past when Katy and I were together, just the two of us?"

"No, but—"

"It didn't bother me when it was just you two, either," Connor interrupted. "So what's the difference?"

"I knew that you were together? I knew that you were goin' out on a date with her? I knew what your relationship involved?

I *knew* about the two of you. She doesn't have any idea of what I wanna do to you, Con." With every statement framed as a question, Levi's voice rose. He'd started pacing again too. Even preoccupied, his reaction times were still lightning quick, catching the clean pair of boxer shorts Connor had plucked from his dresser drawer and tossed to him to distract Levi from the tirade.

"So talk to her. She'll be back soon, you can explain it. We can do it together if you want."

"And if she says no?"

"I'm positive she won't. I get that you're scared. I'm freakin' out too, but I know what I want." Connor paused. He had to do it, but the admission wasn't easy. "And it's not just Katy."

"Katy should be enough. She *is* enough. She always will be." Levi's voice rose, ringing through the quiet house.

Connor blocked his path, standing in Levi's personal space. He needed to make it clear, to put it out there. Levi had to understand. His words came out low, but strong, confident. "But I'm a greedy bastard, and I want both of you."

"How is this even gonna work?" Levi tossed his arms up in the air and sidestepped him. "I need to know. I can't give up everything that's important to me for—"

"For what? Me?" Connor interrupted, his own voice raised too. "I'm sorry I don't stack up to your expectations." He'd put himself out there, gone so far out of his comfort zone that he was walking the plank. He'd been hoping for amnesty—a lifeline to pull him back—but Levi's words were the final kick sending him plunging into shark infested waters, to a world full of hurt. Ashamed that his voice cracked, that he couldn't keep the emotions tightly bottled up inside himself anymore, Connor murmured, "I thought if I was good enough for Katy, I might be good enough for you. I can see that I was wrong." Swiping his cheeks with the back of his hand he added, "I'll save you making the decision, Lee."

Connor bent down to grab his bag. Any other clothes he had there would be staying. He wasn't going to stick around to pack properly. He'd barely hefted the bag onto his shoulder when a force out of nowhere barrelled into him. Like a back-rower in a footy match, Levi crash-tackled him, sending him tumbling into the wall and pinning him there.

"Listen, and just for once, don't run," Levi growled, pressing his palm against Connor's back, pushing his chest against the wall. His bag was yanked off his shoulder and tossed to the floor before the heat of Levi's body blanketed him. When Levi ran his tongue along Connor's throat up to his earlobe and nipped it, Connor shuddered, an achingly hard erection tenting his briefs. "I can't risk everything that's important to me for an experiment. I want you for more than that. I need you to be sure."

The heat of his body was gone. It had Connor turning, searching for him. Levi hadn't gone far. Chest heaving, eyes wild, he looked like a predator, like he would consume Connor if given half the chance. Gazes colliding, they stared at each other for long moments, until Connor's feet moved of their own accord, launching himself into Levi's arms. The second they touched skin on skin, Connor wished he hadn't gotten partially dressed.

Levi twisted him, tossing him onto the bed like he weighed nothing and crawled up over him. It was the sexiest fucking thing Connor had ever witnessed. Rippling, bulging muscle hovered above him, his best friend's face mere inches from his own. But he was more than that too—Connor had lusted over this man, had yearned with his very being to touch him, to love him. And now he could.

He reached out and trailed his fingertips over Levi's pecs, down over his washboard abs. Flicking his gaze lower, Connor watched Levi's semi harden, but resisted reaching for it. Instead, he slid his hands back up to clutch Levi's shoulder and reach around to the back of his neck, pulling him close. Levi didn't resist, lowering himself until their bodies were aligned, every inch touching. All he had to do was reach up and press their lips together, but Levi had him pinned, his gaze searing into Connor. He stared at the man before him, taking in details —the fine laugh lines around his eyes, the freckles along his nose—that he'd never seen so close before. But when Levi's tongue snuck out between those plump lips, licking the bottom one, Connor lost all self-control. Closing the last of the distance between them, Connor kissed him like a man possessed. There were no gentle glides of lips and tongues against each other. It was desperate, primal. Instinctively, Connor spread his legs, nestling Levi between them and moaned when their cocks aligned. Unable to stop himself, Connor touched every inch of Levi he could reach—the broad planes of his back, down his spine to his ass to mould the perfect globes and back up his sides, to his pecs. Pinching the flat discs of Levi's nipples had the other man gasping and thrusting his hips forward in a dance as old as time itself. Connor couldn't help his chuckle when Levi's pained moan sounded.

His laugh was cut short when Levi dragged his strong hand down Connor's body and lifted his leg, wrapping it around his hips. Connor hooked his other leg up too and cried out as Levi punched his hips forward, grinding hard against him. Tongues duelling and teeth clashing, hands clutching and grasping at each other, had Connor riding a wave of endorphins. He was high on this man, addicted in a way he'd never been before. And the sensation was so freeing—finally experiencing who he'd known he was deep down all along. This wasn't some experiment or question about his sexuality. This was Connor. He was bisexual, had been his whole life. He'd just never admitted it. Had never needed or wanted to, because the only man he'd ever dreamed of having was apparently straight. He'd never been happier to have been so utterly wrong.

Giddy, Connor laughed, holding Levi tighter as the other man licked and nipped at his throat. "I'm not doin' it right if you're laughing," Levi grumbled, biting him harder.

"You're doin' everything right, Lee," he whispered before capturing the other man's mouth again. "Let me touch you," Connor begged. With Levi's nod, Connor snaked his hand between their bodies, yanking down his underwear before wrapping his callused hand around Levi's length and stroking. A strangled moan sounded from the other man, which turned into a full-body shudder when Connor aligned their cocks again. The precum leaking from each of them lubricated their way a little, but not enough.

"Fuuuck," Levi cursed before pulling away. "Get those damn jocks off, Con. We need lube." Connor didn't need to be told twice. Lifting his hips, he shimmied out of his underwear and kicked them off while Levi reached over to the side table and rummaged around in the drawer until he found what he was looking for. It was only a second before Levi was settling himself between Connor's spread legs again, squirting the gel-like substance on Connor's outstretched hand.

Reaching up, Connor pulled Levi back down to him. Resting on an outstretched arm, Levi's muscles bulged before him, but there wasn't even a minor shake in his locked position. With his slick hand, Connor stroked Levi's cock against his own. Connor hummed at the sensation—hard against satiny smooth, heat and the cool of the lube. It turned into a drawn-out moan when Levi's hand joined his own, jacking them together.

He couldn't believe what was happening—that he had Levi in his arms, loving him. His touch, his smell, his weight pressing Connor into the bed, surrounded him. He was on sensation overload. They were better together than he ever thought possible, better than he ever dreamed. *Fuck, I hope I'm not wrong about Katy. What if I am and the shit hits the fan? I could never be enough for him.* The more he thought, the more he worried. Connor's cock softened a little, but Levi doubled his efforts, growling at him, "Stop thinking. Just be with me. Lemme fuck you into the mattress. Blow with me, take what we both need." Connor griped their cocks tighter as a surge of heat washed over him at Levi's words. *He wants me. He wants this. He wants to fuck me.*

The words tumbled from his mouth as every dirty dream he'd ever had about Levi flashed before Connor's closed eyes. "I want your cock buried in my arse. I wanna feel you balls deep in me, fucking me until I shout your name. I wanna feel Katy's mouth on both our sacks, around mine sucking me off while you fuck me. I want you to ride me. To own me."

"Oh fuck, yeah." Levi shuddered, thrusting hard against Connor once more, before his dick pulsed and he shouted Connor's name. Thick ropes of cum jetted onto Connor's abs and chest, the slick heat lubing the way and tossing him over the edge. Connor choked out a cry as his orgasm swept through him. An explosion of sensation barrelling through him like a herd of buffalo, he shot stream after stream of cum onto his belly, mixing and mingling with Levi's load. Watching him with awe in his eyes, Levi's arm gave out and he crashed onto Connor's chest and rolled them to the side. He loved the contrast between Levi and Katy—her soft, tiny body compared with Levi's hard muscles and much heavier weight. He loved it, loved the connection he shared with them too.

"I wanna wash you, Con. Take care of you."

"I wanna blow you," Connor blurted out, making Levi's cock twitch between their bodies.

"Huh," he remarked, smirking. "I didn't think I'd get it up again for a week. I might have been wrong."

"You'd better be. Katy wanted us in bed waiting for her when she got back. She probably should have been here already."

Suddenly serious, Levi asked, "What are we gonna tell her, Con?"

"The truth, dumbass." Connor smiled, trying to lighten the mood, but deep down he shared the same fear Levi did.

"Shut up." Levi nudged him with his shoulder, giving him a shy smile. "I wasn't suggesting we lie to her. I meant, *how* do we tell her?"

"Gently, so she understands that she's the centre of our universe. Us doing this—" Connor motioned between the two of them, "doesn't change anything with her." when Levi leaned in and kissed his forehead, Connor nuzzled into him, breathing in the orange and cedar scent that was uniquely Levi, mixed with a healthy dose of sex.

"Come on, let's get cleaned up and check what's taking her so long.

Swinging his legs off the bed, Connor stood and walked toward the light spilling in from the open front door. Katy normally locked up when she left—the predawn cool chilled the air too much otherwise. He walked over to it, checking the latch. It wasn't even closed, never mind locked. Nausea passed over him. *Fuck.* "Lee, you need to get out here."

"What's up?" the other man asked as he wrapped an arm around Connor from behind dropping a kiss on his shoulder, before stepping to the side.

He pointed to the door sitting ajar. "I think Katy might have already come home."

Katy

Katy closed the door to her car gently and rested her head back against the seat. Hands trembling in her lap, she blew out a breath and tried to quell the ache in her heart. She was happy for them, but it didn't make her reality hurt any less, didn't ease the pain. She curled in on herself and cried, knowing she wasn't needed anymore. The realisation had hit her full force when she'd seen them moving together on the bed, hot tears falling before she'd even made it through the front door. Like a category five hurricane had swept through her, everything good in her life, everything that made her happy had been obliterated with the sight of them making love.

She was alone.

She'd lost them. Both of the men she adored with every fibre of her being were gone. Deep down, she'd known it would happen all along. It was inevitable that the attraction between them would spark eventually. She'd secretly hoped it would— how couldn't she? She'd loved Levi for her whole adult life, and if she were honest, Con too. Now that they'd finally given into the yearning, she wasn't needed as the buffer. And like she'd always known, they were beautiful together—masculine grace personified. She'd never forget the image of their intertwined bodies, moving as one.

So now, she had to do one more thing for them. She had to leave—pick up the debris after the storm and hold her head up high. They were happy, that's all that mattered. Her battered heart would survive. Maybe in a million years she'd be able to love again. It was their time now. She'd had Levi for long enough that the memories could carry her through. Wiping her cheeks with the heel of her hand, Katy started the car and looked at the house one more time. Tears welled up again as the memory of Levi carrying her over the threshold when they'd first moved in flashed before her eyes.

It was done, over.

"Katy, suck it up and get the fuck outta here," she chastised herself. *But where do I go?* She needed time to think, time to heal. The airport was tempting as fuck, but she had too many responsibilities to just pack up and leave. People were relying on her to make the happiest day of their lives complete, no matter what havoc was being reeked in hers.

She didn't have a destination in mind when she reversed out of the drive, but ten minutes later she was at the beach. Problem was, it was the same beach that she and Levi had taken Con to when he'd come home, and so many times since. She couldn't do it, couldn't force herself out of the car to head down onto the sand, so she pulled away.

Driving again, she found herself at her cousin's house. Katy didn't know why she'd gone there. Or maybe she did. Con had done the same thing when he'd needed space. Maybe it'd give her peace too. Not giving herself time to change her mind, she strode to the front door and pressed the bell. Chimes sounded in the background, and after a moment, the door swung open. The smile slipped from Emma's face as she took in the hot mess Katy knew she was. Sweaty and dressed in ratty running gear, she'd headed to work to issue a few invoices and check that payments for two cakes she was working on had come in. Then she'd driven home and walked in on Levi and Con making love. Now her eyes were red-rimmed and swollen too.

Silently, Emma opened the door more and ushered her in, waiting until it had swung closed again before she took Katy into her arms. "You okay, honey?" The embrace was all wrong. Emma was too skinny, too soft, her smell too floral. Katy wanted her men. She needed them. She loved them more than life itself.

How the hell was she going to walk away? Her body shook as she cried into the other woman's arms. "God, the three of you have had such a rough trot."

Katy curled into her and cried harder. "It's over," she whispered, her breath hitching on the last word as she choked out a sob. Saying that, putting a level of finality on it, shattered her. Sapped all her happiness, leaving her a mere shell.

"Oh, Katy." Emma hugged her tight, and ran her other hand down Katy's hair, like Con always did, making her cry harder. "You can't work it out?"

Katy shook her head. "No."

When Emma went to lead her deeper into the giant house, Katy wrapped her arms around herself. "Come on in, honey. I'll make us some tea and we can talk if you like."

She wiped the tears from her face and took a fortifying breath. "I don't wanna impose." Pointing to the beach outside, she added, "Can I just go out back for a while? I need some time. I've got no idea what I'm gonna do from here."

"Of course. Take as much time as you need." Emma placed a hand on her stomach and waved her hand around, adding, "And make yourself at home. I'll be in the bathroom if you need anything."

Katy looked her friend over for the first time. She looked drawn, tired. Ill. "You okay?"

"Yeah, just got a tummy bug. I'll be okay when I kick it." Emma motioned with her thumb over her shoulder and headed toward what Katy knew to be the downstairs bathroom.

Katy let her gaze roam around the house. Everything was white—walls, floors, kitchen, furniture—but there were splashes of bright colours everywhere too—the rugs, throw cushions, the paintings Nick's best friend and their neighbour, Cam, had painted. Everything was beach themed, worshipping the waves that were framed by the double height floor-to-ceiling wall of glass serving as the back door. The stacked sliding doors were open, a warm breeze floating in. She could smell the salt in the air, hear the waves rolling in. Pandanus palms framed the view at the end of the garden. The ocean beckoned to her.

Katy slid open the screen door and crossed the small lawn, heading out of the white picket gate to the beach. Here the sound of the pumping surf as it crashed against the sand bar was much louder, it's steady pattern soothing. Katy unlaced her running shoes and tossed them back over the fence when she'd taken them off. The surface of the sand was warm on her bare feet, but cool less than an inch down. She walked directly out to the water, not stopping until she was knee deep in the waves. Crystal clear and cold, the water swirled around her legs, the push and pull from even that depth quite strong. The foamy whitewash from the surf rolling in tickled her. But Katy stayed, letting the wind and waves do their magic. Out on the beach, Katy could switch off and just be. She was at home there. The sun, the surf, the awesome power of nature, of the universe, gave Katy a connection. It grounded her. The ocean healed her, albeit temporarily.

The tide was coming in, the water reaching midthigh before Katy waded out of the water and sat down on the soft sand, letting the sun dry her legs. This stretch of the beach was deserted except for the seagulls swooping on the breeze. A cerulean sky stretched above her, marred only by the gathering clouds on the horizon. A late season storm was brewing. It was a pretty apt representation of her life—everything seemed beautiful and clear, but in the distance was wild weather that could destroy everything. Her storm was a fast moving one. It had swept in well before she was ready, obliterating her world. Her tears had stopped, but the bone-deep ache of loss had enveloped her.

Katy loved both of them. Knowing they were happy would

ease her pain eventually. She wasn't selfish—even though having two men smacked of it. No, she'd realized that she was meant to love both of them. The fact that they'd found each other was great, wonderful in fact, but she was totally redundant now. Why would they need her when they had each other? Katy sat for hours, the sun shifting higher in the sky as she tried to figure out what to do. But everything came back to them. God, her brother was going to have a field day. He was the king of "I told you so," and he'd take every opportunity to remind her of her own failings and how much he disliked Levi. But at least she had family to go to—Nick and Emma, her parents, even Levi's. They were great. Con thought he had no one. It would have broken her heart if it were him that was alone.

9

KATY

"HI," LEVI SAID GENTLY, STARTLING KATY OUT OF HER THOUGHTS. When she looked up at them, he and Con were flanking her, facing the beach and watching the waves roll in.

"Hey," she mumbled. Seeing them had her wanting to reach out, to draw them to her, to beg them to keep her.

"It's beautiful here, so peaceful. Feels like there's no one around for miles," Con murmured as he sat cross-legged on the sand. Levi followed suit, sitting on Katy's other side.

"It is." Katy blinked away the tears, choking on the lump in her throat. Seeing them was eviscerating her. Like stories of the Japanese samurai committing *harakiri,* Katy's insides were being gauged open, yawning holes appearing.

"Katy, we're sorry," Levi started. She turned to look at him. Eyes red and his hair standing on end, it looked like he'd been crying and running his fingers through the blond strands. His mouth, which so often curved up in a smile, was a frown, his lip red as if he'd been worrying it with his teeth. His devastation was easy to read. "We didn't want to hurt you. This morning just happened."

"I get it," Katy replied. "I'm glad you found each other. And I know what you're gonna say now. Like I said, I get it. It just hurts though, you know?"

"Whatcha talkin' about?" Con asked, a mixture of confusion and defiance in his tone. "The only thing we were gonna say is that we're sorry for letting you believe, even for a second, that you aren't as important to us."

"What do you need me for now that you've found each other?" Katy whispered into the breeze. She was never the type to hold back, but voicing her deepest darkest fears was more difficult than she'd ever imagined, especially when it was playing out before her eyes. "You two have known each other for most of your lives. I bet if you think about it, you'll both realize that you didn't wake up this morning in love, or lust, or whatever. Those feelings have been around for a long time—I've seen them grow. Now that you're finally together, you don't need me as a buffer anymore."

"Is that what you think, sugar?" Levi ran his fingers through his hair and tugged on the ends, frustration radiating from him. "Damn it," he swore under his breath. "Why is it that the two people who mean everything to me, have no idea of it? Am I that bad in showing my feelings?" He reached out and took her hand, squeezing it tightly. Moving to his knees in front of her, he opened his mouth as if to say something else when Con interrupted.

"Cupcake, you're not a buffer between us, you never have been." Moving to mirror Levi's position on his knees, he took her other hand in his and added, "I've loved you since I first met you. I ran because it hurt so much seeing you happy with Levi, knowing that I'd never get that chance with you. I didn't realize it at the time, but you're right. When I look back at how I was feeling, I know that it hurt so much because you'd found the one other person in this world that I love." Looking at Levi, he joined their hands. "I'm sorry if this is too soon for you to hear or if you don't feel the same, but I love you, Lee. As much as I love Katy."

"Sugar, I don't tell you this enough, but I love you. So much." Levi brought her hand to his lips and kissed it, a soft, lingering press of his lips against her fingers. When he looked up and their eyes locked, the honesty, the love in his gaze stole her breath. "You're my soul mate. I can't live without you. What you said before—about feeling something more for Connor all this time—it was spot on. I think I've loved him for years." Pausing, he looked at Con. Katy could see how strong the chemistry was between them, but this time she wasn't the outsider. The warmth of their hands on hers, the strength of their grip gave Katy the reassurance she'd needed. They were kneeling so close that she could lean forward a few inches and kiss both of them. There was no hiding anymore. What she saw on their faces, and what Levi reflected back at her when he directed his gaze back to hers was raw, powerful. "But nothing will change what I feel for you."

"You're our cream filling," Con chipped in, a grin lifting one side of his mouth.

"What?" Katy and Levi both asked at the same time. It was a totally random comment, and it was exactly the thing she needed Con to say to make her smile. "Think of us like an Oreo. Lee and I are the chocolate biscuits. You're the cream filling. With it, we're fuckin' delectable." Katy smirked and shook her head at Con's reference to her cake shop, and Levi groaned. "But, without that cream centre, we're just boring, dry biscuits."

Levi leaned forward, pressing a soft kiss to her forehead, just a gentle brush of his lips. "You make me a better man, Katy. You're... you." Moving his mouth to her temple, he kissed her again. "How can I not love you? You're generous and sweet—a firecracker, so sexy." He pulled back and looked into her eyes. "Con told me that you got us, that you could see how we were meant to fit together. I couldn't have even kissed him without knowing I could rely on your strength when I freaked out. I mean, heck, I kissed a bloke."

"You loved it." Con nudged Levi's arm with his elbow and smirked.

"I did." Levi smiled at him, and Katy knew then, without a doubt, that they were in it together—all three of them on the same page. Levi loved Con, but he loved her too. And so did Con —he showed her in every one of the things he did for them, in the way he looked at them. Katy recognized the warmth in his eyes, the love. Her heart beat hard. It was real. It was crazy and insane and exciting, and it filled her heart to bursting.

Whatever Con saw in her expression had him growling in appreciation, a low hum that shocked through her. He and Levi both tugged on her hands, bringing her to her knees too. Con swooped in and trailed kisses along her cheek and down her throat while Levi brushed his lips gently against hers. They hovered there for a moment, soft presses of their lips until Levi licked along the seam of her mouth and she opened to him. Pouring all her heartbreak, all her love for him into her kiss, it went from sweet and innocent to down and dirty in a second.

Con moaned and jostled Levi. When he pulled away from Katy, Con was there, gazing at her with love so raw and so powerful it stole her breath. Their kiss screamed of desperate love, hungry and powerful.

"I love you, too," Katy murmured between kisses. "Both of you. So much." They stayed there, trading kisses and hugging on their knees in the soft sand. When she realized that Levi and Con hadn't kissed, she pulled back, breathing hard. Snuggling into Levi's side, she asked, "You think we can make this work?"

"Are you okay if Levi and I are together too? With you, or just the two of us?"

"I'd really like to watch," she blurted out. This time, instead of the sheer devastation that had coursed through her, heat flooded her pussy. They were gorgeous together. And the thought of watching her two guys loving on each other too got her revved up like nothing else.

"Oh, fuck yeah," Con moaned before kissing her again. Their lips had barely parted when Levi crowded her, his lips crashing down on hers.

"Kiss him," Katy begged, pulling away from Levi. When Levi turned to Con, they stared at each other for a moment before leaning in close and brushing their lips together softly, then pulling away again. It was fast but the love between them sparked like a wildfire in Katy.

"Should we take this party home?" Levi breathed, each word punctuated by a bite or lick to the column of her throat.

They rushed towards the white picket fence and through the gate, stumbling to the screen door. Katy noticed Nick kneeling before Emma's prone form and she shushed her guys' laughter with a wave of her hand. Looking up as they walked in, he smiled and dabbed a wet cloth over Emma's forehead before getting up and padding over to them.

Speaking in a hushed tone, he explained, "Emma's resting. She said you were out back. Is everything okay?"

"Yeah, mate. I think we're good." Con smiled at him, and Katy's insides lit up. She slid her hand in his and hugged Levi tighter.

Looking between the three of them, Nick smiled. "Good. I'm happy for you guys. Em saw it the night that you flew in, Con. I'm just glad that you figured it out before you lost each other."

"Nick," Katy asked, "Is Em all right? She didn't look well

when I got here, and Con said she'd been sick when he was staying here. Has she seen a doctor?"

"She has, but there's nothing they can do. It's morning sickness, but she's sick all the damn time, not just in the mornings. She's exhausted too, but apparently that's perfectly normal."

After congratulating Nick, they headed out, Katy still holding hands with Con and hugging Levi. The trip home passed in a blur, Levi touching and teasing her and Con's heated stares in the mirror turning her on until she was primed to come. They made Katy bolder than she'd ever been before and that confidence was freeing, their love empowering.

Falling through their own front door, they barely made it into their bedroom—the first room in the house. Clothes were tossed left and right as they stripped and caressed, kissing each other like they'd been starved of one another's touch for years rather than hours.

Katy found herself being deposited in the middle of their bed, with Con and Levi positioning themselves on either side of her. Not a single inch of her went untouched by lips and tongues, rough fingertips and gentle breaths. They weren't fucking, they never had been. No, she was being worshipped, obliterating every doubt Katy had ever had that she wasn't needed.

Two broad shoulders made her spread her legs wide as they traded kisses and tongued her clit. With deft fingers lodged deep inside her pussy, Connor sucked hard and she saw stars, her breath catching as she rode the edge of an orgasm. Fighting her way there, she let out a frustrated cry when she teetered on the edge. Connor doubled his efforts while Levi pulled back and licked his palm, then wrapped his big hand around Connor's erection. Breath rushing out of her lungs on a moan, Levi slid a finger into her tight heat with Connor's and stroked her. Katy's body locked and her pussy contracted tightly around their thick fingers, her orgasm crashing through her and lifting her hips clear off the bed. Panting, she laid there, letting the endorphins carry her on a tide of ecstasy, watching while Levi pulled Connor into a scorching hot kiss.

Nuzzling their noses together, they couldn't hide their bone-deep connection even if they tried. How they'd managed it for the months Connor had been home was beyond her.

"Con, lie down on your back. I wanna taste you."

Levi

He'd blurted out the words on instinct. *"I wanna taste you."* What the hell was he thinking? Talk about jumping into the fire. Connor's guttural moan made it obvious what he thought of Levi sucking his dick, but actually doing it? The concept was a little overwhelming. He'd never touched another man's cock until that morning, and while he wanted it—with an almost animalistic need—he was kind of clueless on how to do it. Levi knew what he himself liked. Would Connor enjoy the same? Where did he even start? Connor knew he wasn't exactly experienced in the dick sucking department, but he didn't want to screw it up either.

Thank God for Katy. As soon as the words were out of his mouth, his girl was scrambling onto her hands and knees and reaching for Connor. Looking at Levi while she tongued the other man's length, Levi knew she was teaching him, making it as good as she could. Hesitation gone, Levi kissed his way down Connor's body, stopping at the words tattooed down Connor's side. *Live passionately, fight bravely, forgive readily, love completely, die honourably.* He nuzzled him, breathing in his spicy scent. Straddling Connor's leg, he tentatively reached out, swiping his thumb across the slit of Connor's broad head and, before he could psych himself out, licking the clear liquid off. Salty and not that dissimilar to the taste of his own spunk when he'd kissed Katy after she'd blown him, Levi hummed. Connor's reaction would have been enough, even if he hated the taste—pupils blown wide in his heavy-lidded stare, mouth open and chest heaving, Connor was a sight for sore eyes. A desert oasis.

Damn sexy.

Levi could get used to this, could even love it if he'd elicit the same reaction from Connor again and again.

Taking a breath, he leaned down and tentatively licked around Connor's piercing. The choked grunt from above had him smiling. His man—he liked the sound of that: *his man*—had been reduced to non-comprehensible garble from Levi's touch. It was empowering, giving Levi the courage to close his lips around Connor's shaft and suck gently. His hand wandering, Levi cupped Connor's balls and massaged them, touching for the first time a barbell at the base of his nuts. He moaned, taking Connor's cock a little deeper into his mouth all the while imagining how much extra sensation it would have added. Connor shuddered and fisted the sheets in a white-knuckled grip, making Levi's dick jerk against his stomach.

When he looked at Katy, she was slathering her fingers in lube, just as Connor tried to spread his legs wider. Levi pulled off, moving between his outstretched legs. He had an insane urge to take in every inch of the man before him. So strong, so resilient. Levi loved him, and Connor needed to know just how much. Running his hand over Connor's shaft reverently, he watched as Katy circled her fingertips around Connor's hole, massaging it until he could see it soften and she pressed the tip of her finger in.

"Oh fuck. Fuuuck," Connor groaned as she sunk in to her second knuckle.

Levi needed to be the one doing it, the one preparing *his man*, even if it was just this once. "Katy," he begged, not knowing how to explain it to her.

She smiled, wordlessly pulling out. Levi reached over and pulled the plug out of the drawer, Katy slicking it with lube. He bent over once again, positioning Connor's cock at his mouth and trailing the plug over Connor's balls to his arse. Together, he sucked and plunged the tip of it inside, making Connor go rigid. He froze, not knowing whether Con was on edge or in pain. Katy did too, about to flick her tongue against his pebbled nipple. After a moment, the relentless squeeze of Connor's clench relaxed, and the plug slid in further. He sucked him deep and plunged the plug in, fucking him with it. Connor's whimpers escalated to loud moans when Levi brushed the plug over what must have been his prostate. He'd heard from his gay friends—and those straight friends who didn't mind a little anal play of their own—that blokes had this magic button inside of them, and the way Connor's body lit up the first time he skimmed over it, he had no doubt that it existed. But he wanted to feel it. He wanted—no needed—to be the one giving everything to Connor, not some piece of latex. Levi yanked it out and tossed it aside, trailing his fingertips down the same path he'd taken with the plug. Katy drizzled lube down Connor's balls, Levi wetting his digits on it before circling his hole. Pressing two fingers into him for the first time was revelatory. The tight heat, the stretch, the silkiness of his channel had Levi shivering. The moan that escaped Connor was illicit and so damn hot. Watching his fingers stretch him, penetrate him had Levi's dick pulsing. The desire to possess Connor was visceral, to have that unique piece of him no one else had ever claimed. But, *God*, he wanted to give that same piece of himself to Connor, to show the other man how much of Levi he already owned.

"Stop, stop," Connor demanded urgently, causing both Levi and Katy to pause. "I'm gonna blow. I wanna be in Katy when I do."

"On your back, sugar," Levi directed. Katy stretched out immediately and spread her legs, inviting Connor to join her. Kneeling behind Connor, Levi took him in. The lean muscle of his back tapered into a narrow waist and a tight round arse that he couldn't keep his hands off. Palming the globes, he pulled them apart, putting Connor's hole on display while he sank into Katy. Levi watched as the other man rocked into her gently and kissed her deeply. He wanted to do the same. He needed to—every instinct screamed at him to join their bodies together.

"Con, can I come inside you?" His voice was gravel, full of need and desire. He'd have been embarrassed if he didn't know Katy and Connor were just as worked up as he was.

"Do it," he moaned, the order clear even at Connor's most vulnerable.

Levi lined himself up and blew out a breath. Nerves assailed him. What if it wasn't good for Connor? What if he didn't like it? What if...? *No.* He needed to follow his heart, not his head, not all the doubt and limitations he placed on himself to keep within that invisible set of very straight, rigid lines. Letting go of every self-imposed reservation, he wrapped his hands around Connor's hips and marvelled at how soft his skin was, compared with the taut muscle underneath. Hot and smooth. Levi hummed.

Pressing forward gently, he put enough pressure behind the thrust that Connor's hole began to stretch around his girth. Drizzling a little more lube on his shaft, Levi rubbed it in and pushed in a bit more. Connor went rigid against him, tensing every muscle in his body. Desperate to relieve the pain, Levi massaged the small of his back, and when that didn't work, he bent forward, plastering their bodies together and wrapping his man tight in his arms. Levi kissed along Connor's shoulder inhaling his unique scent and loving the taste of his skin. Petting and caressing him, Levi begged him to relax. Katy did the same, reaching up to pull Connor's face to hers and kiss him again. Levi withdrew minutely and then pushed forward again just a little, the head of his cock popping through the tight resistance. He cried out as Connor's channel strangled his shaft with a silky vice-like grip. It sent him straight into orbit. But Con was experiencing something else. He reared back, gutting Levi—he was hurting him. Wild-eyed, he looked down at Katy and saw alarm in her eyes too. While Katy petted him, Levi swore, "Shit, Con," and moved to pull out. But Connor threw his arm back, gripping Levi's arse and he let loose a growl that was so damn dirty Levi had to grit his teeth together to stop from blowing right there and then.

"More," he gasped after a second, and using his grip on Levi's arse, Connor pulled him forward. The combination of the warmed lube, the tight fit and the knowledge that he no longer had to hide what he'd dreamed of doing with Connor, had Levi barrelling towards an epic orgasm. But there was no way he was letting go without Connor and Katy being right there with him. He stopped moving, breathing hard as he forced his body back from the edge.

"I've got you, Con. Lemme take care of you." Levi was panting, barely able to string a sentence together. This was nothing like the previous times the three of them had come together. This, right now, was something so much more. And he never wanted it to end.

It only took a moment for Connor to relax in his arms, handing the reins to Levi. Nuzzling him, Levi thrust slowly, edging forward an inch at a time. Deeper and deeper he sunk into Connor's body and with every movement, Levi lost his heart to them more. Katy was beautiful, lavishing attention on Connor to calm him and stoke the fire all at the same time and Connor was masculine strength and grace. The scars marring his shoulder only made him more stunning in Levi's book.

Fully buried within him, Levi moaned. *Damn*. He'd never experienced anything like this. Being with the two of them was everything. Not a single thing on earth could compete with this experience. After a few awkward thrusts, they found a rhythm, and when they did, it was exquisite. Delirious ecstasy. Every time Connor drew away from Katy, Levi did the same, then he thrust forward again, sinking into Connor's depths as he pushed him into Katy. Writhing in glorious sensation, Levi marvelled at the lights flashing before his eyes as his world lit up in high definition Technicolour.

Levi's thrusts became harder, more insistent as he neared the edge, but he could tell his partners were close too. Katy clawed jerkily at Connor's back, her blunt nails leaving no marks, while Connor shuddered below him. Their moans and grunts, sighs and whispered encouragements formed a symphony that was imprinted in Levi's memory forever. For life-changing moments, this one was pretty spectacular.

Katy tumbled first into oblivion, crying out and sending Connor over too, his moan a deep rumble. Every contraction of Connor's arse, every pulse of cum he pumped into Katy surrounded Levi. He experienced Connor's orgasm too— touching him in places no one else had as Connor flew. Levi thrust deep one last time and shouted out as he emptied his seed into Connor. Doing this without protection, having them joined completely for the first time was a dream come true. Levi was so damn grateful they'd been tested weeks earlier.

Riding the wave of bliss, Levi tumbled to the side and

pressed their bodies close, never wanting to be separated from them again. The sex was hot—inferno level—but the touches, the affection he could finally show to Connor as well as Katy, was by far the best part. With them together like that, nothing could intrude. Not even the real world.

———

Connor lay between him and Katy. Of the trio, Levi was the only one awake and it was late... well, early. Around three if he guessed correctly. Another couple of hours and the sun would peek over the horizon, but at that moment, it was dark and almost eerily quiet.

Connor's gig from earlier in the night tumbled around in his mind. Connor had been on stage singing, Katy sitting on Levi's lap at the table closest to him. His arms wrapped around Katy, holding her close, Levi breathed her in, but he couldn't take his eyes off Connor. The attraction between them, the desire, it was heady. Then Connor had started singing "Slow Hands" by Niall Horan, and Levi's dick had hardened. Katy was up, the warmth of her small body pressed against his gone, leaving him bereft, but only momentarily. As soon as he stood, she'd wound herself around him, swaying with him as he held her close, his gaze ping-ponging between the two of them for the entire song. Even though they were separate, the three of them were still connected—the memories of mapping Katy and Connor's bodies with his fingertips, his lips and tongue and loving on them still fresh in Levi's mind. The lyrics oozed sex, and listening to Connor's smooth voice as he sang, had Levi desperately wanting to bend them both over the damn stage. He held himself back... barely. Katy was a little more open with her appreciation, blowing Connor a kiss, a smile lighting up her face as Connor touched his fingertips to his lips.

Levi hadn't thought anything of it. Why would he? But the blokes on the table next to them had had a field day with it. He didn't care that they'd called him a pussy for letting his woman cheat on him, but it took everything in him to stop himself from beating the shit out of them for the insults they'd hurled at Katy. And it was obvious that Connor had heard them too. The whole damn bar had, the conversation becoming hushed as their taunts escalated. Connor shot them a death-glare, and Levi ground his teeth, itching to shut them up when Katy rested her hand on his. It was the first deep breath he could take, her touch unknotting his insides, calming him. Logically he knew they weren't worth it, but his inner caveman wanted to rearrange their faces for saying that crap about his girl.

And then it was over, and Levi was left reeling. A few of their friends—Nick and Emma, Mike, Sarah, Dylan and Ashton—had rocked up and pulled a few tables over, outnumbering the others two to one. Of course, the hovering bouncers might have helped too. A few pointed stares and well-placed comments, and it didn't take long for the other group to quieten down and skulk away to a different part of the bar. But the whole episode left Levi antsy. They'd recognized him and used it against him, antagonising the three of them until Levi was ready to snap.

The whole "being recognized" thing wasn't unheard of for him. It didn't happen that often, though he did get asked for an autograph every now and then. But it was surreal listening to them trash-talk him like he was a Cockroach supporter on Origin night. The roller coaster he'd been on those last few days and the revelation that came with finally giving into his desire for Connor, combined with such a stark reminder of his B-list—at best—celebrity status on Aussie TV, had jarred him. The night could have easily turned into an all-in brawl, and it was his lily-white arse on the line. Did he want to deal with that conflict, the stress every day? Could he handle keeping a secret as massive as theirs?

Levi rolled onto his back. *What the hell am I doing?* If anyone got wind that he was in a ménage relationship—one where the happy times went all three ways—he'd be out of a job before he could blink. But now that he'd had a taste of what it could be like, what happiness between the three of them meant, there was no way he'd give it up. *Could I? Would I?* Levi rolled to his side again and sighed as he watched Connor and Katy sleep peacefully in the dim moonlight filtering through the blinds. Unsettled and fidgety, he couldn't lie there anymore. Levi's mind was going a million miles an hour and he'd only wake them if he didn't move.

Slipping on a pair of sweats, he padded out to the kitchen and boiled the kettle. Dropping a teabag in his mug, Levi watched the steam curl into the air while the tea steeped. When it was strong enough, he sat at the table cradling the hot cup between his hands and staring out the window at the stars. Questions tumbled around in his head. *Who am I now? What does the future hold? Can I do this? Is it right to love them both? Am I holding them back from being happy together?* The darkness outside matched the whirlpool of emotions sucking him under inky black waters, and he spiralled downward. Were they doomed for heartbreak?

"Hey," Katy murmured in a sleepy tone when she stepped up to the table. Dressed only in one of his baggy T-shirts, she looked adorably sexy. With Katy in front of him, his light on a dark day, a picture began to form—the answer to all the questions he'd been muddling through taking shape. "You okay?"

"Yeah, just thinking." Levi took a sip of his now cold tea and grimaced.

"About what?"

"Those guys at the pub."

Katy slipped into the chair next to him and reached for his hand. "Wanna talk about it?"

He shrugged, unsure of where to even start explaining the mish-mash of thoughts in his head. "I've just jumped head first into this, and I got a helluva wake-up call tonight. People actually thought you were cheating on me. Can you imagine what they woulda thought if I'd gone and kissed him? I dunno, Katy...." He trailed off, not even knowing what he wanted to say. Those thoughts swirled around again. *Am I worried about what people think? What if they find out? What about my career? Will it always be a constant battle with people's attitudes?*

"I guess I'm not worth it," Connor interjected from the doorway. The sadness in his tone was unmistakeable. Head hung low, Connor turned and went to walk away. *No.* Every protective instinct in Levi flared. That tangled mess of emotions—the muddy waters—suddenly became crystalline. There was no way Levi could let Connor think he wasn't worth it. There was no way he'd let him go, not without a hell of a fight. He was on his feet, vaulting over the couch and sprinting over to his lover before he could think twice. Reacting on instinct, Levi grasped his arms from behind and held tight as Connor made a half-arsed effort to struggle. Levi stepped in front of him and cupped his face with both hands.

"Don't ever think that." Pulling Connor's face down to his own, Levi brushed a soft kiss against his lips. "I love you, Con, but this—us—is an adjustment for me. Gimme time to work through it in my head. We're solid, man. You, me, and Katy— we're good. It's the other dickheads that were the problem."

"You're risking too much," he murmured. "When you realize that, you'll walk. Maybe it's better we stop now."

"We aren't gonna walk. You've lost a lot in your life—your mum and dad, Rob. But me and Katy, we've never left you. We never will. Please don't ever doubt that you're worth it."

Connor looked into his eyes, studied him, and after long moments gave him a single nod. "Okay."

"Okay?" Levi asked, unsure about the apparent sudden turnaround.

"Yeah, okay." Connor nodded. "I've been alone for so long that I don't really know how to be in a relationship. I know I keep fucking up, I know I run and push people away, but I trust you. Both of you." Connor turned to look at Katy who was still sitting at the table, her arms wrapped tightly around her middle, worry etched across her features. When Connor held out his hand to her, Katy's smile lit up the room. "God, she's beautiful," Connor breathed. They pulled apart, bringing her into their embrace when she joined them and Connor rested his head against Levi's temple. "Ever since we were kids, I think I've always been waiting for the other shoe to drop, for you to wake up and say you don't want me around anymore. But you've proved to me so many times that you don't do that—it's always me who runs. I need to stop doing that, so I'll work on it, I promise. I'll talk to my therapist about it, figure it out."

All the stress, all the angst flowed out of Levi. Standing there in that hallway, wrapped around Connor and Katy, his life was perfect. He pulled them both closer, hugging them harder. With these two people in his arms—the two people who were his world—he was home. "Let's go back to bed. I've done enough thinking. Now I need to hold the two of you," Levi murmured, nuzzling Katy's hair and leaning into the taller man's shoulder.

With arms still wrapped around each other, they slowly made their way back into bed, laughing when their legs got tangled, and they stumbled. When they finally made it under the covers, Levi fell between them, being cocooned between his lovers. It was exactly what he needed—to be surrounded by them, to be protected and held close, but at the same time, sheltering Connor and Katy too. A perfect symbiosis.

He woke in the same position they'd fallen asleep in—Katy wrapped around his right side, and Connor on his left. With both of them lying on his arms and their legs thrown over his, he was pinned down, surrounded by them. He didn't want it any other way, especially not when Connor's hand migrated south and closed over his morning wood, making him suck in a breath. It turned into a hiss when Katy bit his nipple and cupped his balls.

10

CONNOR

HE'D PLAYED AT THE SAME PUB TWICE SINCE THE GROUP OF dickheads had nearly got their faces rearranged. He knew Levi still had doubts—it wasn't surprising when he had so much on the line. But there was nothing more Connor could do than keep their relationship on the down low. He hated it, hated being the invisible one, the one who always had to step away, who had to resist kissing either of them, but there was no doubt he'd do it. When they were alone, there were no boundaries, no walls between them. In public, they didn't have that luxury.

The day before had wiped Connor out. He'd finally finished prepping Lee's bike and laid it all out on trolleys ready for the big reveal, then helped one of the mechanics finish the job they'd stopped to guide him. After that, he'd backed up a full day at the garage with a gig afterwards. He couldn't wait to show the bike to Levi, to decide on a colour scheme and then reassemble it together, but it'd have to wait until late in the next week—Levi was travelling up to the Sunshine Coast to film crocodile wrangling at the Irwin family's Australia Zoo. Until then, Connor had a couple of days off. Sunday nights free were a luxury he didn't pass up when his boss offered them.

Rolling onto his back, Connor stretched and yawned. The bed to his left was cold—Katy was already up. Levi lay to his right fully dressed and smirking at him. "Good morning, Sleeping Beauty."

"Shut the fuck up." Connor laughed, his voice still raspy from sleep. "I'm hungry. Feed me."

"In a minute." Levi leaned down and kissed him. Warm skin against his, strong hands on his body made Connor hum, then grumble when Levi pulled back far too quickly. "Your cousin messaged you. Wanted to know if we're still on for today."

Connor smiled, excited about catching up with Ford again. He hadn't seen him in a decade, well before Connor had joined the army. He was meeting Ford's partner too—something he hadn't expected, not only because Ford had prided himself on being single, but because according to the online gossip rags, his partner was a bloke. And not just any dude, but *the* Reef Reid, current World Champion of freestyle snowboarding.

"What time is it?" He pulled Levi down to him again and kissed him slowly, sucking on his bottom lip. Lee shifted his weight, climbing between Connor's legs and wrapping him in his arms.

"Time for you to get up so we can go celebrate Nick's birthday," Levi murmured against his lips between kisses.

"In a minute." Connor bit Levi's throat gently, making the other man moan.

"Boys, as much as I wanna join you, get up." Katy appeared next to them and smacked Levi's arse playfully. Connor hadn't even heard her coming, but without hesitation, Levi reached out to her, and pulled Katy onto the bed next to them.

"No," she shrieked, laughing as Levi tickled her. "I've gotta get the cake to Nick and Em's without anyone seeing it. We can't be late." Connor leaned over and kissed her like he'd done to

Levi and sighed happily, a goofy love-struck smile plastered on his face.

"Come on, boo. Up you get before we're so late we miss your cousin." Katy smiled down at him, the warmth of her smile lighting him up. When she leaned over and kissed him, her soft lips made him want to wrap her up and keep her there forever—in a totally non-stalkerish, non-serial killer kind of way.

It didn't take long for Connor to get ready—anything at Nick and Emma's was always super casual, so he only needed to shower and toss on some boardies and a tee. His thongs were at the front door—not that he'd wear them when they were there. Bare feet were pretty much the norm too.

Eyeing Katy's arse in her cut-off jean shorts as she bent over to strap on her sandals, Connor's grin faded, his libido fighting with the knowledge he couldn't do anything to reveal they were together. Nick and Emma knew, but if anyone else found out? No, distance was the name of the game.

Levi wrapping his arms around Connor from behind had him leaning into the other man. "Hey, you okay?"

"Yeah, just thinking that I can't touch either of you today. It's gonna suck." Connor sighed, and Levi held him closer.

"It will, but I'll steal you away for a few. There's no way I can go a day either, especially when I'm not gonna be here this week." Levi nuzzled his back and dropped a kiss between his shoulder blades. Katy joined them, hugging Connor close.

"My brother will be there too." The disapproval in Katy's tone rang loud and clear. She and her brother, Jonathan, didn't get along. Connor had always wanted a sibling, so he'd never understood how someone as loving as Katy could have it in her to avoid her brother like the plague, especially when she saw her parents regularly. But then he'd met Jonathan, and he understood why. The total opposite of Katy's playful, laid-back feistiness, her brother was high-strung and critical of everything. Judgemental was his middle name. He had hoped they'd be able to put off the inevitable reunion a few more months, but Nick was big on family, and he'd insisted on inviting his other cousin to his party. So now, he not only had to keep his distance, but listen to Katy's brother and his wife brag on about how wonderful their life was, and how he'd need to get himself a career so he could live the great Australian dream, whatever the hell that was supposed to be. If he asked Jonathan, his first suggestion would be to stop living in peoples' spare rooms.

Levi drove as Katy balanced the box containing the cake on her knees and Connor sat in the back. He'd laughed when he'd first seen Katy's creation. Nick was the eldest of the cousins, and apart from Mike who was a few weeks older, he was also the oldest in their group of friends. And apparently, at thirty-two Depends underwear and Viagra were critical. Katy's recreation of both in the form of a two-tiered cake was pretty ingenious and about as photo-realistic as you could get when icing was involved.

Levi had managed to get the cake stored in the cupboard Emma had cleared for them when Nick barged into the kitchen. "Hey, guys. Didn't realize you'd arrived. Come on out back. Con, you can put your guitar down anywhere and that beer'll go in the Esky outside."

Motioning for Emma to go first, Connor followed, Levi and Katy bringing up the rear. Most of the guests had already arrived. Mike and his kids, together with Nick's brother Brett and his twins were in the pool, Jonathan and his wife, Elsie, sitting off to one side. There were a bunch of other people too. Connor didn't know them, but they seemed friendly enough, raising their beers to him as he followed Emma out onto the deck. Lined up in the shade were some coolers filled with ice and bottles of drinks. "Pop your beer in there, Con." Emma motioned to them. On his knees, he opened the six-packs they'd brought and shoved the bottles in the ice.

"I'll get some music on, hey, babe?" Nick asked Emma, holding her close.

"I'll do it, mate," Levi replied. "You enjoy."

"Cool. I'll get the barbie started in a few. Might have a game of footy first though. You up for it?"

"Absolutely." Katy grinned, making Connor shake his head and laugh.

"Great, I'll grab the ball."

Flo Rida's "Good Feeling" pumped out of the sound system Nick had hooked up outdoors. If the little old lady who lived next door to Nick wasn't rocking out in the backyard with them, Connor would be worried she'd complain about the noise. Instead, Connor smiled and wandered across the grass to say hello to Cam and Maxi. But he was distracted by the sight on the other side of the fence. Soaking wet, two men hugged hard, totally oblivious to the world around them as they kissed each other like their lives depended on it. The blond one had his hands in the other's long hair, while the darker-haired dude slid his into the taller one's boardies. They were beautiful together, so fuckin' passionate and full of life and love. Connor's heart skidded to a halt as did his footsteps while he watched them. God, he longed for that—to be able to stand in the middle of the street with Levi and Katy and kiss the ever-loving-fuck out of them. He didn't want to hide. He didn't want to be their dirty little secret, but what could he do? It'd never change. And he knew that going into this thing with them. Didn't mean he couldn't wish for it all.

The men moved, turning towards them and Connor's mouth dropped open. *Holy shit.* He grinned and jogged out of the gate, yelling out, "Ford, my man. That you?"

Connor watched his cousin break away reluctantly, but the smile he flashed at Connor let him know he hadn't screwed up by interrupting them. "Connor, great to see you," Ford greeted him, his British accent not as strong as the last time they'd spoken years ago.

"Likewise." He grinned, so damn happy that his only family —well, the only one he wanted to see anyway—was standing before him. Ford stepped away from the man Connor recognized as Reef Reid and hugged him hard. "It's been far too long."

Taking the other man's hand in his, Ford spoke again. "Sweet, this is my cousin, Connor O'Reilly. Con, my boyfriend, Reef Reid."

Connor laughed when Reef shook his hand, staring between himself and Ford. They looked alike—even more so as they'd grown up. There was no mistaking they were related, even with the height difference between the two of them.

"Holy shit," Katy breathed from behind them. "And you think Nick and I look alike. You guys could be twins."

"Right?" Reef said to her smiling, as she hooked her arm through Connor's. Having her there with him, showing him some affection—it filled him with a warmth that made the butterflies in his stomach flutter hard. He smiled down at her, knowing that the love he had for her was written all over his face. He wanted to pick her up and kiss her, love her, but he didn't. Barely. Reef spoke again, and he looked at the other man, trying to dispel the image that had just popped into his mind of he, Levi, and Katy walking along the beach hand in hand.

"Good to meet you, Con."

"I'm Katy, Con's friend." Connor flicked his gaze towards Katy again, and she instinctively leaned closer. The heat in her eyes was unmistakeable and, God, did Connor want to take her up on her invitation.

"Come inside and meet everyone," Con murmured without

being able to tear his eyes away from Katy. He motioned to the house he'd just come from and began walking.

In a loud enough voice that Cam and Maxi, Nick and Emma and Levi would hear—the closest group to the back gate—Connor called out, "Guys, meet Ford, my cousin, and his partner, Reef. They're here from Kiwiland for a few weeks." Turning to Ford and Reef, he grinned. "We'll test ya on names later, but the only other person you really need to know is Levi, my best mate and Katy's partner." Connor motioned to Levi who sauntered towards them. Connor bit his lip to stop the appreciative hum escaping just as Katy tightened her grip on his arm. Levi was effortlessly gorgeous—ripped muscles, dark blond hair, and smooth golden skin that he wanted to lick.

"Damn, you're all freaking beautiful," Reef muttered under his breath, making Levi break out in a laugh as he held out his hand in greeting.

"G'day, Reef. Hey, Ford, nice to meet you. Nick, Katy's cousin, is gonna throw some burgers on the barbie in a few. Beer's in the Eskies over there. Chuck yours in there too, if you like." Levi motioned to the coolers lined up in the shade. "We're about to play a game of footy. You guys in?"

Reef's wicked grin at Ford, and Ford's smile back was contagious. Levi tossed an arm around Connor's shoulders and squeezed him tight for the briefest of moments before ripping his singlet off and carelessly tossing it onto the grass. Connor almost swallowed his tongue watching the other man jog out the gate.

"Looks like I'm playing against him then, huh?" Katy mumbled. Connor paused and looked down at her before barking out a laugh when she flicked her shirt.

"I'd pay good money to watch you play skins, Cupcake," he teased.

"Shut up, doofus." She nudged him and reached down to slip off her sandals before shouting, "Okay, boys, let's do this."

Connor followed her in a daze out the gate and onto the sand. Ten of them—five on each side—were lining up to play, Mike in the centre holding the ball. Placing it on the ground, he used his foot to roll it back into Levi's waiting hands, and the scrambling began. Katy ran behind him as Connor charged for Levi, readying to tackle him. The ball was passed away and Connor diverted, running for one of the other players. Sand flew in the air as they sprinted across it, racing after a ball being tossed between players. Wind in his face, salt in the air, his heart beating hard as he pumped his legs fast, Connor grinned. This was life. Friends and family, having fun. This is what he'd been defending, sacrificing those years for. The war wasn't over—hell, it'd probably continue for decades as the world tried to rid itself of those crazy bastards—but Connor wanted to live. He wanted to love.

Reaching long, Levi got his fingers on the ball, barely three feet from the makeshift try line. It was a shoe-in that he'd cross the line, but it didn't stop Connor going in for the tackle. Bending, he wrapped his hands around Levi's middle and let his weight drop, pulling the other man down with him. Levi slammed the ball down on the ground and yelled out in triumph.

"Lucky pass," Connor muttered as he stood and dusted himself off.

"Superior skill, babe." Levi slapped his arse and winked at him before sauntering off back to the middle of the field. The few people around him didn't bat an eyelid, but Connor's skin prickled in awareness. Blowing out a breath, he picked up the ball and kicked it toward his team's try line, aiming for Nick's outstretched hands. The other man caught it easily and passed it to Katy, who tucked it under her arm and sprinted. She was small but fast. Dodging the bodies of the men hurling themselves at her, she crossed the line and planted the ball down, arms raised in victory as she shook her cute little arse.

Soon they had Cam and Maxi, and two people who he learned were Emma's sister-in-law and her PA, join them on the makeshift field. There were a few tries The King would be proud of, but the rest were disastrous. And the plays? God awful. But it was hella fun. Sweaty, out of breath and covered in sand, Connor needed water, so he was relieved when Nick called a time-out. Making their way back through to the yard, Connor brushed off all the dry sand he could, before stripping off his shirt and standing under the outdoor shower to rinse off the rest.

"So how're you settling in since you've been back?" Ford asked him as Connor handed them both a bottle of water from the Eskies.

"Yeah, good." Connor nodded, smiling as they stood in the sun to dry off. "I've got regular gigs at a couple of pubs and cafes a few nights a week. I'm living with Katy and Lee, and that's working out great."

"And Lee's the same Levi who you've been friends with since you were a kid?" Ford queried.

"Yeah. We've been mates since we were five." Connor looked over his shoulder at his lover and smiled, Levi grinning back. Steering the conversation away from himself, he asked the two of them, "Ford said you two met on the slopes. How'd that happen?"

A longing filled him when Ford wrapped his arms around Reef from behind and pulled the man back against him. Nuzzling their heads together when Reef turned side-on, the snowboarder smiled. "He was my heli-skiing guide when I holidayed in New Zealand. We got stuck in a snowstorm while we were on the slopes and we camped out in a ranger's hut for a few days while the blizzard passed. Then this one got hit by an avalanche and the rest is history."

He'd heard about the avalanche, knew that Ford was injured, but not too seriously. "So what, cabin fever?" Connor teased his cousin.

"Hey, don't knock the D until you've tried it." Ford gave as good as he got, making Connor choke on his drink, but his demeanour had changed on a dime, becoming defensive, and maybe a little aggressive. "Dude, if you've got a problem—"

Connor held up his hand, halting Ford in his tracks. The other man had tensed, the opposite of what Connor wanted. "Mate," he whispered, grabbing Ford's arm and dragging him away from the others into a more private nook in the yard. Reef followed, standing shoulder to shoulder with Ford, clearly backing his lover up. "I'm bi, you don't need to convince me. I'm not judging you, dammit." Connor scrubbed his face and looked around. "But keep it to yourself. Not many people in this crowd know, and I'd like to keep it that way."

"Do Katy and Levi know? You're not hiding from them, are you?" Ford asked, concerned.

"Yeah, they know." Connor let out a breath. "Can I ask you a question, Reef? About when you came out?"

"Sure, anything."

"Why'd you do it when you did? Why not earlier? Or not at all? Why not keep your relationship a secret?"

Reef smiled, his dimples showing, and Ford nuzzled closer. "No, I'd done enough hiding." He paused and looked at Ford, the love in his gaze palpable. "And we were ready to move on." Reef pressed a soft kiss on his man and turned back to Connor. "I'm actually surprised we didn't get outed earlier."

"You wanna come out, Con?" Ford asked him gently, then shook his head. "Sucks that we even have to do that. Straight people don't have to make some grand announcement, but apparently, the rest of us do or we're closet cases. And it happens every time you meet someone new." Reef stroked his fingers through Ford's hair, comforting him without even realising it. God, Connor wanted what they had—so much so it hurt—but fuck, that was so damn selfish. Why couldn't he be satisfied with what he had? Levi wasn't hiding him because he was ashamed of him; it was because the world wouldn't understand and Levi would lose everything he'd worked for. Connor got it. He agreed that Levi didn't have much of a choice. But it still hurt.

He shook his head and shrugged his shoulders. "Nah, no point. It's just hard, ya know? Our relationship is everything to us, so we're good there, but I hate hiding. I wish we could be more, put it out there, but it's just not possible."

"He must be pretty special for you to protect him like this," Reef added.

"Without a doubt." Connor smiled sadly. He didn't want to kill the mood. This was supposed to be a party, and instead, he was being a sad sack.

"Let him know you'll be there when he is. It's the only thing you can do if you aren't prepared to walk away."

"Yeah, I will. Thanks, guys." He smiled at them, this time not having to force its genuineness. "If you'll excuse me for a minute, I'm gonna help get the barbie started. I'm starvin'. I'll be back in a bit." He capped his empty bottle and tossed it in the makeshift recycling bin before heading inside.

His heart pounding, Connor closed the bathroom door behind him and splashed water on his face. Resting his hands on the sink, he looked at his reflection in the mirror. Messy curls, suntanned skin, a tattoo on his arm that curled up and over his bare shoulder, a short beard and dark eyes stared back at him. *Get it together, mate.* Seeing Ford and Reef together had made him yearn for a relationship like theirs with Katy and Levi. They were so open and loving, so uncaring of what the judgement of others held. And there was judgement. Jonathan and Elsie had stared at them, their disgust evident in their turned-up lips and exaggerated shudders when they hugged or kissed. Another reason to hate the stuck-up couple.

The door opening startled him until he saw Levi's reflection in the mirror as he entered and closed the door without a word. Connor turned to face him, ready to explain. He was sure Levi would know. He always did.

Instead, he crowded Connor, pushing him back against the sink and stepping between his spread legs. "Please talk to me," he whispered. "You're miserable."

"We can't change it. I want what they have, but I'll settle for it in private." Levi sighed at Connor's words and closed the distance between them, brushing their lips together.

"I dunno what else to do." The sadness in Levi's eyes tore at Connor's heart. His man was hurting just as much as he was. No doubt Katy was going through the same thing too. He cupped Levi's face, warm, smooth skin against his cool hands. They gravitated towards each other, their lips touching, gently at first. Need overcame him, and Connor deepened the kiss, thrusting his tongue into Levi's open mouth. The taste of Levi's drink—whiskey, dry, and lime—and that unique Levi flavour burst onto his tongue, making Connor moan. He wanted this man, yearned for him. Needed him closer. Moving his hands down his boyfriend's firm body, Connor brushed his fingers over Levi's nipples making the other man gasp.

"Damn, you're sensitive there." Connor smirked against the other man's lips and laughed when Levi bit him. Slipping his fingers under the other man's shirt, he hummed when the firm muscle quivered under his light touch. Warm, silky smooth skin met his fingertips and Connor was suddenly ravenous. He needed a taste of him. Needed everything. Grasping the bottom of his shirt, Connor ripped it off Levi, bringing them chest to chest.

He kissed him hard, their tongues tangling together as Levi yanked Connor's boardies down as far as they would go before stepping back and falling to his knees. Levi licked his lips, and Connor nearly came on the spot. *Damn.* Levi nudged his legs closer together and slipped Connor's shorts down to his ankles. He sucked in a breath when Levi's warm palms skirted up his legs and around to his arse pulling him forward until he buried his face in the crease between Connor's leg and his pubes. He ran his fingers through Levi's hair, watching as the other man mouthed his abs. When Levi licked up his length, Connor let his head fall back and he moaned. He shuddered, his hips thrusting forward of their own volition when Levi closed his mouth around his shaft and sucked. Over and over again until Connor couldn't stand it any longer. He was riding the edge, so damn close to coming. Tightening his fingers in Levi's hair, Connor moaned incoherently trying to pull back. He didn't want to come yet. He didn't want it to end.

Then Levi's mouth was on his, kissing him. Ravaging him. His hands on Connor's back, he held him close. Con reached between them and grasped their shafts, fisting them together.

The door slammed open, and he froze. Levi did too. *Oh fuck.* He dared not open his eyes, but he didn't need to. He knew that voice anywhere. "What the...?"

Katy

Katy had just sat down with Ford and Reef when the words,

"You cheating piece of shit," rang out. She stiffened, her heart sinking. Like a house of cards, she could see everything toppling down around her, bursting the little bubble of blissful happiness she, Levi, and Con had been living in.

Her brother was angry, and that was never good. He reacted like a cut snake whenever someone ticked him off. And by the one-sided shouting coming from inside the house, Katy knew it had to be that he'd walked in on Levi and Con.

"What the?" Ford asked, confused.

Katy pressed the heel of her hand against her forehead. "It's Jonathan. Sorry, guys, I need to get in there."

"Yeah, sure," Reef said, standing and taking Katy's bottle of beer from her. She wiped her suddenly sweaty palms on her jean shorts and headed inside. But she wasn't alone. Elsie was already rushing in there too, her long white linen vest and loose skirt billowing behind her. Emma too. Katy followed third, the sounds of the insults being hurled by Jonathan getting louder and louder, and not just because she was getting closer. He was ranting, giving a sermon that he didn't really believe. Or maybe he did. He'd always been a judgemental prick, being homophobic wouldn't be a stretch.

When she stepped around the corner, Katy skidded to a halt. In the bathroom stood Con and Levi, and just outside the door was Jonathan. Con was struggling to pull his still-wet boardies up but they were tangled, his shirt balled up next to the sink. Levi was fully dressed but flustered as hell. Trying to calm her brother, Levi placed a hand on Jonathan's arm, but Jonathan jerked it away. "Get the fuck off me, you—" he shouted, stopping abruptly when Con sidestepped Levi, getting in Jonathan's face.

"Watch it, mate," he growled, standing over him with fists clenched. Audible gasps of shock sounded from the onlookers gathered around them. Time slowed, the rushing in her ears too loud to hear her sister-in-law's shocked screech when she realized what was going on. And then it sped up again, the force of Elsie's disgust hitting her like a slap to the face.

"Or you'll do what, faggot? You make me sick." Seeing he had a crowd gathered, Jonathan almost preened. It made her nauseous. "Kaitlin, do you know why you haven't got a proposal yet? Why he's been stringing you on for so many years? He's cheating on you. With him." Jonathan pointed to Con, looking at him like shit on the bottom of a shoe. "Another five minutes and one of them would have been bent over taking it up the arse." The hatred in his tone, the accusation, had tears welling in her eyes. His words were like the stab of a knife, wounding her and drawing out the pain with each one, killing a piece of her one jab at a time. "See what you've done? You've broken her heart. You're disgusting, both of you."

Con staggered back like he'd been struck, Levi catching him in his arms. Her eyes connected with theirs and the heartbreak in each of their gazes eviscerated her. They didn't deserve her brother's wrath. She had to fix this. She had to make him stop. Katy wiped her tears and stepped forward, wanting to go to them. Only a few feet separated them, but it could have been the entire Pacific Ocean. Jonathan blocked her way, and cool bony fingers snaked around Katy's bicep, pulling her back. She looked to the side and met Elsie's haughty stare. That bitch always thought she was better than everyone and she was in her element now. Katy shook the other woman off, anger pulsing through her at their interference and judgement.

"Kaitlin—" Elsie started.

"Stop it. Both of you just stop." Katy held her hands up, her tone hard as she spoke. She was done with pussy-footing around. The cat was apparently out of the bag anyway, so she was dealing with this shit head on. How dare they judge her men? How dare they judge her?

"Kaitlin, you're coming home with us. There's no need for

you to see them anymore. I can take care of getting you moved out, getting you your fair share of the house."

Katy blinked, unbelieving of what she'd just heard. "What?" she spat back, her voice rising indignantly.

"Jonathan, why don't you calm down," Emma spoke from behind, always the peacekeeper. "You don't know what's going on here, and I think you need to leave judgement out of it. Let them explain."

"Butt out, Emma. This is between us. Family. Not you."

"Emma is my family," Con said stubbornly, his arms crossed over his chest, looking deadly. Unsuccessfully trying to pull him back, Levi wrapped an arm around Con's middle and used his bodyweight to shift him. Even outside of Jonathan's personal space, Con was imposing. "Watch how you speak to her."

Stepping closer to Con, Emma squeezed his forearm, smiling at him, before turning her attention back to Katy's brother. "You're right, Jonathan. This is something you should speak with these guys about, but first I think you need to leave. You can come back and talk once you've had a chance to calm down."

"You think you can kick me out when my sister is here?" Jonathan's eyes flashed angrily. He was like a raging bull, ready to charge. "I'm not leaving her so she can be taken advantage of."

"My wife asked you to leave," Nick snarled, suddenly standing beside Katy. "Now do it."

"Nick, you have no idea what's happening here." Jonathan's tone morphed instantly from angry and aggressive to placating, then again forceful when he continued. "I'm not in the wrong. I just walked in on those two"—he pointed with his thumb over his shoulder at Con and Levi—"half naked in the bathroom. They're cheating on her. Together." Jonathan paused his accusations and faced Con. "You're a disgrace to this country. Terrorists shoulda killed you when they had the chance."

Katy watched everything like it was in slow motion: Levi wheeling around, his hand curling into a fist, the other reaching for Jonathan's shirt, murderous intent darkening his face, Con throwing himself at Levi, wrestling him back and away from her brother, Katy herself instinctively moving forward, the roar she let rip drowning out the animalistic growl coming from Levi. And suddenly she stopped moving, hauled back again by strong arms, pinning her against a thick body. Powerless, frustration welled in her as Con wrestled Levi back, pulling him away from the piece-of-shit-for-a-human former brother. Katy twisted, trying to break free, but the arms pinning her tightened, holding her fast. "No, Katy," Ford whispered in her ear. "He's not worth it. Trust me, he's not."

No one was holding Nick back. He'd pinned Jonathan to the wall with fists balled in his shirt. The always smiling, always laughing Nick was gone, and in his place a dominating and downright scary man stood. Her brother visibly withered when, in a deathly calm tone, Nick spoke. "You have no idea how fucking wrong you are, Jonathan. Get the fuck out before you say something else you'll regret. You're no longer welcome here." Nick pulled him away from the wall then immediately slammed him back against it before letting Jonathan go. He didn't move though, still towering over her much shorter brother. With barely a couple of inches between their chests, it was a picture of opposites—Nick's long body hard from the workout regime Mike had him on and Jonathan standing half a head shorter, his middle rounder.

Elsie gasped in horror at Nick's move, while Katy silently dared Jonathan to push his luck again. One more crack and she wasn't sure Con would be able to hold Levi back. One more crack and he'd probably find himself on the receiving end of her fist too.

But Jonathan wasn't entirely stupid. Unfortunately. Straightening his shirt and stepping out of Nick's immediate reach he shook his head. "Come on Elsie, Kaitlin, we're leaving." Turning to Nick he added, "I don't believe you'd side with them."

Ford's arms around her didn't loosen, and Reef was shielding her with his body too, putting as much distance as possible between her and her sibling. For that, Katy was grateful. But it wasn't necessary, she wasn't leaving with him. "I'm not going anywhere, Jonathan. I'm staying here with *my* family. *My* guys."

"You knew about this?" Elsie asked, shocked and completely appalled. When understanding dawned, she added incredulously, "You're fucking both of them. You slut."

Katy smiled. She couldn't help it. She wanted to cackle insanely and sing "nah nah nah nah nah." Dance a jig even. She might have been going slightly insane. Elsie huffed disbelievingly and turned on her heels, following Jonathan out the house. The front door slammed and Katy flinched, the sound ricocheting in the silence. The smile slipped off her face and her bravado from a moment earlier left her in a rush. Ford was no longer hugging her, but she didn't want that anyway. She wanted her guys. Nick was between them, and he stopped her before she could rush into their arms. "Go upstairs into our bedroom if you want. You can talk up there and no one will interrupt you. Stay as long as you need." He squeezed her arm and Emma smiled, nodding in encouragement as they followed the others out into the late afternoon sunshine, leaving her alone with Levi and Con.

"Sugar, I'm sorry—" Levi started.

"Don't," she replied, resting her face on his chest and wrapping an arm around his waist. His furiously beating heart was a testament to the anger boiling inside him, the tenseness in his body not having dissipated. She laid a kiss on his chest, grateful that he hadn't hurt himself knocking Jonathan's block off. "Don't ever apologize to me for loving each other. That arsehole..."

Katy blew out a breath, trying to calm herself down. It was done now. She was done with him. No matter what he said or did, she no longer had a brother. There was no way she'd stand for him treating either—all—of them the way he had. "His opinion means nothing. I don't give a fuck about what either of them said." Katy reached up and cupped Con's cheek. "They're meaningless. But you? You're everything to us." She dropped her hand, wrapping both arms around their waists and stepped in close to them, tears welling in her eyes. The anger and frustration, the sorrow for the words spoken to Con were overwhelming. She wanted to protect them, to wrap them in her arms and hold on tight. She wanted nothing more than to make this right. Through a half sob, half laugh she added, "But seriously, lock the fucking door." Connor huffed out a humourless laugh and held her tighter, Levi doing the same while she regathered herself. Their touch—as simple as stroking her hair and kissing her temple was—was comfort. It was home.

"I'm sorry. God, they were so mean," she whispered, biting back a fresh wave of tears. They'd tried to hide it, tried to keep what they had between them and now it was out there in front of a whole party of people. "What the hell are we supposed to do now?"

"Now we go outside and fess up, I s'pose." Levi shrugged, trying but failing to hide his nerves. "Maybe eat some cake?"

Katy tilted her face to look at him, and Levi captured her lips in the most innocent of kisses. Squeezing him tightly, she turned to Con, waiting for his opinion, "I'll do whatever you want, Cupcake."

She nodded, a smile stretching her lips. "I could do cake. And beer."

"Cake and beer it is." Taking their hands in hers, Katy led them through the house and out back.

Ford held out a beer, Reef handing them two more. Katy

took one and smiled at him before turning her gaze to the rest of the group sitting down around the fire pit. "I guess we, um, have some explaining to do."

"No. You don't," Nick replied, standing up and moving over to her. "You don't need to justify yourselves to us. All you need to know is that we love you guys. You're our family, and we'll stand by you no matter what." Hearing those heartfelt words filled her heart with happiness and love—for Nick and Emma who were more family to her than Jonathan ever was, or would be. She hugged Nick hard. His acceptance of them, and the knowledge that at least one person in her family didn't judge them, meant the world.

"We need a toast," Cam called out. "To love and three-somes... And Nicky's birthday. Happy birthday, mate."

A chorus of, "Here, here," and, "Cheers," rang out around the crowd.

There was a bit of shuffling and a space large enough for them opened up. Con dropped her hand and stepped away. Confused, she turned to follow him, realizing what he was going for—his guitar. It was never far away from him.

Levi sat down and pulled her onto his lap while Con made himself comfortable next to them. Joining hands with Con, Katy smiled and snuggled into Levi's broad chest. Warmth and love surrounded her, her heart full to overflowing. "How did I get so damn lucky?" she murmured. "I love you."

Con pressed his lips against hers and Levi kissed her temple softly, his stubble brushing against her cheek, before he turned his face and pressed his mouth to Con's. "And we love you." Con smiled at her, the crooked grin lighting up his face, his eyes sparkling. It had the butterflies in Katy's belly fluttering.

After settling back, sitting cross legged on the cushions surrounding the fire pit, Con repositioned his guitar on his lap and started strumming.

"Miley," Lexi, Mike's little girl squealed. She'd been quiet until then, resting her head on her father's lap. She was adorable, long dark hair in pigtails swaying wildly as she snapped up. Lanky and in love with everything netball, Lexi could recite the stats of every player in her favourite teams. She was rarely out of her netball uniform too, the short yellow and green dress part of her daily wear.

"You know this one, hey?" Con grinned at her.

"Every word," Mike moaned. Katy couldn't help but laugh. She'd been exactly like that growing up. When she loved a song, she'd learn every word of it, playing it endlessly until the next one piqued her interest and she'd move onto that.

Con sang. The lyrics resonated within her—being free and loving life on a perfect beach was apropos, poignant as they sat there on that cool autumn night, the waves crashing in the distance. She watched the flames dance in the shallow iron pit on the deck while the sun set. Early evening was upon them, and Con's deeper voice, mixed with Lexi's sweet alto created a bubble around them, winding romance through the air.

"Sing us a classic, Con," Maxi asked when he'd strummed the last note. He nodded thoughtfully for a moment and then sung the slow opening of INXS's "Never Tear Us Apart." Katy loved the song, loved the imagery of a man finding love and no matter what intervened—worlds colliding, a thousand years passing, absolute chaos—he'd never let them be torn apart. Katy was swaying in Levi's arms, humming along, when Nick stood and held his hand out to Emma, dancing slowly with her in the dying sunlight of the day. Reef and Ford were soon up too, Ford's front to Reef's back as they swayed as one, Ford holding Reef tight.

Con followed, standing up and walking around the couples, stepping over outstretched legs and coming before her and Levi again. Holding out his hand, he helped Katy up. "Dance with our man, Cupcake," he murmured, before pressing a lingering kiss to her lips. Katy sighed, all the happy feels coursing through her veins when Levi took her into his arms, and they watched Con sing the rest of the song. She was enraptured, so damn lucky to have not one, but two men who loved as hard as Levi and Con. They gave everything to her, to each other—all of their hearts.

"D'ya know this one?" Con asked as he bent and fished a pic out of his guitar case. "Stupid question, everyone knows this one."

Katy was preoccupied, staring at his arse and long, strong legs as he bent. *Damn.* What a view. Katy giggled at Levi's rumbling groan and snorted out a laugh when Con stood back up and winked at her.

"You shit," she playfully chastised him. "You're torturing the poor guy."

"Eh, I try." Connor shrugged, and using the pic, strummed the unforgettable first strains of The Kinks' "All Day and All of the Night." Cheers went up through the group and with all of them standing and dancing, they shout-sang the lyrics. Wildly out of tune, they were all laughing and jumping around as Con continued to play. It was freeing, the weight of her brother's vitriol being shaken off all their shoulders. Katy's heart was light, love and laughter in her soul. Spinning around, Katy raised her arms above her head and belted out the lyrics. They totally described how much she wanted her men—she was insatiable around them. She twirled in Levi's arms, laughing when he dipped her low. God, she'd needed this, needed to be able to show the world just how much they meant to her.

Only a short song, it ended quickly, but Katy wasn't disappointed. Con took her hand in his and kissed her fingertips, his other hand wrapping around Levi's neck and pressing their foreheads together. Breathing hard, Con crushed their lips together.

It was quick, but scorching hot, melting Katy's insides. He grinned wickedly at both of them and strummed down the strings, stopping to adjust the tension on a couple. While he did that, he began singing. He got three words in and she knew it was "Thinking Out Loud" by Ed Sheeran. Katy looked around her. All the couples were cuddled together. Levi's warmth pressed against her, his strong arms cradling her as she rested her head on his shoulder. Katy smiled at Jaxon, Mike's youngest, as he looked around disgusted at all the people surrounding him, none of whom would throw the footy to him. Spinning it on his finger, he huffed out an exaggerated sigh and rolled his eyes. Katy pointed to him and Levi murmured, "Poor lil' dude."

"I'm gonna play with him. Why don't you dance with Connor?" Levi's hum was all the confirmation she needed. Katy stepped out of his embrace and held out her hands to Jax. His little face lit up like he'd won the lotto. Catching the ball he threw to her, she snapped her gaze to her men when the music abruptly stopped.

"Nick, get a radio on," Levi's low voice rang out clearly among the quiet group. "I wanna dance with my man." Katy smiled and tossed the footy back to Jax, all the time watching as Levi held the neck of Con's guitar and lifted it over his head, setting it against the wall. When Levi stepped into Con's arms, they melted together, holding tight while they joined their lips in another scorching kiss. Right then, she wanted Con to have Levi more than anything. She was so ridiculously happy, so damn ecstatic that her guys could finally love each other in the open. She knew how hard it was for Con to be kept hidden, even if he wouldn't admit it to them. Katy couldn't help her goofy smile and the giddy happiness at full bloom in her.

11

LEVI

Connor pulled up into the drive, and Levi's gut sank, its contents very nearly coming back up when he saw the car sitting there. He'd been riding a high after Jonathan left the party, everyone's unflinching support and acceptance freed him from the weight of Jonathan's words, his hatred. But that four-by-four parked there, and its occupants who were waiting for them, undid it all. He could see Katy's father sitting on the front step—his dark brown but greying hair was neat as usual. He was dressed casually but sat ramrod straight, his jaw clenched tight and his mouth drawn into a thin line. Levi looked around for Katy's mother and, sure enough, she was there too, inspecting the grevillea that Katy's parents had gifted to them for their housewarming.

He took a deep breath and wiped his suddenly sweaty palms on his shorts, a fine tremor in his hands. He'd been through the ringer that night, and he was tired, emotionally spent. Levi didn't have it in him to do anything more than curl up in bed with his lovers and hold them tight, but Rich clearly had something on his mind. It didn't take a genius to guess that Jonathan had called them.

He remembered back to "the talk" that Katy's father had given him years ago—the one that went "if you fuck my daughter over, I'll cut your balls off with a rusty knife and watch you bleed out with a smile on my dial." God only knew what Jonathan had said, but even a toned down version would easily count as one of those "I'm gonna cut your balls off" scenarios.

None of them spoke as Connor turned off the engine. With a final glance at each other, he and Katy opened their doors. Connor was right behind them. As soon as Katy stepped out from the passenger side, Rick had his hand on her arm, dragging her across to his car. "Dad, what the hell?" Katy fought him, pulling her arm away, but his grip visibly tightened. She winced, and it kicked both he and Connor into gear, both of them racing to her side. "Dammit, Dad, that hurts. Let go."

"I spoke to your brother tonight. You're coming home with us." He tugged on her arm again with a sense of urgency and Katy stumbled, Rich catching her before she fell. In his peripheral vision, Levi saw the front lights of their neighbour's house turning on, the screen door opening and their neighbour Ying walking outside in her PJs and holding a cricket bat. But she was the least of his worries. Connor's expression was murderous, rage boiling in his dark eyes, every muscle in his body vibrating as he clenched his fists ready to attack, and Levi was right there too. Rich putting his hands on his daughter and hurting her? Not in this lifetime.

"Dad," Katy ground out, fighting to pull free of his embrace. "I'm not going anywhere."

"Kaitlin, now isn't the time to do this. You're coming home."

Levi saw red, blinding rage filling his every pore. Her father was as delusional as his son, judging them for something he knew nothing about. "Let her go, Rich." Levi's words were deceptively quiet and calm, but anger bubbled just below the surface, like a volcano about to erupt. He and Connor were a united front, standing shoulder to shoulder, working together as a team. Levi took Katy into his arms and Connor reached out, pressing down on a pressure point on Rick's wrist until the other man dropped his hand. Rubbing it, Rich looked at Connor horrified, but Connor's attention had already turned to Katy, gently caressing the red mark her father had left on her arm.

"You bruised her," Connor gritted out, clenching his fist again and stepping closer to Rich. Panic filled Katy's mother's face, and she stepped between them, placing her hands up to stop Connor, halting his progress on a dime.

"Katy, honey, are you okay?" Andrea, her mum, asked.

"I'd be better if we weren't arguing about bullshit after my bedtime on my damn front lawn. I'm drunk and I'm tired. Jonathan almost ruined our night and he's an arsehole, so if you're here because of him—and of course you are, because why else would you be here at nine at night—you can just leave." Katy was ranting, and Levi couldn't help his smile. God, he loved this woman. She was feisty and fiery and called it exactly as she saw it. "Can we at least go inside?"

"I think that's a good idea," her mum replied. When Levi looked to Connor and nodded, his lover strode over and opened the door, ushering everyone through. Katy's parents went on ahead, walking into the living room while Levi hesitated, putting some distance between them.

"Cupcake, you okay?" Connor asked, his voice filled with concern as he lightly fingered the quickly fading mark.

"Yeah, boo. I am now." She reached for him and hugged him hard without letting go of Levi's waist. The three of them stood there wrapped around each other just inside the front door, the cool night air wafting in on the breeze. Something in Levi relaxed, clicked into place, let him breathe again. He was home —and it wasn't being inside the walls of that house that did it. No, it was being with the two people who meant everything to him. His heart was full, his soul complete because of the man and woman in his arms. One of the songs Connor had sung earlier flashed back into his mind—Armageddon could happen around them, but no matter what happened from there on out, Levi knew down to his bones that they'd be okay.

He could have stood there for hours, just holding Connor and Katy, but his girl was wavering on her feet. He knew they needed to get this conversation with her parents over with and right on cue, Katy broke away and stomped into the living room. Levi followed, Connor right beside him, and he bit back a smile upon seeing Katy's stance. Arms crossed, legs apart and chin up, she didn't beat around the bush. "What exactly did Jonathan say?"

Looking Levi in the eye, Rich voiced his worst fear. "He believes Levi forced you into something you aren't comfortable with and he's worried about your safety." Turning his attention to Katy, he added, "Jonathan said that he tried to talk to you this afternoon but Connor—and I'm assuming this is him—" Rich motioned to the man standing rigidly next to Levi, "physically threatened him. He felt like he had no choice but to leave to protect Elsie."

Katy's laugh held no humour. Levi wanted to punch something—Jonathan preferably. It was so typical of Katy's brother to twist the truth of what happened to suit his own agenda. "Jesus, I need another drink," she huffed out and shook her head. "Mum, can you please help me make some tea."

Katy's dad sat in the middle of their three-seater couch, leaving only the recliner for him, Connor, and Katy to sit in. Levi hesitated, but Connor directed him into the seat. Levi perched on the edge, unable to relax into the chair, and Connor sat down behind him on the armrest, absently massaging Levi's shoulders, keeping a constant connection between them. Levi needed it, needed him in the moment. He leaned into Connor's touch, reaching out to squeeze his knee, to try and say with that simple touch, thank you—for knowing him, for falling in love with him, for being his best mate.

Carrying a tray of mugs filled with steaming tea, Katy set them on the coffee table, her mum following with sugar and milk. Katy stood beside Connor, the other man instantly wrapping his arm around her, his other one not leaving Levi. All the mugs were left untouched while Rich stared at them, his gaze hard, cold. Levi tried to ignore Rich's eyes on him, but he couldn't. They'd been solid. Actual mates. But apparently, a rumour was enough to destroy any friendship that'd grown over the years. Levi knew he wasn't worthy of Katy—his girl was a shining light in a sky full of dull grey—but he'd tried his damnedest to be the best person he could be for her. He thought her father had seen that; it killed him knowing Rich's opinion was so easily swayed.

"Katy, tell me what's going on—" her father growled.

"Rich." Andrea chastised her husband's harsh tone. In a much softer one, she asked, "What's going on, Katy? We're worried about you. We've been waiting out here for hours with the worst thoughts possible going through our heads. Your brother scared us."

Katy groaned. "He crossed a line today, Mum, and he can't come back from it. I don't wanna have anything to do with him again."

"So tell us your side of the story," Andrea pleaded. "It took us a good hour to calm your brother and Elsie down after they left Nick's to get the story out of them. We tried calling you over and over. Then when you didn't answer, we came over to see you for ourselves. We were just about to come to Nick's. Your brother is convinced that you're in danger."

"Oh, for God's sake, I'm not in danger." Katy tossed her hands up in the air. "*Come on*, you two know Levi; he'd never hurt me." She ran her fingers through Connor's hair and smiled down at him. "And Connor wouldn't either. I'm happy, we all are, and I'm not in any danger despite what Jonathan said."

"That's what victims of domestic violence say. You know that, don't you?" Rich challenged.

"Watch your fucking mouth," Connor snarled as both of he and Connor jumped up off the armchair. White-hot fury raged through Levi. Rich's accusation was a strike below the belt. Levi had never laid a finger on Katy. He never would. Why would Rich say something like that now? Why, when Connor was sitting there, did he have to act like a dick when in truth, the man was good people?

"*This* is exactly what I mean." Rich pointed at them, making Levi's heart sink. Jonathan had poisoned Rich's opinion of both of them. Levi could handle his own reputation being slandered, but not that of the beautiful man in front of him. Especially not before Rich and Andrea had even met Connor. "I say something you don't like, and you both jump up, beat your chests and measure your dicks. What if it's Katy who says something that makes you angry? You gonna threaten her like you're threatening me?" Levi looked down, shame dousing the anger flooding through his veins. Sure, Rich was acting like a dick, but Levi was reacting in exactly the same way. And there was no denying that he was doing exactly what Rich had pointed out. When neither he nor Connor answered, Rich continued. "Are you a violent man, Connor? Are you someone who I can trust living in the same house as my daughter?"

"I don't consider myself violent, Mr Daniels, but it depends what your definition is. Will I hurt someone for the sake of it or in anger? No, never. Have I killed before? Yes." He nodded. "Under orders in the line of duty. Will I kill any bastard that hurt Levi or Katy, or tried to, even if it meant giving up my own life? Without hesitation. So I dunno, Mr Daniels. Am I a violent man? As for whether I can be trusted with your daughter, I'd say that's a decision she needs to make."

"I agree, Connor, and for the record, I don't think that you're a violent man." Andrea answered for him, and Levi blew out a breath. "Nor you, Levi. Young and impulsive, yes, and protective too, but not violent. Question is then, why did Jonathan say Katy's in danger?"

Levi scrubbed a hand over his face. He had to man up. He had to do a solid by Katy's parents and let them hear the news from him, because Jonathan wouldn't give him a second chance to fess up. He sat back down and clasped Katy's hand, drawing strength from her rock-solid grip, her unwavering support. "I love Katy more than I can put into words. That hasn't changed and it won't. My life is pretty damn perfect with her, but there's always been something missing. Until Connor came home, I didn't realize it wasn't some*thing*, but some*one*. Him. We're together—"

"Lee, no. This isn't only on you." Katy turned to her parents and without a shred of hesitation, blurted out, "We're all together. The three of us. I'm with Connor too. Jonathan walked in on Con and Lee and assumed they were cheating on me. Then when he found out I knew, he figured they were forcing me into it." Katy shook her head. "But he was wrong. I love both of them."

Shock rendered Rich speechless; Levi didn't expect it to last long. He was waiting for the explosion, Vesuvius's second coming—the eruption to end all others. But like a guppy, Rich opened his mouth and closed it again, then repeated the action. He ran his fingers through his hair and sat back on the couch, then after a moment, asked, his tone disbelieving, "You're serious?" Levi nodded and winced when the other man shook his head. "How do you expect me to accept this? It isn't right."

"We're not doing anything wrong, Dad." Still holding his

hand, Katy reached out for Connor's and held tightly. Levi looked across at both of them, the three of them sharing a glance. It was one tiny moment in time, but Levi's breath caught in his throat. He could see the love written on each of Connor and Katy's faces and he reached out, touching Connor's face before bringing Katy's hand to his mouth and kissing her fingers. Her parents had to see that this was no whim—it was written all over their faces. All they had to do was look. "I love them and they love me."

"Do you hear how naïve you sound, Katy? *I love them and they love me.*" Her father uttered sarcastically. He grimaced and stood, pacing the length of the couch. Tossing his hands up in the air, he shook his head and huffed out an exasperated breath. "There are so many things you haven't considered. What are people going to think of you walking down the street with two men on your arm? Have you thought about how your business —everything you've worked for—could be destroyed? And what about you, Levi?" Rich motioned to him. "You might as well say goodbye to your job if this gets back to them. How will you explain to some kid why you're with the two of them? What sort of role model will you be?" Rich was being realistic, stating things how he saw them. Levi had done the same thing, had thought through every one of the issues the other man had raised, but he couldn't fight it anymore. He couldn't hurt either of Katy or Connor by ignoring what was there between them. He wouldn't.

"So what, Dad?" Katy huffed out a breath and pursed her lips. She was trying hard to keep a lid on her temper, but she was failing. Levi squeezed her hand in support. "We live our lives in misery because we're denying a fundamental part of ourselves so we can fit into the little box society has made for us? No thanks. I'd rather be labelled a slut." She raised her chin in the air defiantly. Pride at her defiance, and horror at the possibility of her being branded a slut by more than her brother and his wife warred within him.

"We were gonna keep it quiet," Connor added softly. "We didn't want to risk any blowback. So in public, I'm just their friend. It was stupid of us letting things get as far as they did at Nick's." He shook his head. "I screwed up."

"We were both in that room, Con. This isn't your fault." Levi reached out and took his hand, squeezing it. Connor's callused fingers, rough from playing his guitar, closed around Levi's and he held onto him, that small connection between them enough to ground Levi.

"Mr Daniels," Connor added. "I agree it's unconventional, but it's real. Whatever you think about Levi and I being together, we both love Katy. She'll always be the most important person in the world to us."

"I'm sorry you found out like this. I wish it'd happened differently." Levi gave him a sympathetic smile. "It's taken us months to come to terms with what's happening between us, and it's been thrust on you in one night after you'd already had a rough one."

The room was quiet, Rich watching their interactions like a hawk and Andrea absently stirring her tea.

"Mum, you haven't said anything." Katy prompted quietly, her voice breaking on the last word.

Andrea put her mug on the coffee table carefully and took a moment before speaking. "I'm not particularly happy, but it's not because the three of you are seeing each other. Well, it is, but you're old enough to make your own choices. I *am* upset because you didn't trust me enough to tell me." Andrea stood and waited for her husband to get up too. They were part way to the front door when Andrea added, "We deserved to know, even if you were keeping your relationship a secret from the rest of the world." That parting shot was like a stab to his heart. Disappointing her parents wasn't an option for Katy. She loved them dearly. Knowing she'd let them down, hurt them, would break Katy's heart, and Levi ached for her.

She was in his arms the second they'd turned their backs again, curling into him and crying silently. Her body shook and her tears quickly dampened his shirt. He wanted to protect her, to save her heartbreak, but it was his stupid actions that had put Katy in that position in the first place. He should have locked the door. *Why didn't I?* Was there some sick part of him that wanted to be caught?

Levi hadn't realized he'd closed his eyes until Connor held them both close. He leaned into him, breathing him in. "Come to bed," Connor murmured.

They stumbled into bed like that, wrapped around each other, holding tightly, moving together until they each came hard. Katy fell asleep quickly after that, but Levi lay awake in the darkness. He wasn't sure whether Connor was staring into the night like him, or whether he'd found enough peace that he could rest, but the other man was quiet. He stayed like that, thinking about their future together and what it would mean for them if they did come out to the world. There'd been a lot of fanfare and speculation, and just as much criticism of Reef and Ford, but the dude was an international star. Levi wasn't anywhere near as famous. But still....

Levi wiped the sweat from his brow. It was hot standing in the afternoon sun, watching while the handlers entered the crocodile enclosure and laid out their gear within easy reach. Ropes and blankets, a roll of thick tape and what looked like a spinal board. The next day, Levi would be one of them. He swallowed hard. Yeah, he was a little nervous—the hairs at the back of his neck standing on end and gut churning even thinking about getting up close and personal with an animal as deadly as a saltie.

He watched the test run—the final practical lesson on how to go about roping and restraining one of the crocodiles. Jack, the head trainer, called out, "Levi, you'll be right next to me tomorrow. You need to be aware of your surroundings, like I've said. Saltwater crocs are fast bastards. They can run at nearly thirty clicks in short bursts—that's a lot faster than you." Jack's gaze never strayed from the reptile sunning itself on the edge of the pond. Jaws open, the white on the inside of its mouth was visible. Its powerful legs tipped with claws sharp enough to gut a man if he got too close made Levi swallow. His mouth was dry as a desert. The croc was about the same size as the one they'd be moving the next day, and it was freaking huge. *What am I doing? Am I insane?*

They worked efficiently—short, sharp moves and clear directions spoken calmly, but loud enough that there was no mistaking them. He watched as the handlers spread out, moving down the length of the rope that Belinda, another trainer, would lasso him with. Levi was awed, watching as she got close enough to the croc to use a rod with a hook on the end to manoeuvre the heavy rope noose over his top jaw.

Where the reptile had been still as a statute a moment before, suddenly it was thrashing. Belinda had yanked on the lasso, tightening it around the croc's snout and within a millisecond, it was doing a deathroll into the water, splashing and fighting to drag her in.

"Levi, we grab the rope and haul him up now. You'll be behind me." Speaking more to the other trainers in with him, Jack said, "Remember, don't loop it round your hand." They worked seamlessly, each of the five men and women pulling until their muscles strained. Cedric, the crocodile, fought hard but the handlers were experienced and knew how to get him up to the clearing with the minimum of fuss.

The growls the croc let loose when he hit the shore had Levi breaking out in a cold sweat. He'd done some crazy things in this job, but this was madness. Fear prickled through him and his heart raced. White-knuckling the railing, he sucked in a breath and jumped out of his skin when DJ, their location manager, clamped a hand on his shoulder. "Lookin' forward to this one, mate?"

He didn't answer. He couldn't. He was too busy staring in horror at the monster being dragged unceremoniously up the embankment. One of the handlers tossed the small blanket over the croc's eyes and suddenly they were all launching themselves on top of it while Belinda held the rope as steady as she could.

"Levi, tomorrow if you're near a leg, you'll need to grab it and pin it up and back, like this," Jack called out, showing him the position. "Watch the claws or you'll cut yourself open." Jack asked Belinda, "We secure?"

"Yep, jaw is taped."

"Okay, boys and girls, let's get Cedrick on the board, then we'll check him over and release."

It was only a few minutes later that Jack dusted his hands off on his khaki pants. "How was that to watch, Levi?" he asked with a grin.

"Terrifying." He shook his head. "You guys were impressive, but I'm not so sure about getting in there."

"You'll shit bricks the first time, but we'll be right there with you. It's dangerous, but as long as you keep a cool head and follow directions, we'll keep you safe." Jack clapped a friendly hand on his shoulder and called out to the group. "Right, let's take a smoko break. We're nearly done for the day."

Sandwich in hand, Levi sat on a large boulder in the shade of one of the many gum trees and cracked open his bottle of water. He took a swig and listened to the sounds around him —birds sang in the branches above, the distant sounds of the show in the Crocoseum entertaining park-goers. The dazzling blue sky stretched out, cloudless, above him. Levi checked his phone for messages. He had a text from head office: *Levi, you're needed for an urgent meeting at the studio. Please telephone immediately upon receiving to advise of your expected arrival time. Eva McLaughlin is travelling from Sydney to meet with you in person.*

"What the hell?" Levi mumbled, dialling head office's line. The receptionist picked up on the first ring, and after the usual, impersonal greeting, he spoke. "Hi, I'm Levi Flaherty. Apparently, Ms McLaughlin is flying up to the Gold Coast studio to meet with me this afternoon. Is that right?"

"Yes, Mr Flaherty. That's correct. Should I telephone the studio to let them know you're on your way?"

"We have at least another hour left before we wrap up here, so I won't be there for at least four. I'll hit peak hour traffic coming through the city."

"Mr Flaherty, I have strict instructions to advise you to leave immediately upon getting the message, not to wait for the day to wrap."

"Oh-kay," Levi replied slowly. "Any idea why the urgent meeting has been called?"

"Can't say, sorry," she answered dismissively.

"I'm sure you can't," he mumbled under his breath. Louder, he asked, "Is anyone else required to be at this meeting or is it just me?"

"Everyone on set."

Levi pulled the phone away from his ear and looked at it as if it'd miraculously give him an answer. He shook his head and looked up, searching for the director. Sure enough, she was on the phone too, rushing over to where DJ was sitting. "Yeah.

Yeah," he said, distracted, "Okay, I'll help get everyone organized, then we'll leave."

"Mr Flaherty, I just said that you needed to leave immediately upon getting the message. Never mind the others, they've got their own instructions. You need to meet Ms McLaughlin. She's already on her flight. She won't appreciate being kept waiting."

Something wasn't right. Never in all the years that he'd worked on TV had he been called in the middle of a shoot and ordered to a meeting with top level management. He'd heard that the network had financial problems—everyone had, it was national news—but they'd also been assured by the administrators that no jobs would be lost. He blew out a breath and hung up, then yelled out to DJ, jogging over to him and the director locked in conversation. "Hey," he called, getting their attention. "I need to go. Apparently we have a meeting back on the Coast, but my instructions are to leave straight away rather than help you guys pack up."

"Yeah, no worries. We were just told the same thing. Good luck, yeah."

Levi froze, an anvil settling in his gut. "Do you know something?"

"Nah, mate, I don't." DJ shook his head. Levi was clueless, but he nodded in response and bumped fists with his friend and nodded to the director before jogging across to his car. Pulling out to begin the two-hour drive back to the Gold Coast, his mind churning, he dialled Katy. "Hey, sugar," he greeted her when she picked up and said hello to him. "I won't keep you. I'm heading back, I'll be home tonight."

"How come?"

"Some sort of meeting at the studio. We've all been ordered back. No idea what's going on. You haven't heard anything on the news about the network, have you?"

"Nah, babe. But I haven't really been listening either. Hang on, I'll ask Ash." A shuffling noise came through his speaker and muffled words before Katy spoke to him again. "Nope, Ash hasn't heard anything either."

He made good time back to the studio, missing the peak-hour rush. He smiled as he stepped away from his car, reading Connor's message—**Glad to have you home tonight. We would have missed you.**

Opening the door to the studio, Levi smiled at the receptionist waiting there. She picked up her phone and dialled, speaking in a hushed tone as he made his way through the long and narrow space. They had a simple setup in the onsite offices, a desk, couches, and a large wall-mounted TV. Signage for the station adorned the wall behind the large desk and pictures hung along each of the others, one for every show filmed on the Gold Coast.

"Go straight on through, Levi. They're waiting for you."

"Ms McLaughlin here yet?" he asked, wiping his sweaty palms on his jeans, his nerves getting the better of him. When Allison nodded, he swallowed, hoping the bad vibes he had were over exaggerated.

Levi entered the meeting room after hearing, "Come in," when he knocked. Three people sat across the long boardroom desk from where he stood—Eva McLaughlin and two others, a man and a woman, neither of whom he recognized. A thin manila folder was the only thing sitting on the desk.

"Mr Flaherty, thank you. Please, take a seat," Ms McLaughlin said, pointing to the vacant seat before him. Levi blew out a breath and sat. There were no introductions to the others sitting in the room. He didn't know whether to be grateful or more nervous. Either way, he just wanted to get things over and done with.

Shuffling into his seat, Levi tried to tamp down his nerves. "So, this is highly unorthodox. Mind telling me what's going on?"

"We find ourselves in a highly unorthodox situation, Mr Flaherty," Eva began. "But it's manageable with some discreet handling, if that becomes necessary."

Levi stared at her, clueless as to what she could be talking about. She saved him asking, speaking to him in a tone that was completely devoid of emotion. It unnerved him more with every passing second. "Mr Flaherty, can you please explain this photograph to us?" She slid a printout of an image to him. It was pixelated, as if it had been enlarged, but there was no question what it was.

"It's me kissing my girlfriend goodbye. Looks like it was from this morning. Who took this? Why is it even an issue? We've lived together for years."

"It's not the issue, Mr Flaherty. This one is." She slid another sheet of paper to him. This one had two images. In the first, Connor was standing naked inside the doorway from the house into the garage, with Levi walking towards him. The second had had been taken sometime after the first. In it, Levi was lifting Connor up, pinning him against the wall. Wrapped around each other, lips connected and every inch of their bodies pressed together, it was obvious what they were doing. Levi flipped the papers over and closed his eyes. Mortification and cold fury warred for top place within him. No, it wasn't that. He felt violated, creeped out by someone having captured he and Connor in a moment which was meant just for them.

"These pictures were found online today. Your personal profile was tagged in them. I'm guessing you haven't seen them?"

When Levi shook his head, she continued. "The good news is that they haven't gone viral yet, but it won't take long for people to make the link between your personal and professional personas. We've petitioned the social media sites to have them taken down pending an order from the federal court. A few of them have been pulled because of the sexual content, but the other is taking longer. It's only a matter of time before the shit storm hits."

Levi nodded again, unable to find the words to reply. It was as if his mind and body were disconnected. He couldn't process what was happening before him. He couldn't get past the fact that someone had been spying on him. It wasn't easy to see into their garage from the street. The land sloped down, away from the road. Whoever it was had been close. That and the lack of light left him with only one conclusion—it was an intentional shot. There was someone out there spying on them.

His skin crawled and worry pricked at him. If they were being watched, who knew what that person was capable of? Who the hell was it? Would they try to hurt Katy or Connor? He needed to call them, needed to make sure they were safe. He held up his phone. "I, um, need to call Katy and Con. I...." He trailed off, not even knowing how to begin to explain what he needed to do.

Oblivious to his struggles, the man beside Eva began talking, "You might be best off taking a proactive approach on this—get your friend to find a bloke who'll stand in as his boyfriend for a while and put up some pictures of them online. You'll have to make some comments congratulating them, something like that. That way there'll be an explanation if the images do get circulated more broadly. Worst case, you can do a press release stating that the images were of your friend and his boyfriend."

"I'm sorry, but who the heck are you?" Levi asked, annoyed that they'd barrelled on, regardless of the turmoil coursing through him.

"Francis Medley, PR for the network." The other man held out his hand and years of ingrained manners had Levi standing and reaching out.

"I'm Louise Arcadia. I'm in Human Resources." The lady beside Eva stood and reached over the boardroom table. After shaking her hand, Levi sat down and scrubbed a hand over his face.

"I need to get Connor to pick up Katy from work. If there's some psycho taking pictures of us, I can't have her alone. Give me a minute, okay, then we'll talk about these." Levi motioned to the two pieces of paper in front of him. He dialled Connor's number and stood to walk out of the room.

"Levi, stay in here, please. You walk out there and anyone can overhear. This needs to be handled delicately," Francis chastised when Levi reached for the doorhandle.

Ignoring him, Levi opened the door and walked out into the hall, crossing it to use one of the empty offices. Connor's phone rang out, clicking over to his message. Frustrated, Levi spoke after his recording finished. "Hey, I need you to do me a favour. I need you to pick up Katy from work. Something's happened here and I'm..." He paused, blowing out a breath. "I'm freaked out. Please don't leave her alone. I need to know she's safe." Levi's voice broke on the last words and he breathed deeply, forcing his fear down. "Call me as soon as you get this. I need to know you heard it." He hung up and walked back inside the meeting room, placing his phone on the desk in front of him.

"Is there any way of finding out who took the photos? Or even who posted them?" Levi asked the three people sitting impatiently across from him.

"We aren't sure. It's not really relevant," Francis replied bluntly.

"Ah, yeah, it is. Some crazy bastard is out there taking pictures of us at four in the morning." Levi's voice rose as he grew more angry and frustrated. "Of course it's relevant. What if Katy was alone out there and that maniac hurt her?"

"I'm sure that's an issue the police will want to talk to you about," Louise replied, shooting a look at Francis. "It's not our focus, but it's obviously important."

"Levi, we need to set a plan in motion. If the federal court denies the application—and there's a distinct chance they might —or the news or current affairs outlets get a hold of the pictures before we can get them pulled off the web, you must have deniability."

"Deniability?" Levi asked incredulously. "You did look at the pictures, didn't you? It's pretty damn obvious it's me in both of them. For god's sake, I'm wearing the same clothes here in this office."

"Mr Flaherty, we're trying to give you some options. You're a children's TV presenter, and not just any presenter, but a Logie winning one. Your private life is private. However, it also needs to be discreet."

Levi pounded his fists on the table in frustration. "Stop giving me HR speak. Say it straight," Levi ordered.

Eva nodded and Louise spoke, "Purely off the record? You can't work as a children's television host when you're cheating on your girlfriend. It's immoral and inappropriate for someone with your role."

The pieces started to click into place. He was the only host of the show. It would cost them time and money to change, two things the network didn't have, so they were giving him a way out in the hope it'd all blow over. But he needed to hear it, needed confirmation that's what they were thinking. "You want me to stick with Katy, to deny being with Connor so we can continue filming. What if I don't? Or what if I continue seeing him?"

"We have your termination letter here. Effective immediately," Eva replied, her clipped tone not permitting any discussion on the point.

Levi sighed. He'd worked hard to get this far, proving every day that the network hadn't made a mistake when they'd chosen his video audition over hundreds of other applicants. And he was happy there; he loved his job, loved the adventure and the challenges. Every day was different and he got to work with great people. It was everything he'd dreamed of in a career and with the success that the show had achieved, he knew he could do it for at least a few more years. The money was good, and there were a few perks that he enjoyed too. But there were downsides with it too. His whole life was wrapped up in his work persona. He'd had to become the part he played, the clean cut role model. It wasn't just what he did anymore.

"Mr Flaherty, you appreciate that we need to take action on this, don't you? You're a valued part of the network's team. Your show is a centrepiece of our children's entertainment programming, one of only a few with uniquely Australian content. We want to keep growing it and we firmly believe that you are the right person to do it. But you have to work with us on this. It's the sort of controversy that could be career ending."

Levi nodded. He got it, he did. And he wished things were different.

12

CONNOR

CONNOR DROPPED THE BASKET OF CLEAN LAUNDRY ON THE FLOOR and kicked the door shut. Noticing the light flashing on his phone, he picked it up and listened to the message Levi had left, then replayed it again. Whatever had happened in his meeting had left him rattled. Swallowing down his worry, he dialled Katy. "Cupcake, hey," he greeted her when she picked up. Connor was relieved just hearing her voice. "I'm forwarding you a message from Lee then I'm coming to the shop. I need you to close it down and lock the doors. Make sure Ash and Dylan both stay there with you, okay?"

"What's going on? What's happening?" Katy asked, indignant. "I can't just close."

"Please, Cupcake," he begged. Trying to keep his voice calm was an effort. He'd be lying if he said Levi's message hadn't freaked him out. "I'm not sure what's going on. I don't know any more than you do, but whatever is happening, Levi needs you safe."

"Yeah, okay," she relented. "But I'm just working out the back. No one needs to be here with me. I'm not gonna ask them to stay if we're closing. I'll just lock the front door when they leave."

Connor scrubbed his hand over his face, anxiety and frustration welling up inside him. He wished she had the same sense of urgency he had. "Please, Katy, if you won't do it for me, do it for Levi. He's really fuckin' worried."

"How about I pack up and meet you at the studio? We can speak with Lee there, get an idea of what's going on."

"Good, yeah, that'll work, but I want someone with you the whole time. Until I know what's got Lee freaked out, I'm not taking any chances. I'll swing by, then we'll head on over together. Gimme ten and I'll be there."

Connor threw on a clean tee from the washing basket, laced up his boots and rushed out of the door. His phone pinged with an instant message. It was from his former commanding officer: **Now I get why you've fallen off the face of the earth. Message me. It's been too long since you checked in. I wanna know my brother's still in one piece.**

Connor smiled at the playful gruffness of his CO's message, even if he was clueless on what he was talking about. Either way, it could wait. He needed to get to Katy first, then to Levi. Reversing out the drive, another message came in, then another. He didn't check them, not while he was driving, but curiosity was a bitch. What was going on?

He'd barely pulled on the handbrake when his phone rang. "Holy shit, anyone'd think I'd won the lotto." Fishing it out of his pocket, Levi's grinning face lit up the screen. "Hey, Lee. I'm at Delectable now. Just about to head on in."

The phone was quiet for so long that Connor pulled it away from his face to check the connection. "I need you, Con. And Katy." His voice was soft, broken, and it shot a knife through Connor's heart.

He nodded and clicked off his seatbelt. "We're coming, Lee, we'll be there soon. Sit tight, okay."

"Yeah." Another pause. "And, Con? Thanks."

"Anything for you." The line went dead, and with a sense of dread, he dropped his phone on the dash and ran over to the shop, banging on the front door. "Katy, it's me." Dylan opened up after a moment and Katy, Ash, and finally Dylan all emerged into the late afternoon sunshine. It'd started to cool, the clear skies providing no blanket to keep the day's warmth in during the night. Autumn on the Gold Coast was like that—perfect days, clear nights, fresh breezes and a crispness that you just didn't get in summer.

"Hey, Cupcake." He took her into his arms and held tightly. Pulling back a little, he kissed her forehead gently and spoke just loud enough that only she could hear, "Lee needs us."

"Let's go." Speaking to the other men, she added, "See you tomorrow, guys. Sorry about the schedule change. I'll pay you for your normal hours."

"Never mind that, Katy." Ash waved her off. "Just call us if you need us, yeah?"

"Thanks, boys," Connor murmured. "Catcha."

They drove in silence, the peak hour traffic crawling slowly. Connor turned off the main road and hit the backstreets, winding through them until they could finally see the massive Green Lantern symbol on the roller coaster in the main park. Turning into the studio lot, Connor squeezed Katy's hand and steered his car to the security checkpoint. Making it through easily enough, Connor continued on, following Katy's directions until they reached the studio offices of the network. Connor's heart constricted when he spotted Levi leaning against the wall of the office. His hands were in his pockets, his shoulders slumped. He was looking down, his gaze riveted to the ground. Misery rolled off him.

"Oh, Levi," Katy breathed from the passenger seat, her voice cracking on his name. She was out of the car sprinting to him as soon as Connor had rolled to a stop. Her hands on Levi's face, she pulled him down into her arms. Levi clutched her, crushing her in his embrace. Connor spied the gym bag at Levi's feet, the same one he always kept in his car, and his gut twisted. *What happened?* It took everything in Connor, every ounce of his strength, to hold himself back from taking them into his arms. But all hesitation fled when Levi looked up at him, absolute desperation clouding his face as he held out his hand. Connor slammed the car door shut and strode over to them, stopping close and bracing a hand on Levi's shoulder. But Lee wasn't having it. Apparently, the "no touching in public" rule was being shattered. Levi wrapped his hand around the back of Connor's neck and pulled him close, kissing him like he was the oxygen he needed to breathe. Levi feasted on him, kissing him long and hard. Rough fingertips, sharp stubble, and Levi's masculine scent overwhelmed him, and Connor melted into his touch. Any question of whether they were intimately familiar with each other was utterly decimated. Connor's head spun, his legs went weak, and he held onto the two people dearest to him as Levi claimed him.

Clutching at Connor and breathing hard, Levi's desperation radiated from him. Whatever had happened was making Levi crazy. Every protective instinct in Connor flared brightly. He needed to fix it, to stop Levi from hurting. Too soon, Levi broke away and kissed Katy, this time much slower and gentler. Connor couldn't stop, couldn't break away. He licked and kissed, nibbled on his man's neck, loved on him the same way Katy was doing. Katy's breathy moan and Levi's much lower growl had Connor pulling back, watching them. They were beautiful together—big blond Levi, all smooth muscle and clean skin against Katy's tanned complexion and even darker hair. Both blue-eyed and gorgeous, Connor loved them endlessly.

"Let's go home," Levi murmured. "I don't wanna be here when the others arrive for their meeting."

"What was it about?" Katy asked him gently, her arms wound around his waist.

"Pics of us are on social media from this morning. Me kissing you, and me and Con together." They'd done so much more than kiss. Feeling adventurous and crazy horny, Connor had strutted into the garage starkers and tried to bait Levi, or at the very least, say goodbye before he'd left for work. And the other man had delivered in spades, making Connor see fireworks he'd come so hard. Pinned up against the wall, Levi had thoroughly dominated him, and Connor had loved every second of it. But some bastard had seen it, seen him riding Levi's fingers? If there were pictures on social media and Levi had been called back, there was one obvious conclusion—they knew.

Connor blanched and stumbled back. *They know. No, I can't do it to him.* The world was closing in on him, his head spinning. He struggled to take a breath. How could he have been so stupid? How could he have pushed Levi into risking so much? He would lose everything he'd worked for—Connor couldn't let Levi ruin his career for him. He couldn't stand by and do nothing.

"No, Lee, surely there's a way."

Levi looked at him, his eyes not holding their usual spark. But he reached out to Connor and pulled him back into their fold, holding him tightly. "They were trying to get the images pulled, trying to get me to say that it wasn't me. They thought if I said we aren't together and we distanced ourselves it might blow over."

"So we do it. I'll move out, get my own place. We can take a break. We can... we'll work it out." The words tasted bitter on his tongue, but if that's what it took for Levi to keep the job he loved, he'd do it.

"No," Levi replied quickly. "They wanted you to find a replacement boyfriend." In a softer tone, but one that was still filled with steel, he added, "I already told them, no. I loved my job, loved the people I worked with. It made me happy, but it was just a job, a pay cheque. You're everything to me, the two of you are my whole world. I love you both. Quitting wasn't even a choice I needed to think about. I wouldn't have changed this morning for anything, especially not a job that tells me I can't love both of you." Those final walls, the ones that caused the lingering self-doubt in Connor crumbled into dust. Right there, right then he fell in love with Levi all over again. His parents had left him, Rob had left him, but true to his word, Levi hadn't.

"So what, that's it? You're done? You can't do anything?" he asked, hopelessly disappointed and in love and hurting and happy all at the same time—a whirlwind of emotions buffeting him from all directions.

"I can take you out for dinner and we can celebrate?" Levi paused, clearly thinking something through. "I don't have a ride anymore—they took the company car back."

"Good, that piece of shit was awful," Connor muttered.

"I've got a better idea than going out for dinner." Katy smiled at him, her grin infectious. "Come on, we've got something to show you." Connor smiled despite his inner turmoil.

"What?" Levi asked, curious.

"It's a surprise. Let's go." Katy motioned to Connor's car.

They headed straight to his father's garage, Connor calling ahead to make sure the workshop was still open. Even if it hadn't been, he would have done a detour, picking up the keys before heading on over. The bike was in pieces, but each part was primed and ready for painting. As much as Connor had wanted to assemble it and give Levi a completed bike, he hadn't. It was something they'd wanted to do together since they were kids, and there was no way Connor was jumping the gun and finishing it without Levi's involvement. The parts lay underneath a sheet, protecting them from the dust and grease in the workshop.

"What have you done, Con?" Levi asked as they stopped in front of the covered-up mound. The sound of rattle guns and clinking metal from the other mechanics stopped, the heavy thud of their work boots surrounding them.

"Katy and I decided for your birthday that we needed to do something with the boxes of parts in the garage. So here it is. It's ready for us to paint and assemble. Happy birthday, Lee." Connor swallowed. He hoped like hell that Levi liked what he'd done. Tugging on the thick sheet, he pulled it away and balled it up, haphazardly tossing it to the side. He couldn't take his gaze of Levi, watching, hoping that he'd show some sign that he liked what he saw. The other man's eyes widened and his mouth opened and closed a couple of times. A nervous laugh and a hand scrubbing through his hair followed. Connor's stomach was in knots, his heart in his throat. Then Levi stepped forward. Reverently, the touch almost sensual, he ran his fingertips over the gleaming chrome of the engine block that was resting on a trolley. Levi's head fell forward, and as he turned away, Connor saw him touch the heel of his hand to his cheeks. Connor stepped forward, watching as Levi's chest rose and fell. He didn't really know what to do—he hadn't expected Levi to be so subdued. He thought the other man would whoop and scoop Katy up in his arms, laughing, his excitement bubbling over. But this quiet contemplation was scaring him.

Connor placed a hand on Levi's shoulder, and it seemed to kick-start something within Levi, his friend and lover turning in Connor's arms and burying his face in the crook of Connor's neck. Trembling, shaking like a leaf, Levi took one heaving breath then another. His arms around Connor's waist were crushing him, so Connor held Levi tighter too. Running his fingers through the short spikes on his head, their prickle soft against his palm, Connor breathed Levi in, laying a gentle kiss on his temple. Orange and cedar and something uniquely Levi filled his senses. He squeezed tighter, burying his nose in Levi's hair.

"You didn't finish it without me," Levi whispered, his voice thick with unshed tears. "Wait, what's in our garage? It's still full of boxes and parts."

"Boxes are empty and half of the parts aren't even from bikes." Connor shrugged. Massaging his shoulders, he added, "You kept it, you waited for me, didn't you?" It was a question, but not really one at the same time. Levi loved bikes, and when they were growing up—starry eyed kids—they'd made a pact that they'd both get their dream car and bike and do them up together. It hadn't quite happened like that, at least not with Connor's car, but there was no way he was finishing Levi's bike without him.

Levi nodded. "It's always been you and Katy, Con. Even though I was too blind to see it, it's always been you."

"I love you too," he whispered. Levi pulled Connor's face to his and kissed him. Slow and sweet, Connor poured his heart and soul into their connection. Not even the clearing throats and muttered comments put a dampener on his ride on cloud nine, but Katy's snarky, "You got a problem?" had Connor laughing.

"Chill, Cupcake. These boys had no idea I'm bi."

"Screw 'em. If Lee kissed me, they would've wolf whistled, but with the two of you, they get all uncomfortable. It's attitudes like that," Katy muttered, frustrated, while pointing around the workshop, "that have me getting two hundred messages in the last fifteen minutes—most from complete strangers—telling me what dogs you and Lee are."

"Babe." Levi pulled Katy into their circle until she stood between the two of them. "I don't give a fuck what anyone else thinks. I love the both of you. That's all that matters." He kissed her and Connor stared open mouthed at his boyfriend. *He swore. He actually cursed.* It was something small, but Levi never would have done it before. He was filled with guilt over Levi having lost his job—hell, if he'd kept his dick in his pants... well, if he'd had any on, Levi would still have the job he loved—but at the same time, he couldn't be too sad about it either. Not when he was standing in a workshop full of guys, openly and intimately holding the two most important people in his world.

Connor stretched, lazily waking up, his muscles pleasantly aching. The warm hard body pressed against his didn't budge, but that didn't surprise him. Levi had gone through the ringer the day before. The four hours of driving up to the Sunshine Coast and back and a full day at work would take it out of anyone, but to have lost his job and have their world turned upside down by all the craziness was exhausting. And that wasn't mentioning the two-hour detour they'd made to Levi's parents' house. It hadn't been at all bad though. Levi's father admitted he'd seen the longing between them years before, but had dismissed it when Levi began dating Katy. Levi's mum had hugged him tightly and whispered, "Now both my boys are happy. I'm so glad you came home to them." It'd shocked the hell out of him, but it shouldn't have—Levi's parents were pretty fucking awesome.

Once they'd finally managed to get out of there, they'd had to fight the news vans and intrusive reporters camping outside

Levi's childhood home to get to the car. It was crazy—it'd only taken a few hours after the photos were leaked to go viral. Social media had exploded and the network's press release didn't help, subtly making out that Levi had been fired because of his indiscretions, rather than having quit. The worst of it was that the whole show had been put on an indefinite hiatus. Every one of the crew was effectively out of work, a situation that the network's administrators were probably ecstatic about. What better way to save money and stop the company getting into deeper financial difficulty, than have the star's relationship exposed and the whole show canned? The weight of the knowledge that his friends were soon going to be lining up for the dole crushed Levi.

The mainstream media had quickly jumped on the "blame Levi" bandwagon, making him look like an angel fallen from grace, screwing up in the worst possible way. Katy was the innocent victim—Connor was kind of glad she'd been portrayed as that, rather than as a whore. It was the one saving grace of the whole damn debacle. They'd laid the worst of it on Connor—he was the drifter, the homeless ex-soldier who'd done the dirty on his best mate and screwed up his relationship, not by sleeping with his Mrs, but by leading him astray. It would have been comedic had it not been playing out on a worldwide stage. Especially because none of the news outlets had voiced the obvious question—why were the three of them still being seen together?

By the time they'd made it home and Levi flicked on the tele, Katy's brother was being interviewed by some late night current affairs "alternative fact" type program. Watching him accuse Connor of bringing sin into Levi and Katy's happy home and ruining their relationship had been a lesson in self-restraint. Connor had wanted to beat the shit out of him, but he'd held it together.

Barely.

Jonathan wasn't religious at all, but was clearly happy to pull out the God-card when it suited him. But the Church had lapped it up, the hypocritical bastards getting their say in too. It made sense, Connor supposed. Their misfortune gave the Church an excuse to focus on something other than the fact that their highest-ranking official was facing child sex charges. They'd turned their relationship into a political issue too, the Church using the platform as another reason why marriage equality shouldn't be allowed in Australia—you let "the gays" marry, and they'll corrupt everyone, tempting them into sin and ruining the sanctity of marriage. Hell, some dumbarse was saying that you allow marriage equality, people would be able to marry the Harbour Bridge, so nothing really surprised him. How there was a link between the three of them and the marriage debate, Connor had no idea, but the church were good at fire and brimstone—they'd had centuries of practice.

Like masochists, the three of them had stayed up most of the night watching TV and seeing the updates scrolling across the bottom of the screen. Their phones had gone into meltdown, notifications completely out of control. All three of them had been analysed and commentated on like they were in a damn goldfish bowl, every Tom, Dick, and Harry having an opinion on them. But they'd had an incredible amount of support too. As soon as they'd heard, Ford and Reef had headed over, Katy's friend Sarah too. Nick and Emma were on the phone for half the night, and Mike had visited at four in the morning, when Katy was ready to head to work, to help them navigate through the circus gathered just off the front lawn.

They were on strict instructions from Nick and Emma not to say a word, and being lawyers, Connor figured they knew best. He and Emma had penned a press release, and Levi—with Reef's help—had written a statement. His boyfriend was still tossing up whether to read it out, but whatever he decided,

Connor and Katy would be there beside him. Even though they were quiet, the rest of their friends and family weren't. Neither were the complete strangers—thousands of people on the web and every LGBT+ organisation around—who'd all stood by them, commenting and tweeting their support and trying hard to turn the hate around.

But all that was too heavy for Connor to think about on a quiet Tuesday morning. After they'd followed Katy to work, he and Levi had made sure she was safely ensconced in the shop with Dylan and Ashton. Given that none of them wanted Connor and Levi to stick around—the news crews following them were a little distracting—they'd headed home, to get some much-needed sleep.

Connor slipped out of bed and smiled at the Post-it note Katy had left: *Don't let him be too hard on himself. I'll be home early —think up something fun we can do for him.* Connor pondered the idea as he padded out to the kitchen to make a coffee.

Steaming mug in hand, he turned to look out the window, resting his elbows on the kitchen bench. The sky was a brilliant blue already with no clouds in the sky. And still too—there wasn't a breath of wind. It'd be the perfect day for the beach. Still a little chilly, but beautiful.

He startled when Levi's warm hands touched his skin, the other man pressed against his back as he nuzzled Connor. "Mornin'," Connor murmured, twisting in Levi's hold so he could hug him. Levi hummed and snuggled in closer while Connor ran his hands up and down his boyfriend's broad shirtless back.

"I need coffee," Levi mumbled. "Gotta make some decisions."

Connor slipped his hands into Levi's boxers and gripped his arse, pulling him closer. "Not today. Today I'm gonna find some way to outrun the cameras and the three of us are goin' to the beach, even if we have to go to Straddie to do it. Katy'll be home any minute now. We can pack a picnic and then go." Levi smiled and leaned in to kiss him, nodding after they eventually pulled apart. "Actually, there was another beach I found down south a while back too—no one there, super quiet. We could go there—swim, lie in the sun, rub sunscreen on each other, run around naked for a while—you know, the usual."

"As long as it's just the three of us, I'm in," Katy spoke from the doorway, startling both of them. He hadn't heard her come in. "I like the naked bit too."

"Yeah, sugar? You'd be up for that?" Levi asked. Connor smiled. His man wouldn't deny Katy—neither would he if he were honest—so if she wanted it, that's what they'd be doing.

It didn't take long for them to get organized and on the road. The lack of news vans sitting outside the house gave Connor hope that they'd already found something more interesting to report on. It was almost too good to be true, but he wasn't going to look a gift horse in the mouth. Twenty minutes later, as Connor was turning onto a dirt track which led to the tiny bay, he looked in the rear-view mirror, checking again that no one was following them. Relief washed over him. It looked like their luck was holding out. Maybe the three of them could have a few moments of peace.

The trees opened up and the sight before him instantly calmed Connor's frayed nerves. A strip of perfect white sand framed by gentle waves and tall palm trees greeted them. He'd found it by chance, looking for an entirely different road, but he was glad he'd stumbled on it, visiting the quiet spot a few times over his months living back on the Coast.

The weight lifted off Connor's shoulders the minute their bare feet hit the sand, letting him take a breath for the first time since the shit had hit the fan. Levi looked calmer too, staring out at the water with a small smile lifting his lips. Katy laid out their towels, and Connor ripped off his tee, tossing it onto the soft sand. The salt in the air and warm sun had Connor stretching his arms above his head, looking up at the bright blue sky. They really did live in paradise. But even though it was perfect there, he could have been in Siberia or the Sahara and he still would have felt the same. As long as Levi and Katy were with him, his life would be perfection.

"Last one in!" Katy yelled out as she dropped her jean shorts on the towel and sprinted towards the water. He smiled, watching Levi chase after her, whooping when Katy pulled on the string of her bikini, sending it sailing from her body. There was no way he was going to sit this one out. Connor dropped his shorts, running naked into the ocean after them.

The water was like ice on his skin when he first hit it, taking his breath away and making Connor squeak embarrassingly. The cold didn't last long though, especially when he was tackled by both Levi and Katy, being dragged underwater and coming up laughing.

The sun rose higher in the sky, the time passing quickly as they laughed and kissed, splashing and swimming together. Connor's stomach rumbled while they floated and body surfed in the small waves. "Come on, mate. Let's get some food in ya." Levi kissed his throat, and Connor moaned softly, it coming out as a pained gasp when Katy closed her hand around his hard-as-fuck shaft. The teasing bastards left him there though, cackling as they walked out of the water to their towels.

Levi sat between them and rested his elbows on bent knees, watching the water and taking a swig from the bottle of water he'd uncapped. Katy plucked the sunscreen out of her bag and rubbed down his arms, crawling in front of Levi to get his chest. Connor looked after his back, and when he'd finished, he held

Levi tightly, kissing a line down his throat and along his shoulder. The three of them sat there like that—Connor hugging Levi, Levi holding Katy until she shifted, getting out her phone and snapping a selfie of them. He looked at the shot. They were wet, Katy's hair still slicked back. Her bright bikini top—which she'd slipped back on once they were out of the water—was a contrast against Katy's darker skin. He was smiling, a serene, goofy grin on his face. If he didn't already know it in his heart, it'd be obvious from the shot that Connor was head over heels in love. Levi too. The other man was looking at him in the photo with such adoration it took Connor's breath away. Levi's lips whispered over Connor's bearded cheek, while he held Katy close, her back against his chest, his thumb gently caressing her cheek. Connor had held one of her hands, but he couldn't see it in the photo.

"This one's a keeper." Katy smiled at Connor before leaning up to kiss him.

"He is," Levi murmured. "Same with the pic. We can keep that too." Connor couldn't help his happy laugh as he held them tighter. Whatever happened from there on out, it was the three of them. They were the perfect match, an unbreakable trio, and despite all the craziness going down, life was fucking good.

EPILOGUE

Two months later

Levi had just about finished setting up the screen and projector on the back deck, fiddling with the speakers that would project the sounds of the final Origin game. Katy dropped the last of the beanbags down and surveyed the area, smiling. Levi and Con had worked tirelessly, building the deck and a railing around it and she now had her view back. The lights of the Surfers Paradise skyline in the distance had always captivated her. She'd fallen in love with the view when they'd first seen the house, but since then the trees had grown and blocked most of it. Trimming back a few strategic branches had solved the problem and Katy spent many an arvo out there, doing paperwork or reading, curled up in her men's arms. She breathed in the perfume of the evening jasmine just starting to bloom in the planter boxes Con and Levi had also built.

Since he'd quit, Levi had done a lot. She was damn proud of him. Getting behind some of the local LGBT organisations who'd spoken out in his favour, he was now actively supporting them, speaking out to promote acceptance and understanding. He'd attended every one of the pride events during June and raised tens of thousands of dollars for their youth initiatives. Somewhere in between Levi had managed to start a killer tattoo as well; the Japanese-style phoenix rising from the ashes covered most of his arm, his shoulder blade and his pec. The outline had healed enough that he was starting on the first of the sessions to have it coloured in a few days. And on top of all that, he was getting his career back on track, looking at going into business with Mike.

Con had struggled when they'd been under the media spotlight. He'd had an episode in front of the paps, their flashing lights and shouts sending him back to the battles he'd fought. He hadn't left the house for days after that, only venturing out when the temptation of playing at the pub was too strong to resist. The trauma would always be with him, but he was mostly managing it. His music, and the regular gigs he got were good for him. It was his safe space; getting paid for it was a bonus.

Her own business hadn't seen much of a change, except for the drop in sales of over the counter cakes—it was hard to move them when customers were avoiding the store because of the interviews they'd have to give. But since the speculation had died off, things had bounced back. Dylan had been her lifesaver throughout, pulling some long hours for her and giving her some much-needed time away from the prying eyes of the camera crews. They'd left them alone for all of a day, and that was only because the paparazzo who'd leaked the pics spilled the beans on who'd tipped him off—her brother. Once the other news agencies had made the familial connection between them, they'd hounded the three of them for weeks. The only good thing to come out of the whole damn debacle was the confirmation of just how slimy Jonathan actually was. Finding out it was him had been the catalyst for Katy to start speaking with her mum and dad again. She was earning their trust back, and they were making the effort to get to know Con. For that small mercy, she would be forever grateful.

Katy smiled as Con dropped the fluffy blanket from their bed on top of the beanbag and took her into his arms. He grumbled as the doorbell rang and Katy laughed, playfully squeezing his arse. Their visitors had arrived—Mike and his kids, Nick and a very pregnant Emma, Dylan and Ash from the shop, and a few of their other friends who'd stuck with them through the last few months.

They watched the game—as frustrating as it was to see the ref's shitty decisions cost Queensland more than one try—and mowed through the masses of popcorn and beer, hot dogs, and pies that Katy had made. Yelling and cheering rent the night air from their own yard as well as their neighbours'. State of Origin was always a big deal, but it was the first time they'd hosted it. It wouldn't be the last.

"Oh, come on," Levi shouted when Queensland was penalized on the half-time buzzer, slamming his beer bottle down, while Emma cheered. As the only Cockroach supporter, she was happy for New South Wales' chance to get points on the board to narrow Queensland's lead. Katy was still mumbling insults at the referees as she stepped over the bodies sprawled out on their deck. Dessert was ready to be dished up and she could do with a hot drink. Even being sandwiched between Con and Levi and covered with a blanket wasn't enough to ward off the chill in the winter air.

She'd just poured steaming milk into the mugs spread out on the bench, dropping marshmallows into the hot chocolates when Con joined her, stepping behind her and wrapping her in his arms. He nuzzled into her, pushing away the collar of her Maroons jersey and kissed her throat with cool lips. Shivering, she laughed, batting him away, but he held tighter and sighed happily. Katy turned her face and kissed his temple, noticing that he was staring at the photographs on the wall. "I love those pics of us at the beach. Nearly seven years between them, but you're both still my best friends," he murmured to her.

"A lot's happened between them, hasn't it? Would you change anything?" Katy asked, turning her attention back to him.

"To get here? Right now?" When Katy nodded her answer to his questions, Con shook his head and pushed her hair off her neck, brushing his lips over the sensitive skin there. "No, I wouldn't change a thing. That pic—the one from when we were too young and stupid to see what we could have? That was our beginning. My deployment, your lives together before me—that was our middle, how we found our way back to each other. And now? Now we have our happy ending."

"Never mind the ending," Levi murmured, coming to stand with them, his big hand resting on her hip as he stood shoulder to shoulder with Con. "Endings and goodbyes are too fucking sad. Just gimme a happily ever after and I'm sweet."

Katy laughed and snuggled into her men. He was right. She hated goodbyes. Nope, she was happy living her ever after right in that moment.

The end

SONG LIST

"Everlong" Foo Fighters
"Wonderwall" Oasis
"Skin" Rag'n'bone Man
"Back to December" Taylor Swift
"Lay Me Down" Sam Smith and John Legend
"Slow Hands" Niall Horan
"Malibu" Miley Cyrus
"All Day and All of the Night" The Kinks
"Never tear us apart" INXS
"Thinking Out Loud" Ed Sheeran
"In The End" Linkin Park

ABOUT ANN GRECH

By day Ann Grech lives in the corporate world and can be found sitting behind a desk typing away at reports and papers or lecturing to a room full of students. She graduated with a PhD in 2016 and is now an over-qualified nerd. Glasses, briefcase, high heels and a pencil skirt, she's got the librarian look nailed too. If only they knew! She swears like a sailor, so that's got to be a hint. The other one was "the look" from her tattoo artist when she told him that she wanted her kids initials "B" and "J" tattooed on her foot. It took a second to register that it might be a bad idea.

She's never entirely fit in and loves escaping into a book—whether it's reading or writing one. But she's found her tribe now and loves her MM book world family. She dislikes cooking, but loves eating, can't figure out technology, but is addicted to it, and her guilty pleasure is Byron Bay Cookies. Oh and shoes. And lingerie. And maybe handbags too. Well, if we're being honest, we'd probably have to add her library too given the state of her credit card every month (what can she say, she's a book-worm at heart)!

She also publishes her raunchier short stories under her pen name, Olive Hiscock.

Ann loves chatting to people online, so if you'd like to keep up with what she's got going on:

Like her Facebook page: https://www.facebook.com/pages/Ann-Grech/458420227655212

Follow her on Facebook: https://www.facebook.com/ann.grech.9

Join The A-Team (Ann's street team and fan group): https://www.facebook.com/groups/1871698189780535/

Instagram: https://www.instagram.com/anngrechauthor/

Twitter: https://twitter.com/anngrechauthor

Visit her online: http://www.anngrech.com/ (while you're there, sign up for Ann's newsletter. You'll get a free read)

Olive Hiscock's Facebook page: https://www.facebook.com/OliveHiscockErotica